IRRATIONAL NUMBERS
Robert Spiller

Gold Imprint
Medallion Press, Inc.
Printed in USA

DEDICATION:

My wonderful wife, Barbara, who makes all things possible. To my daughters, Laura, Nikki, and Jenny, for their support and encouragement.

Published 2008 by Medallion Press, Inc.

The MEDALLION PRESS LOGO
is a registered trademark of Medallion Press, Inc.

If you purchased this book without a cover, you should be aware that this book is stolen property. It was reported as "unsold and destroyed" to the publisher, and neither the author nor the publisher has received any payment from this "stripped book."

Copyright © 2008 by Robert Spiller
Cover Illustration by Arturo Delgado

All rights reserved. No part of this book may be reproduced or transmitted in any form or by any electronic or mechanical means, including photocopying, recording, or by any information storage and retrieval system, without written permission of the publisher, except where permitted by law.

Names, characters, places, and incidents are the products of the author's imagination or are used fictionally. Any resemblance to actual events, locales, or persons, living or dead, is entirely coincidental.

Typeset in Adobe Garamond Pro
Printed in the United States of America

ISBN: 9781933836881

10 9 8 7 6 5 4 3 2 1
First Edition

ACKNOWLEDGEMENTS:

My critique group: Bill Mason, Barb Nickless, Maria Faulconer, MB Partlow, and Beth Groundwater.

The community of writers at Pikes Peak Writers.

The town of Ellicott, Colorado, which may not be East Plains but comes darn close.

My editor, Kerry Estevez, who has always been patient with me even when I've been crazed.

PROLOGUE

"Slow down, Spoon."

Moses Witherspoon took a loose-gravel turn stupidly fast. The Trans Am slid sideways sending up a cloud of dust. "What's the matter, angel boy? Wings on too tight?"

Gabe Trotter wanted to slap the idiot. "Cut out the angel-boy bullshit. I hate that, always did."

Red-eyed and looking halfway to shit-faced his own self, Dwight Furby giggled. "Gabriel, Gabriel, come blow your horn."

Gabe couldn't believe he'd let Dwight talk him into cruising East Plains' back roads in Mo Witherspoon's Trans Am. Both assholes had been drinking before Gabe crawled in and had since put away even more brew. Spoon's straw cowboy hat sat cockeyed on his shaggy blond head.

In the three years since graduation, Gabe had successfully avoided being subjected to the angel-boy nickname. Hell, he'd mostly made it a point to avoid

Mo Witherspoon altogether. He couldn't believe he once thought Spoon cool, when now it was obvious the asshole had his head so far up his colon he could deliver a singing telegram to his pancreas.

Yet, here I am just like in high school, sidekicking along with Dwight-can't-find-my-butt-with-both-hands-Furby. Chalk one up to a bad memory, boredom, and having no wheels on a Saturday night.

A not-so-still nagging voice reminded Gabe if he'd gotten a job like his mom and Missus Pinkwater kept telling him, he'd have wheels and long ago would have moved out of East Plains and away from Spoon and Dwight. He shrugged off the admonition.

No, Goddammit, this entire shit-fest is Dwight's fault. If I survive this round of high speed idiocy, I swear to God I'm going to kill the imbecile.

"Unlax, bro," Dwight said in his nasally whine. His own shoulder-length dark hair stuck out from beneath an oily Pennzoil baseball cap. "Just having fun with ya. You remember fun?"

Gabe forced a smile. "Yeah, I remember."

He had to admit, there had been fun. Hanging around with a football star and bull rider like Spoon had its high points—the parties, the chicks, the drinking, even the fights. You couldn't hang around Mo Witherspoon and not get into fights. The combination of loudmouth and bigot rubbed a lot of people way past static discharge. But Spoon always came out on top, and by association so did Gabe and Dwight.

What the hell. Might as well make the best of it. "Give me a beer and slow it down to warp one, you gigantic scrotum."

Spoon guffawed and slapped the wheel. "Now that's the Gabe Trotter I remember. Sure thing, buddy. Warp one it is. Hey, lookie there." Spoon pointed with his chin.

Illuminated by the Trans Am's headlights, a tall figure carried a gas can.

"Is that who I think it is?" Dwight asked.

"Damn straight." Spoon decelerated as they approached. "Prom Queen himself."

Long before they came to a stop, the figure stopped. Shielding his eyes from the glare, he waited as the car pulled alongside.

Spoon rolled down his window. "Leo, Leo, Bo Beo, climbed any Brokeback Mountains lately?"

Leo Quinn set down his gas can and sighed. "It seems they let anybody drive these back roads. How you doing, Spoon?"

"Don't you mean, how's it hangin'? That's more your style, Hoss."

Leo wearily shook his head.

Gabe could see a dozen comebacks swim across Leo's freckled face. In the space of a few seconds, he seemed to reject them all. He just gave Spoon a look that declared,

You ain't worth the breath it takes to put you in your place, dickhead.

"As fun as this is, I'm going to go." He picked up the can.

"Hold on there, Girly Man. We'll give you a lift."

"I don't think so." He started to walk.

Spoon turned to Dwight. "You believe this shit? This fairy thinks he's too good for my Trans Am."

Dwight nodded like a bobble-head doll. "It sounded like that to me."

Gabe let a mixture of excitement and dread wash over him—something of the old days. Something that said, *Who the hell knows where this might lead?*

Spoon rolled up alongside Leo. "I think I'm offended, Girly Man. I make an offer in good faith, and you throw it back in my face."

Leo kept on walking. "If that's how you want to interpret it, be my guest. I got problems of my own."

Spoon stopped the Trans Am and popped open his door. "You're right about that, Hoss. And I'm about to add to 'em."

CHAPTER 1

Sunday morning Bonnie Pinkwater awoke unable to breathe.

"Get off me, Euclid," she mumbled, spitting out cat fur. "I swear, you little fuzz ball, one of these days I'm going to learn a recipe for pussycat potpie. If you don't kill me first."

The cat blinked at Bonnie with a look that asked, "You talking to me?"

Bonnie tossed the black Burmese onto the floor. "Why don't you park your rear end on Armen's face every once in a while?"

"I heard that." Armen Callahan rolled toward her. "An alarming and disgusting suggestion to say the least."

Bonnie gave him a kiss on his nose. "Good morning, you."

"Good morning, yourself, pretty lady. What say you and I make a day of it, starting with French toast?"

"Sweet talker. I think I'll have you bronzed."

"Like a pair of baby shoes?"

Bonnie kissed him again—this time on his white goatee. "You're just as cute as a baby shoe, my Sweet Baboo."

Armen rolled his eyes and smiled, despite an obvious attempt to hold the grin in check. "Noooo! Not the dreaded cutsie nicknames. Not at this crucial juncture of our relationship."

She nestled into his arms, back to his front, a pair of spoons in silk pajamas. "I'm sorry, but it's hard to resist a superhero, Señor Mighty Mouse." She felt his breath blow warm into her hair and shivered.

Don't go getting schoolgirl, Pinkwater. You're fifty-three years old, for God's sake. Take it one breakfast at a time.

"Here I come to save the day," he whispered in her ear.

Oh, what the hell. She rolled to face him. "I intend to plant a big wet one on you, sir."

"Madam, do your worst."

The kiss felt so good she held it despite a cold nose prodding her derriere. "I've got cold snout stabbing my rear," she said when she could stand no more.

"I recognize this. We're spies exchanging passwords, right? Okay. Okay. I got the countersign. I've got a cold stout filling my ear."

Bonnie chuckled. "Callahan, you're weird. Good

combination, weird and cute."

She turned and perceived accusing golden retriever eyes staring up at her. Hypatia had her chin resting on the pad of the water bed. "Hypatia, my love. Are you suggesting we have been abed long enough?"

Bonnie sat up and stretched. She stroked the soft fur of Hypatia's brow. "I'll bet you're hungry, sweetie." Bonnie reached behind her and dug a playful knuckle into Armen Callahan's ribs.

She jumped as he reached for her. "You gonna lay around all morning, cowboy? In these here parts we take a promise of French toast mighty serious." She stuck out her tongue.

"A completely unprovoked attack, followed by a shamelessly perverse gesture. Pinkwater, you don't know who you're messing with. Behavior of this ilk demands immediate retribution." Armen threw off his covers and was on his feet in one fluid motion. He caught Bonnie by the back of her silk pajamas before she could reach the bedroom door.

She fell back into his arms. "You're quicker than you look, Callahan. Now that you have me, what are you going to do with me?"

Before Armen could answer, the phone in the kitchen rang.

"Let the machine pick up," Bonnie whispered.

Despite her intention, Bonnie stood frozen in Armen's

embrace waiting for the caller to identify himself.

"Missus Pinkwater, it's Byron Hickman. Please get back with me. It's about Leo Quinn."

Bonnie offered a kiss by way of apology. "I need to take this."

She slipped out of Armen's grasp and picked up the receiver. "Byron?"

"Missus P, am I ever glad I caught up with you."

Bonnie felt more than a little awkward. Byron was a former student, now deputy for El Paso County. When they last parted company, more than a year and a half ago, she'd been a witness against Byron's nephew, Greg. Her testimony promised to send the boy to prison. As it turned out, a plea agreement was reached, and she'd been spared that ordeal. Still, Byron knew she would have testified against Greg if it had come down to it.

Damn straight. The little bastard tried to kill me.

"You mentioned Leo Quinn."

"Correct. I wonder if we could get together some time today."

Annoyance replaced the awkwardness. However curious she was about the new kind of trouble Leo Quinn had gotten himself into, it was Sunday for crying out loud. "Is this important? I've got plans, youngster."

"Yes, ma'am, it's important. Leo Quinn has been murdered."

Bonnie stared out the passenger window of Alice, The-Little-Subaru-That-Could.

"Leo Quinn is dead." She heard herself whisper the words, but felt like they were coming from someone else.

"I'm sorry, Bon," Armen placed his hand in the no-man's-land on the seat between them.

Absently, she laid her hand on his. *Goddammit all to hell, I let that extraordinary young man slip out of my life without a phone call in over three years.*

Bonnie tried to tell herself she had a lot going on in those three years—the death of her husband, almost being killed on four separate occasions, to say nothing of breaking her foot, and getting a concussion, falling in love—but all of her excuses rang hollow. She could have called. Damn it, she *should* have called.

Now, she would never hear Leo's sweet baritone again.

Bonnie scooted across the front seat until her leg touched Armen's. She needed the contact, needed to remind herself she could make contact.

Armen wrapped an arm around her and squeezed. "If there's anything I can do, remember I'm not just a pretty face, I'm a superhero."

She smiled thinly. "I don't think you can fix this one, Mister Mouse."

"This Leo Quinn, he was one of the special people? The ones who crawl inside you and you never forget?"

She swallowed, blinking back tears. "You could say

that. Do you know anything about Leo?"

Armen shook his head. "He was before my time. Good math student?"

Bonnie regarded this man she'd known a mere three months. She was grateful he was here, but still she hesitated to share.

Let it go, Pinkwater. You know you need to talk.

She decided to leave Armen's question unanswered. How good the boy was in math could wait. "Four years ago, when I was student council sponsor, Leo, myself, and a few others went to a weekend multischool symposium. STUCO kids from all over the state met at the University of Colorado in Boulder. East Plains was one of the smallest schools represented."

"That probably happens in just about every setting," Armen offered.

"Just about, but even more so at this thing. Most of the kids I brought with me were intimidated, taken aback by the size of the event or how big the other schools were, you name it. Not Leo. He had a way about him, a style."

Leo's toothy grin swam across Bonnie's synapses, and she found herself having to swallow before continuing. "Here was this big handsome junior. Girls falling all over themselves to get next to him. Guys saving him a place at lunch tables. Even the sponsors took to him."

"He sounds too good to be true."

"In a way he was. Anyway, at the end of the weekend, we all gathered in this immense auditorium. Over a thousand people packed stadium seats while a former professional football player down on the floor went motivational about school spirit. He was good. Shouting. Waving his big muscular arms. Flashing his pearly whites. Threw autographed footballs into the stands. Adults and kids ate his shtick right up. Every time this palooka stopped to take a breath, applause thundered. When he was done, he asked if anybody had a question. Leo stood."

"Why am I tempted to say uh-oh?"

"Because you are a student of humanity and a bit like Leo yourself."

"Okay, you got my attention. What did Leo ask Mister NFL?"

"In a voice that betrayed absolutely no sarcasm, Leo asked, *What is the average rainfall of the Congo Basin?*"

Armen's half smile betrayed a hint of admiration. "I'll bet that didn't go over so well."

"You'd win that bet. With that simple question, Leo traded away all the goodwill he'd won for the entire weekend. You could hear people whispering, *asshole* and *bastard*. I thought he might not get out of there without a fight."

"You've got to admit, it was a wiseass thing to do."

Bonnie sighed, wishing she hadn't dredged up this

particular memory. "I do admit it. In fact, on the way home I asked him what in hell he was trying to prove. He just looked at me and said, *I needed to know how Oscar Wilde felt.*"

"What?"

"Oscar Wilde, author of *The Portrait of Dorian Grey* and *The Importance of Being—*"

"Woman, you try my patience. I know darn well who Oscar Wilde was. What I want to know is what did Leo mean?"

"He wouldn't say."

Armen glanced at her before returning his eyes to the road. "He wouldn't say?"

"Nope. And it took me the better part a year to figure it out. By then it was too late."

"Have a sit-down."

Byron nodded to two soft-seated metal chairs. He folded his own frame into a rolling chair behind his gray metal desk. Once ensconced, he opened the top drawer and pulled out a yellow legal pad. His gray-blue eyes regarded Bonnie affectionately for a long moment before he spoke. "Thanks for coming."

"I'm not really sure why I'm here, youngster," Bonnie said. "I haven't spoken with Leo Quinn in over three years. Not since he graduated."

"Class of two thousand one, right?"

Bonnie nodded, feeling slightly peeved with Byron. He'd deftly sidestepped her implied question. "That's right. Leo was salutatorian."

"Bright boy, second in his class."

"Very bright. Straight As all the way from seventh grade."

Byron whistled. "Not too shabby. Tell me more."

Bonnie locked eyes with her former student. "Cut the crap, Byron. I was one of a couple dozen high school teachers who taught Leo Quinn. Have you called any of them in?"

"Not yet."

"Sooooo, why am I being singled out?"

Byron reddened and turned his attention to Armen. "Any chance at all of her just answering my questions without making me feel like I'm back in ninth grade?"

Armen cocked his head as if he were judging Bonnie's emotional barometer. "I wouldn't count on it."

"Stop stalling, youngster," Bonnie said. "Why am I here?"

Byron reached into a drawer of his desk and pulled out a ziplock bag. It contained a swatch of lined paper. Byron pushed the baggie across the desk. "You recognize this?"

Strangely enough, she did. She even remembered

giving the paper containing her name and phone number to Leo Quinn at his graduation. *Another bit of good intention that didn't fail to bare its teeth and bite me on the derriere.*

"I recognize the damn thing. What of it?"

"We found it in Leo's pants pocket. Not in his wallet, mind you, but in his pants. The boy either called you recently or was meaning to."

Bonnie took several breaths to settle her temper. It wouldn't do her cause any good to lay into Byron for intimating she was a liar. If she were in his size twelve Nikes, she'd make the same assumptions.

"He never called. I haven't heard from him."

Though Byron nodded, Bonnie was unsure if he was merely moving on with his questioning or really believed her.

Screw you, Deputy Hickman. She gave Byron the frosty smile she usually reserved for students she wanted to throw from a precipice.

Byron tapped on the baggie. "Do you have any idea why he might have wanted to talk to you?"

Her first thought was to reply with something sarcastic, but she thought better of it. Leo Quinn was dead. She needed to do anything she could to help. "No idea."

Byron nodded again, clearly unsatisfied with her answer. "Do you know of anyone who might wish Quinn harm?"

"Only about half of East Plains."

IRRATIONAL NUMBERS

"You got my attention."

Bonnie peered at Byron, wondering how he could have lived in East Plains in 2001 and not heard of Leo Quinn.

Although there was that pesky business at the World Trade Center.

She decided to give Byron the benefit of the doubt. "To really appreciate the turd Leo threw into everyone's punch bowl, you need to know the kind of unique individual Leo Quinn was."

"To be salutatorian, he had to be some kind of special."

"He was. But that's not all. He'd played varsity basketball since he was a sophomore, lettering all three years and taking the team to state in his senior year. President of his class both as a junior and a senior."

"Sounds like an exceptional young man. Did you know him well?"

Bonnie nodded absently. *Did anyone really know Leo Quinn well?*

"I'm not finished. The boy rode in the homecoming parade and was on the royal court for all four of his high school years, was the homecoming king as a senior. Not to mention prom king that same year—took Seneca Berringer, the most popular girl in the school and valedictorian. His selection as a salutatorian was only natural. A lot of people thought he, and not Seneca, should have been valedictorian."

"I heard he went a little crazy at graduation?"

So you did hear what happened. Stop playing games with me, Byron.

Bonnie gave him an icy stare. "Depends on how you define *crazy*. Some people believed what Leo did might have been one of his saner moments. Certainly, it was one of his braver."

Bonnie peered down at her hands while she gathered her thoughts. This promenade down memory lane was proving harder than she thought it would be, if for no other reason than what had ultimately happened to this wonder boy.

God damn you, Leo. Why the hell didn't you get your thin ass out of East Plains?

"On the day of graduation, I was in my classroom. I think I was putting the finishing touches on a few presents I had to wrap. Anyway, someone knocked at my door. I opened it to find Leo standing there. I'd never seen him so flushed, so agitated."

A sudden thought brought Bonnie up short. Ben, her late husband, had been with her cooling his heels until the ceremony in the gym. The first signs of the cancer that would ultimately kill him were just starting to raise their ugly little heads.

"Bon? You okay?" Armen asked.

Bonnie blinked at the question. "Yeah, I'm fine. Anyway, Leo told me what he meant to do, and why dropping his bombshell in such a public venue was important. In the months leading up to graduation, we'd grown close; you could even say we were confidants. Not that he was asking my permission or even soliciting advice. He'd already made up his mind."

"What did you think of his decision?" Byron's blank expression betrayed nothing.

Again, Bonnie wanted to throw something at Byron for playing the innocent. He obviously knew about Leo and what transpired that long-ago day.

Okay, you little shit-head. We'll go on playing this game. "I disagreed with it. I asked him if he'd told his father. His mother being long since dead."

"Had he?"

Bonnie shook her head. "Leo just smiled. *You kidding?* he said. *Dad would have to blow something up, probably with me strapped to it.* Leo got this faraway look. He damn well knew what was about to happen between him and the father who had been so proud of him."

"What did happen?"

"As far as I know, Alf Quinn hasn't spoken to the boy since that day. Leo moved in with an ailing uncle, who I believe eventually died."

"What about the speech itself? Was it the bombshell everyone says it was?"

"You have no idea. Leo started in with thanking everyone for all they'd done for him. He talked about the future, colleges, careers, all the standard stuff. Then with a shaky voice, he said, *I need to tell all of you something I should have told you years ago. I'm gay.* Two words that changed everything, in not only his life, but the lives of dozens of other people. You could have heard a pin drop. I think a lot of people were waiting for Leo to start laughing like he'd told a joke and was going to take it all back. Instead, he picked up his speech, straightened the pages, and walked out of the gym."

CHAPTER 2

BONNIE GAVE BYRON A KNOWING SMILE. "I DON'T NEED to tell you how much emotion a place like East Plains invests in its local heroes. Small towns can teach Gila monsters a thing or two about how to hold on and not let go. Hell, youngster, fifteen years ago you were a golden boy."

"Thanks, Missus P, but even on my best days I wasn't in Leo Quinn's league. But I know what you mean. I have baseball fans buying me drinks to this day—remembering scores of games I've long ago forgotten." Byron chewed on his lower lip. "I got to tell you, a lot of East Plains' ideals went belly-up when Leo came out of the closet. Folks looked on that graduation announcement as a betrayal."

"You think?" Bonnie remembered the stunned silence, the incredulous stares, first at the podium then at one another. The disbelief that quickly turned to anger. "Back in Leo's senior year, when the basketball team went to state, we closed school early, took three school buses up to Denver—two for the kids, one for the fans in the community. Even when we lost, no one blamed Leo. East Plains loved that boy. For that type of loyalty, people expect things of their heroes. Telling the world you're gay in your graduation speech isn't on the menu."

Byron drew in a long breath and let it out through his teeth. "Those same good citizens ended up hating him—hating him enough that three years later maybe one of them killed him."

Bonnie pursed her lips. "You don't have to go back three years to find folks willing to do ragged mischief on homosexuals—not in East Plains, not in a lot of small towns. You've lived around here long enough to know what I'm talking about."

"Normally, I'd agree with you." Byron shook his head slowly. "Not this time. Not the weird way it went down."

Bonnie wasn't sure she should ask the next question. Did she really want to know? Her voice had a mind of its own. "How did Leo die?"

Byron hesitated so long Bonnie felt he might not answer. "We found him out on Squirrel Creek Road. You know that stretch going toward Pueblo?"

Bonnie nodded, cognizant Byron wasn't really looking for an answer, just an excuse to keep talking. Now was not the time to interrupt with a geography question.

Byron inhaled deeply, then let the breath go with a sigh. "Someone, probably several someones, stripped him down."

"Naked?" Armen asked.

"As a mole rat. The funny thing is, they folded his clothes, his pants, and his shirt, even stuffed his socks into his shoes. Made a neat little pile."

"That's just bizarre." Bonnie could picture the scene. A remote stretch of dirt road. A pickup full of drunks. What she couldn't fathom was what Leo was doing out on Squirrel Creek. Maybe his murderers snatched him somewhere else and took him there. You couldn't ask for a more isolated place to do dirty work.

But what the hell is up with the folded clothes? Did they play some sort of game with him before they killed him?

"What did they do to him, Byron?" Bonnie heard the strain in her voice but was beyond caring. "What the hell did the cowards do once they humiliated him?"

Armen pulled her close. "Maybe we shouldn't ask."

She shrugged out of his embrace. "I have to. I need to know."

Byron glanced from Armen back to Bonnie. "They tied him to a section of barbed wire, like that kid up in Montana, or was it Wyoming?"

"Matthew Shepard," Armen offered.

"Yeah," Byron agreed absently. "But different from the Shepard case. There's no evidence of beating. Don't get me wrong. Leo struggled and has bruises to prove it. And you don't get stripped and tied to barbed wire without getting cut up, but nothing on his face, no contusions, no black eyes, no bloody nose."

"Real gentlemen." Bonnie spat the words. "I guess that brings me back to my first question. How did Leo die?"

"Three shots to the chest. A tight pattern around the heart."

Bonnie clutched the cup of black coffee like she wanted to strangle it. Open on her breakfast island were four yearbooks—the Leo Quinn years.

Armen licked his thumb and turned a page. "Camera certainly loved the lanky son of a buck. He has . . . had a Jimmy Stewart quality—chewed up the scenery even in still photographs."

In frozen images, the evolution of a small town hero played out—pimply faced freshman to handsome young man ready to take on the world. Memories masquerading as photographs. Winter Spirit Week—Leo dressed as a cheerleader kick-stepping with the basketball squad. Leo, his face covered in whipped cream after a pie-eating contest. Leo dancing with Seneca Berringer. Leo dribbling a basketball staring steely-eyed into the camera.

The senior yearbook might as well have been titled the Quinn Edition. *Oh, God, we loved you, Mister Quinn. Did we love you to death?*

The truth of her musing struck Bonnie full in the face. Or was it the heart? If Leo hadn't been the golden boy, he never would have been at that podium, never given that ill-advised speech. For that matter, if he hadn't been the embodiment of East Plains' hopes and dreams, no one would have given a rat's furry derriere about his preferences, sexual or otherwise.

Don't kid yourself, Pinkwater. There would have still been those who would have despised him—just maybe not as much.

"And why in hell did you have my name and number in your pocket?" The whispered question was out of Bonnie's mouth, like it needed to be heard out loud.

And answered.

"I've been thinking the same thing myself," Armen said. "Byron's right, you know? Leo Quinn was at least toying with the idea of contacting you."

Bonnie couldn't deny the high probability. "I guess what's drilling a hole in my psyche is why. After three years, why would Leo Quinn decide to call me?"

"Then get murdered before he does it." The thought was heartbreaking. "Maybe we're jumping too fast here, Mister Mouse. There's got to be an explanation that doesn't lead to Leo Quinn considering a hypothetical phone call to his old math teacher."

"Sure." The look on Armen's face couldn't exactly be interpreted as skeptical. Even the sound of his voice would make a stranger think he agreed with her.

But he didn't fool Bonnie. "I'm full of crap, ain't I?"

Armen showed her a centimeter gap between his thumb and index finger. "Only a little."

"Okay, okay, try this one. Our clothes-folding murderers go through Leo's wallet and find the scrap of paper with my name and number. To throw off the police, they transfer the paper to Leo's pocket, knowing the cops'll find it and have to haul me in." She'd been avoiding Armen's stare. Now she risked a glance. "How am I doing?"

Armen's expression was noncommittal. "Go on."

Cut me some slack, lover. "You got to admit, an hour spent interrogating me is an hour not spent looking for the real killers. Plus, it muddies the motive waters."

"How so?"

Bonnie could feel the soil gathering near her armpits as she dug herself deeper and deeper.

In for a penny.

"On the face of it, we have a hate crime. Now Byron has to consider another possibility. He has to figure me into the mix." She fixed Armen with a direct stare, daring him to refute her.

Armen nodded slowly, but without conviction. "A

nice theory, but it all starts with a redneck shooting a homosexual."

"I don't see—"

Armen held up a silencing hand. "Yeah, you do, Bon. You detest the thought Leo was killed senselessly, but that's likely the case. Now put yourself in the killer's pointy-toed boots. I don't care how isolated Squirrel Creek Road is. You just fired a gun not once, but three times, after spending a good ten minutes stripping and tying your gay victim to a fence. Unless you got ice water in your veins, you're looking over your shoulder right about now. The best thing you can do to save your homophobic rear end is to skedaddle."

Bonnie didn't have the energy to defend a hypothesis she herself had trouble believing. "I could bring up the possibility our clothes-folding killers had found the paper before they killed Leo, but I won't. Occam's razor demands we consider the simplest explanation."

"Leo put the note in his own pocket."

She nodded in resignation. "Leo put the note there himself."

Bonnie flipped a page in the senior yearbook. "Damn, damn, damn."

"What?"

She stabbed a photo with her finger. Mugging for the camera, Leo had his arm around Seneca Berringer. The girl's hand was poised over Leo's head making rabbit ears.

Bonnie let the bittersweet memory take her away. She could hear Seneca's laughter. Smell her perfume.

You sweet girl, how are you holding up? Did you keep in touch with Leo?

The last Bonnie heard, Seneca had married some cowboy, a bull rider from over in Punkin Center. The match made sense, considering Seneca herself was a champion barrel racer.

Absently, Bonnie let her eyes sweep over the calendar hanging by the sink. She'd blocked off the dates of the El Paso County Fair, half-intending to go. Armen had never been to a rodeo, and tomorrow night was barrel racing.

"Mister Mouse, I would consider it an honor if you would join me for a hefty slice of Americana pie."

When her clock went off Monday morning, Bonnie was tempted to throw the damn thing against the wall. Instead, she hammered it into submission, then peered at Big Ben, blearily trying to focus.

Six thirty.

Back in May, it seemed like such a great idea to teach an accelerated Women in Mathematics class to gifted high school students. Now that the end of July had come, Bonnie would gladly have endured a high colonic if she could just have one more hour of sleep.

Dear God, what was I thinking?

"At least you get to stay in bed." She rolled over to give Armen a kiss.

His side of the bed was empty. The memory of last night's reasonable decision—which didn't seem so reasonable in the light of day—came flooding back. Armen had gone home. After all, she had to work, and he didn't. She wouldn't see him until tonight when he picked her up for the fair.

In disgust, she threw back her duvet and swung her feet over the side of her water bed. Hypatia nuzzled against her leg. Absently, Bonnie stroked the dog's silky fur.

"Hypatia, my love. Stupid as it sounds, I miss him. How could one man, in such a short time, wheedle his way so far into this hard heart of mine?"

The golden retriever snorted as if to say, *It does sound stupid. You got me. What more do you need?*

Bonnie roused herself and stood. "You're right. I am a capable, fully functioning, independent woman. And I have a class to teach."

Bonnie finished taking attendance and set down the computer sheets. She sat atop one of the student desks in her room.

"All right, here's the deal. Because we have a limited amount of time, I've boiled down our fun and games to six female mathematicians." Bonnie let a smile creep onto her face. "But they're good ones. Another decision I've made on your behalf is that I'm not going tell you their names."

As she expected, the announcement elicited excitement and side talk. Like a wave at an athletic event, energy swept through her baker's dozen of brilliant female students.

Let it grab hold of you, cuties.

"We're talking about a scavenger hunt, using any method at your disposal—the Internet, reference help at the library, whatever. Shoot, I don't care if you work in teams, but here's the deal. By this time tomorrow, I expect you to deduce the names of all six mathematicians. If you're interested in extra credit, pick one of them and do a report."

She sat back. Silent, and not-so-silent alliances were established across the room.

"Wanna team up?"

"My dad's got math history books."

"We can go over to my house after school."

Bonnie clapped her hands. "All right, here's your first clue."

She wrote *France* at the top of her chalkboard. Next to this she wrote *1706–1749*. "The first of our mathematicians was married to a French nobleman, making her a marquise in her own right. But neither this nor the brilliant mathematics and science she produced is how she is remembered. Before the ink on her marriage license dried, she became the lover of none other than Voltaire."

Titters of laughter erupted.

Gotcha.

From long experience, Bonnie knew if she could either make her students laugh or connect her subject matter to an area of fascination, in this case sex, she had them. In one stroke, she'd done both.

Below *France,* Bonnie wrote *Greece fourth century* A.D. "Ready for your second clue?"

A chorus of high-pitched voices complained that she hadn't written all the first clues on the blackboard.

Bonnie turned back around and stared at the near empty board. "You know, I believe you're right. Whatever are you going to do about that?"

Writing furiously, they began to exchange information.

After about a minute, Bonnie tapped on the board. "Clue number two."

Pens in hand, they stared at her with their unlined upturned faces.

"Here goes. Our Greek mathematician, legend has it, was the product of eugenics."

Hands shot up requesting a definition of *eugenics* and its spelling.

She wrote the word on the board and underlined it. "Eugenics is the science of selective breeding. Theoretically, our mathematician was the end result of generations of controlled reproduction. She was a designed human being—designed to be brilliant, beautiful, strong, and articulate. Like Mary Poppins, she was practically perfect. And like most perfect human beings this planet has produced, someone murdered her. What makes her different is that the person who ordered her death was one of the first popes of the Catholic Church."

From the back of the room, a thin black girl whispered, "Cool."

Again, Bonnie waited while they scrambled to write down their collective thoughts. This time they were quicker. Bonnie was always amazed at the adaptability of the human species, especially the young.

She wrote *Germany* followed by *1882–1935*. "Ready?"

Every head nodded yes.

"Our next genius had to flee her native Germany. She was Jewish, and at times, this normally civilized country turns from Jekyll to Hyde. Our mathematician and her family came to the United States, only to find that discrimination could speak English as well as German. Overcoming extreme prejudice, this time sexist discrimination, she eventually taught mathematics at Princeton."

Next came *Scotland* and *1780–1872*.

When everyone signaled their readiness, Bonnie began. "This woman astounded the mathematical community of England, first for her brilliance, then a second time when it was learned she was self-taught. At a time when education was thought to be detrimental to the health and well-being of females, this particular female taught herself to read Latin, even before she could adequately read in her native tongue. Her parents were so upset by this turn of events they sought to put an end to her self-education by first denying her heat and light in her bedroom. When this didn't work, they took away her clothing. When that didn't work, they married her off to an uneducated man who barely tolerated reading, let alone mathematics."

A blond girl front and center raised her hand. "How did she get around that?"

Keeping a smile from her face, Bonnie replied, "She outlived him and inherited his fortune."

To a girl, Bonnie's students nodded their approval of this solution.

Bonnie wrote *Italy 1718–1789* on the board.

"This lady could speak five languages by the time she was nine years of age. Her father was a university professor, and she entertained his learned guests with her knowledge of mathematics, science, philosophy, politics, and art. Although she did most of her work in geometry, she is best known because a single word from one of her manuscripts was mistranslated. Because of this error, later generations would mistakenly believe she was a satanist."

Bonnie wrote *Russia* and *1850–1891*.

"It was reported that the last of our women learned mathematics initially because of wallpaper. Whether by design or just because he was too cheap to purchase real wallpaper, our mathematician's father papered her bedroom with copies of Isaac Newton's manuscript pages delineating integral and differential calculus. She spent hours poring over the strange symbols on her bedroom wall. When she was old enough to attend university, our mathematician showed a facility for analysis she attributed to the time she spent studying, not just in her room, but studying her room itself."

Bonnie stifled a yawn and returned to the desk she'd been sitting on earlier. "We're going to quit early today, so you can get started with your scavenger hunt. Before we go, I want to leave you with a parting thought. How many of you have read *Alice in Wonderland*?"

Bonnie wasn't surprised when no one raised a hand. "Well, you should. Lewis Carroll, whose real name was Charles Dodgson, was a mathematician."

Several students groaned as though she had just told a bad joke.

"Get over it. You might as well get used to the fact

I've got a one-track mind."

Bonnie opened a book she'd left lying on the seat of the desk. "The passage I'm going to read, really just one line, is the Red Queen talking to Alice. There aren't too many lines from literature that describe better the plight of the historic female striving to make it in the predominantly male-dominated field of mathematics."

You have to run as fast as you can just to stay in one place. If you want to actually get somewhere you must run twice as fast as that.

CHAPTER 3

WHEN THE LAST OF HER SCAVENGER HUNTERS HIGHtailed it out of her room, Bonnie collected her fanny pack and dragged her now even more tired body into the hall. She waved good-bye to the black girl—Emily, Bonnie recalled—who thought Hypatia's death was so *cool*.

"Remember, Emily, I'm a math teacher, and this is a math class. Don't just gather a lot of juicy history facts. Come back with at least a little math."

The girl nodded in that absentminded way teenagers do when they're giving you about 11 percent of their attention.

Give the girl a break, Pinkwater. It's summer, after all.

Bonnie checked her Mickey Mouse watch. 9:10.

Thank You, Jesus.

She still had most of the day. Maybe she'd give Armen a call.

"Bonnie," a shrill voice from behind her called. Marcie Englehart.

Oh God, oh God, oh God.

Before Bonnie could consider any possible evasive action, the school nurse was upon her, hard into Bonnie's space, perfume and cigarette breath at twelve o'clock.

"I thought I heard your voice." Her gray-blond hair and pink cheeks not six inches away, Marcie trapped Bonnie against her classroom door. "You must be a glutton for punishment, Pinkwater. Didn't anybody tell you school doesn't start for three more weeks?"

Marcie's horsey laugh culminated in a snort.

Bonnie didn't think Marcie really gave a good Goddamn about a summer math history class, so she didn't attempt to explain her presence at the school. Besides, an explanation would only extend the torture.

"Hi, Marcie."

Bonnie slipped past the woman to the relative expanse of the open hall. "I could ask you the same thing. What's the school nurse doing at an empty school?" Bonnie immediately regretted the question. No telling what avenues of information Marcie would feel compelled to share now that Bonnie had primed the pump.

Without warning, the nurse poked Bonnie in the forehead with her index finger.

What the hell?

"Earth to Bonnie," Marcie said. "I sent you an e-mail in May. Today's the day of the sport physicals. We had a couple of docs in here from the Springs. Checked out the kids. Got them all set up for fall sports."

Bonnie rubbed her forehead, wanting to smack the odious woman. She thought better of it and concentrated on making her escape. "I remember. Well, listen, I got to fly. Going to the El Paso County Fair." No need to tell this forehead-poking harpy she wasn't going until six o'clock that night.

None of her damn business anyway.

Bonnie hadn't gone three paces when Marcie's voice froze her in her tracks. "Too bad about Lloyd."

Every molecule in Bonnie's being screamed that she keep going, run in fact. To say that Marcie was the school's gossipmonger was akin to saying Hurricane Katrina was a bit of bad weather. The woman had inroads to information that would astound the CIA.

But Principal Lloyd Whittaker was perhaps Bonnie's best friend on the planet. Against her better judgment, she asked, "What about Lloyd?"

Marcie actually smacked her lips in preparation of dishing some juicy dirt. "So you haven't heard?"

Now the woman was playing with her. "No, Marcie, I haven't heard."

"Well, I was at the Stop and Go day before yesterday, when who should pull up in that old pickup of his but our fearless leader himself." Marcie chewed her lower lip in a transparent effort to look concerned. "The man looked awful. Eyes red and puffy. Lips cracked. Face all white and gray stubble. Ratty old T-shirt with tomato sauce stains—"

"I get the picture, Marcie. Lloyd has shamelessly let himself go. But what harm is there in that? The man's on vacation, for Pete's sake."

"I said the same thing to myself, but I still put out a few feelers, asked a few questions of some friends."

Marcie's clearinghouse of *friends* was legendary. She could give Sherlock Holmes's Baker Street Irregulars a run for their dinero.

"And?"

"And, it's Marjorie. She hasn't been around East Plains all summer. Not in church. Not at any cookouts. Not at women's softball. Not even at any of her bridge clubs."

This last revelation struck home. Lloyd's wife, Marjorie, was addicted to bridge, played in no less than four clubs. "Maybe there's been a family emergency."

Marcie shook her head in slow, seemingly sad arcs. "You know Vickie O'Malley?"

"Pastor's wife at the Baptist church?"

"That's her. She was at the city market, the one over in Henshaw, where Marjorie works? Anyway, Vickie asked about Marjorie and was told she quit and moved up to Denver. Been gone since the beginning of June."

Bonnie cast about for an explanation to toss back at Marcie—anything that would deny that Lloyd and Marjorie were having trouble.

Before she could voice a possibility, Marcie shut her down. "She's gone, Bon. Marjorie has left Lloyd. And the man is falling apart."

Bonnie hopped in Alice, The-Little-Subaru-That-Could, and turned on her cell phone. With any luck, she might be able to catch Lloyd at home. A blinking envelope icon told her she had a message.

She punched in the icon. "Missus Pinkwater, this is Alf Quinn. I need to talk to you. Come on by the range."

Same old Alf. No wasted words. No—*if you got the time*. Not even a *please*. It was a wonder Leo hadn't had a falling-out with his dad long before he did.

Bonnie knew she'd end up going. What else was she supposed to do? Say, *I'm too busy* to the grieving father of a murdered son?

But is he grieving?

Bonnie immediately rejected the question and its implied answer. Of course the rude bastard was grieving. Probably even more so if he never patched things up with Leo.

Oh, what the hell.

The Quinn place was only a couple of miles from the school anyway, in a remote section of East Plains. And *remote* was the operative word. Alf, or as he called himself, Rattlesnake, ran what might be considered a shooting range and paintball course. He also gave demonstrations of exotic weapons—jeep-mounted machine guns, fifty-millimeter cannons, miniguns that fired nine thousand rounds a minute.

The man was a legend. *And the father of a dead homosexual boy*, Bonnie reminded herself.

At the corner of Highway 84 and Jackson Road, in the shade of a Russian olive tree, stood an oaken sign with the words *Rattlesnake's Shootin' Range*.

Bonnie turned Alice's nose down Jackson. Immediately, washboard ridges shook the ancient Subaru until Bonnie thought either it or she would fall to pieces. Little by little the rattle of the car was joined by the rat-a-tat of automatic weapons. Before she reached the turnoff onto Rattlesnake Road, the gunfire ceased.

"The range is cold," a familiar voice sounded over a loudspeaker. "Place your weapon on the table in front of you. Please do not fire while the red flag is hoisted."

Bonnie turned the dirt-road corner and pulled in front of a white stucco office. Six-inch green letters declared this, indeed, was the world-famous Rattlesnake's Shootin' Range.

As soon as Bonnie exited her car, she saw Alf Rattlesnake Quinn standing hands-on-hips. He was about a hundred feet away, but he was hard to miss. At six-six he towered over the gaggle of grade school children behind the tables of the firing line. On the closest table lay a half-dozen firearms.

Alf removed his military-style baseball cap and scratched his bald pate. "What we got here is the newest generation of noise suppressors, what the movies call silencers."

Rattlesnake replaced his hat and picked up a pistol with a cylinder affixed to its muzzle. He waited until the red flag was lowered, then drew a bead on a target fifty yards away.

"Listen." He squeezed the trigger.

Bonnie expected at least a puff à la gangster movies. Instead the gun seemed to whistle. The click of the trigger was louder than the discharge of the gun. She was impressed.

Rattlesnake held up the pistol and, with a press of a button, released the magazine into his hand. "Custom-designed technology allows even more of the muzzle noise to be masked."

As she trudged closer, Bonnie began to make out falsetto questions.

"Who makes better ammo, us or the Russians? My dad says the Russian stuff is crap."

"How come we had to wear those ear protectors?"

"How many tattoos do you have?"

"You said the minigun fires nine thousand rounds a minute. How many is that a second?"

Bonnie strode up and stood in their midst. "That's

one hundred fifty rounds a second or one round every point zero zero six seven seconds." She made a point of emphasizing the *zero zero*.

Every face turned in her direction, including Alf's. "Ladies and gents, this here is Missus Bonnie Pinkwater. She's one of the math teachers at East Plains, and if you ask me, the best of the bunch."

Bonnie offered Alf a grateful smile, already regretting her earlier assessment of this shameless flatterer. "Thank you, kind sir."

"You had my brother last year," said a chubby freckle-faced girl with an almost spherical head. "Bobby Raintree."

Several other children chimed in with relatives who populated her classes in the recent past.

"Whoa, slow down, you guys." She turned her attention to Alf. "What is all this?" She waved a hand in the general direction of the round-headed girl.

Before Alf could answer, Miss Roundhead piped, "We're from the day camp. Tomorrow we're going swimming."

From the girl's tone, Bonnie had no doubt that if the girl had her way they'd be swimming right at this moment rather than at a dusty old shooting range.

A boy, who could have been the girl's brother, shook his equally round head in disagreement of this unspoken assessment. "Paintball is way cooler than swimming."

Robert Spiller

The girl stuck her tongue out at the boy.

Alf's smile never dimmed despite this minor melee. "Every two weeks we get a different group from the Rec Center. I was just showing them some weapons and the firing line before we suit them up for paintball. We'll only be another couple of minutes. I want to show them a few more pieces. Why don't you wait for me in the office?" He pointed with his chin back the way she'd come.

He turned back toward the firing line leaving Bonnie staring at the two words he had tattooed at the base of his shaved skull—*Semper Fi*.

Rattlesnake's office was as messy as his firing line had been neat. Spent brass casings littered the floor. The barrel of an air-cooled machine gun lay diagonally across a stained desk blotter, which in turn sat askew on a gray metal desk. A black military stencil declared the desk to be *Property of Camp Pendleton*. Propped against the wall, looking like it might teeter and fall any minute, was the windshield of a Jeep.

Kicking through the brass, Bonnie made her way to the only seat in the room, a matching gray rolling chair behind the desk. As she sat, she noticed two framed pictures. Dressed in olive drab military fatigues, Alf Quinn had his son in a headlock. They were both mugging for the camera, their tongues protruding, their eyes wide.

Happier times, Bonnie thought. The picture had to be at least five years old—pre-graduation-declaration. *Definitely happier times.*

The other picture showed Leo and Seneca Berringer, her in a powder blue sleeveless gown, a white corsage wrapped about her wrist—a prom picture.

Bonnie was musing over Alf's decision to display the second photo, when the big man himself walked in.

His broad shoulders filled the doorway. "At ease, smoke 'em if you got 'em." He laughed and signaled her to stay seated.

Bonnie squinted up at Alf, wondering how much longer he intended to keep up the façade of the jovial host. *Your boy is dead, Rattlesnake. It's okay to show it.* "Got your message."

Alf removed his cap and scratched his head as if he was somehow lost in his own office. He pointed with his chin toward the photographs. "Loved that girl. Thought Seneca and Leo would end up together, make me a few grandbabies. Take over the range when I took to the rocker."

He chuckled mirthlessly and leaned two-fisted onto the desk. "I guess that's what I get for thinking."

For one horrific moment, Bonnie was convinced this Gibraltar of a man might break down, then he inhaled mightily and recovered. "Since they were kids, they were inseparable. Used to drive me nuts the way they were always underfoot around the range."

From the sound of his voice and the faraway look in his eye, Bonnie could tell the man was painting the scene in the sepia tints of fond memories.

"They played on the range?" she asked, immediately picturing buffaloes.

Alf shrugged. "Only behind the tables, although as they got older I let them do some shooting as well." Alf shook his shaved head as if to bring himself back into the land of the here and now. "Leo called me last Thursday."

Bonnie sat upright and gave Alf her full attention. "How'd that go?"

"I was an asshole, as per usual. I handed the phone over to Oscar, one of my managers." Alf slammed a meaty paw down on the desk. "I should have spoken with my boy."

You poor bastard. A prisoner of your own persona.

Bonnie remembered the slip of paper in Leo's pocket. "What did Leo want to talk to you about?"

Alf blinked at her and slowly shook his head. "He wouldn't tell Oscar over the phone. Said he was coming by"—the big man paused as if a thought had struck him momentarily insensate—"today. Even with me acting like I had a stick up my ass, Leo was coming by to talk to his knucklehead of an old man. Would have been here today."

Now the big man's breathing was coming in short rasps. *Any moment he's going to lose it.*

To her shame, Bonnie wanted no part of Alfred Rattlesnake Quinn's breakdown. She groped for something to say. "I think Leo meant to get a hold of me as well." She told him of the paper in Leo's pocket, successfully avoiding how she obtained this information or how Leo died.

Alf stared as if he were looking right through her. "I think it was a nine millimeter."

At first Bonnie had no idea what the man was referring to. Then she understood what he was seeing with that glassy stare. "You mean the shots . . ." Bonnie couldn't finish the sentence.

"That killed him." Alf nodded. "Three to the heart. They were only going to let me see his face, identify who he was, but I made them show me his wounds. Tight pattern. A steady hand."

Alf stretched out his arm, eyeing his own hand, which wasn't nearly so steady. He crossed the room and drew a pistol from a holster hanging on a coatrack.

"Whoever killed my boy, he was just like me." He smacked the barrel of the pistol hard against his chest. "Knew his way around a gun."

He pulled back the barrel, feeding a round into the chamber. "Did they really think it would be that easy? Kill my boy and then just waltz away?"

Time to go, boys and girls. "Listen, Alf. I've got some

45

errands—"

"Not yet." The big man looked at the pistol in his hand as if someone else had placed it there.

"Sorry." He placed the gun on the desk. "I need to ask you something."

Bonnie's mind raced, wondering what this giant Looney Tune of a man wanted to quiz her about. She hoped to God she knew the right answer.

She had to swallow before she could speak. "Yeah?"

"Leo's funeral is the day after tomorrow. It would mean a lot to me if you would give the eulogy."

CHAPTER 4

THE EULOGY? BONNIE TURNED ONTO HIGHWAY 84. *There's a land mine waiting for someone to trip over. A land mine with Bonnie Pinkwater spray painted on the side.*

What bothered her most was Alf's choice of a minister—Harold T. Dobbs. No one ever suggested the T in his name stood for *tolerance*.

Truth be told, the pastor of the Saved by the Blood Pentecostal Tabernacle had a burr under his saddle when it came to homosexuals. Last spring, he'd led a contingent of the SBTBPT faithful to a Colorado Springs high school when that errant learning establishment had the temerity to consider a gay student club.

Standing with bullhorn in hand, Harold had put in a full day lambasting students and faculty alike.

"Fags go to hell!"

"God hates homosexuals!"

"An abomination in His eyes!"

"Gays are godless!"

Bonnie, who had taken a mere half day off from school to view the spectacle, had to admit the alliteration in *Gays are godless* had a catchy, almost hip-hop ring to it.

I'd give it an eighty-six, Jerry. You can dance to it.

Unfortunately, she hadn't been able to remain a spectator for long. She'd challenged the good pastor on his Jesus' compassion coefficient. She and Harold then enjoyed a major skirmish—even had their ten seconds of fame when the Colorado Springs/Pueblo news station, KCOL, aired the two of them, both red-faced, shouting at one another.

And damn, I certainly hadn't extended any olive branches when I sent Harold that gold-engraved invitation to the Gay Pride Parade in downtown Colorado Springs.

Now she was supposed to share a podium with the damnable, stick-up-the-rear end, son of a buck. Every permutation she could imagine of that eventuality played out as a disaster.

Still, she could halfway see Alf's logic in choosing Harold. The pastor's son, Jason, had been Leo's best friend all through high school. Point guard to Leo's forward. Leo and Jason had double-dated at the prom.

Last Bonnie had heard, Jason was running the summer Bible camp for the Saved by the Blood folks. She couldn't imagine Jason's calling mixing comfortably with Leo's revelations.

Would Jason even come to the funeral?

She reached for her phone. Armen could get her thinking of something other than funerals and maniacs. She hit his number on her speed dial.

Busy.

Damn.

Since she had the phone out already, she called up Lloyd on the speed dial. Even as the phone rang, first one then two times, she could picture her good friend sitting in a dark room, maybe drinking, deliberately not picking up. His answering machine kicked in. Marjorie's melodic voice encouraged Bonnie to leave a message.

". . . we promise we'll get right back to you."

As soon as the beep finished, Bonnie said, "I know you're there, Lloyd. This is Bonnie. You can either pick up, or I'm coming by. I'm not five minutes from your house."

When there was still no answer, she turned Alice's nose toward Lloyd's place.

Two minutes later—she'd sped just a tad—Bonnie found herself staring with halfhearted satisfaction at Lloyd's truck.

At least the man's vehicle is in residence.

Bonnie quick-stepped to her principal's front door and gave assault—rapping hard five times and after a two-second interval having at it again. She stepped back to see if perhaps Lloyd was peering at her from behind a side-window curtain. Sure enough, a jaundiced eye met hers.

"You might as well let me in, Lloyd. I'm not going away until we talk."

She could swear she heard a groan as the small aperture in the curtain closed. An eternity later, the front door opened a crack. "Bonnie? What in God's name are you doing here?"

"Lloyd Whittaker, are you going to just let me stand here like some sort of salesman? Invite me in, for Pete's sake."

With a reluctance you couldn't cut with a Ginsu, Lloyd opened wide the door.

"Forgive the mess," he grumbled.

A mess hardly described the family room. Pizza boxes, most with hard-curled slices stuck to their bottoms, were stacked in high, random piles. Empty, ripped-open cardboard twelve-packs of Coors and Bud—mute testimony of Lloyd's impatience to sample the contents—were everywhere. Crushed cans, like aluminum commas, punctuated the remaining space.

Bonnie tiptoed through the rubble and began collecting the dead soldiers.

Head down like a child caught reading a dirty book, Lloyd followed behind doing the same.

In the kitchen, Bonnie located a box of large garbage sacks. With an efficiency born of practice, she popped open a bag, dumped her burden, and held the sack for Lloyd.

Her longtime friend refused to meet her eyes as he

IRRATIONAL NUMBERS

unloaded his armload of boxes.

Bonnie wrinkled her nose. "You, sir, stink. Go grab a shower. I'll finish cleaning up and then we can talk." She took his elbow and walked him to the bathroom.

Without complaint, Lloyd let himself be led. At the door, he turned back, leaning on the jamb. "Thanks, Bon."

She reddened at the naked gratitude in her friend's face. "Yeah, yeah, just don't forget to shave. You look like a Santa Claus wannabe."

Lloyd smiled for the first time since her arrival. "Woman, you're not one to pull punches, are you?"

She returned the smile. "You've never been someone who's needed me to. Now get. You're giving smelly a bad name."

He shut the door.

Twenty minutes later, as she was tamping down the last of the pizza boxes in the fourth garbage sack, Bonnie heard the squeak of the bathroom door. She was tempted to take a gander, but resisted. The last thing Lloyd needed was to be caught bare-assed scurrying from his own bathroom.

By the time she'd returned from tossing the sacks, Lloyd was dressed and sitting on a raggedy overstuffed chair—a twin of the one in his school office. He'd even combed his hair.

He licked his lips, obviously ill at ease. "I suppose you've heard."

51

Bonnie nodded. "I had a confab with Marcie. I'd hoped it wasn't true."

"It's true."

She crossed the room and took Lloyd's hand. "How you holding up?"

A flicker of indecision passed over Lloyd's craggy face—the possible consideration of a lie. "Crappy pretty much covers it."

"I've never been a huge fan of crappy myself. You got a recovery plan that doesn't include barley, malt, and hops?"

Lloyd stared mutely up at her.

She squeezed his hand. "I'll take that for a no."

Using her other hand for leverage, Bonnie hoisted Lloyd to his feet. "You're coming with me."

Bonnie pulled up at her house. She'd fully intended to give Lloyd her full attention, to hear the Marjorie story in its entirety and be appropriately supportive. But when she mentioned Leo and realized Lloyd, who'd been holed up like a hermit, knew nothing of the boy's death, the floodgates opened. She was just beginning to tell of the trip to Rattlesnake's as she shut down the engine of Alice, The-Little-Subaru-That-Could.

"I'm sorry, boss. This was supposed to be your time."

Irrational Numbers

Lloyd shook his head. "Fact is, I'm not anxious to bare my soul just yet. I'm going to need to work up to it. But I am grateful for a chance to think about something else besides me and Marjorie. I can't believe Leo is dead. I remember that graduation like it was yesterday."

"I know what you mean." She snapped her fingers. "I almost forgot." She told him of Wednesday's funeral, the eulogy, and the Reverend Harold T. Dobbs.

Lloyd whistled. "That should be good. As I recall, you and the good pastor got a bit of history."

Bonnie popped open her door. "I'm glad you think it's so funny. Me, I'd rather be bent over a pool table and spanked with a rusty colander than face that man again." She led Lloyd through her garage into the house.

"I've never seen you play duck and cover with anyone. I'll bet there's a part of you that can't wait to mix it up with old Harold."

Bonnie turned on the bank of houselights. Immobile as an Egyptian statue, Euclid sat in the long hall.

Lloyd leaned close to Bonnie. "Don't take this wrong, Bon," he whispered, "but that cat gives me the creeps."

Bonnie scooped the Burmese into her arms and rubbed her face into his ebony fur. "Don't listen to the mean old man, Euclid. He just doesn't understand royalty."

She pointed with her chin. "Go ahead into the kitchen, Lloyd. I'm going to let the dogs in."

Still holding Euclid to her face, she opened the wood and aluminum door to the dog run. Almost knocking her down, her three canine housemates bounded into the hall. Hopper, the black lab, and Lovelace, the border collie, ran past with scarcely a backward glance. Hypatia, the golden retriever, stopped and licked an offered hand.

"I love you, too, sweetie." Bonnie scrubbed her fist across the dog's head, stopping to softly stroke the pink scar behind the right ear.

In the kitchen, the collie and lab had surrounded Lloyd. They had him backed up against the breakfast island, each demanding a fair share of his affection and perhaps any food he might have hidden on his person. For his part, Lloyd was administering rough love in the form of gentle and not-so-gentle slaps to the dogs' jowls. He looked up from his play.

"You got a message."

The red light on the phone by the microwave was blinking. Bonnie set the cat on the breakfast island, crossed the room, and punched the message button.

After the whirr of the tape, she recognized Armen's voice. "Bon, I'm going to need to beg out of our date to the fair. Something has come up." Abruptly, he signed off.

Bonnie stared at the phone, more disappointed than she wanted to admit. *Doggone-it, he sounded strange.*

A red-faced Lloyd Whittaker tried to pretend he hadn't been eavesdropping.

"No big deal," Bonnie said. "We were just going to the El Paso County Fair."

Lloyd's expression carried just the right mixture of sympathy and casualness. He shrugged. "I ain't been to the fair yet this year. How 'bout we go together?"

Bonnie exhaled and released an increment of the tension she hadn't realized she'd been holding. She nodded her acceptance. "I would be honored, kind sir."

Bonnie slid off the camel and took back her cotton candy from Lloyd. "Now that's something you don't get to do every day. You should give it a try."

Lloyd took her elbow and led her past the petting zoo. "So is peeing on an electric fence, but I ain't got a hankering to do that, either. Besides, the dang things spit."

"Chicken."

Her principal shook his head. "Nope. Now, there's a chicken."

Behind a wire-mesh fence a gigantic rooster with a red cocks comb that covered most of its face stared malevolently.

"My God, the thing looks possessed." She dipped her head and took a sticky bite from her cotton candy.

"Keep your voice down," Lloyd whispered. "That critter is some little girl's pride and joy."

Sure enough, a chubby girl in long braids and flowered overalls gave Bonnie the evil eye. She grabbed Lloyd's arm and quick-stepped into the dusty throng of the fair. Soon they'd lost themselves in the crowd surrounding the twin lines of booths.

Her guilt monitor hummed, albeit subsonically. She knew she should be feeling at least a little bit melancholy. After all, a former student was dead and Lloyd was in the process of losing his wife of thirty-four years. The truth was, the only regret she owned at the moment was wishing she'd bought a funnel cake.

As far back as she could remember—and for her that meant almost into the womb—she loved county fairs. And for some reason, the El Paso County Fair never failed to make her positively giddy.

She'd checked the schedule at the gate. Besides the rodeo, this week the fair promised a demolition derby, a greased-pig competition, a pie-eating contest, bad hair and bad Hawaiian shirt judging, a wiener dog race, and a vintage car display.

The only problem was the heat. Bonnie's tie-dyed T-shirt—ALGEBRA: AN UNDERGARMENT FOR A MERMAID—clung to her like a second skin. *Ye gods, it's almost seven and still the temperature has to be close to ninety. How come these cow and horsey thingees are always so damn hot?*

"And how come you're not sweating?" she demanded of Lloyd.

"I'm an administrator. We don't sweat."

"Bull crap." She took a quick look-see to make sure no one in the crowd was listening to their conversation. "I've seen The Divine Pain in the Ass dripping like a cheap faucet. And he's the bull-goose administrator in these here parts, hombre." She dropped her chin, doing her best John Wayne.

Lloyd shook his head in mock frustration. "One of these days you're going to push that man too far and then—"

"And then what?" She giggled maliciously, remembering what she had called Superintendent Xavier Divine—to his face—when they'd last locked horns. "Will all the king's horses and all the king's men forget how to put that potato head back together again?"

Lloyd gave her a dirty look before his face broke into a full smile. "You got a mean streak, Pinkwater." He gave her a wink.

"You better believe it. Want a bite?" She offered the cotton candy.

"No, thanks." Lloyd shook his head. "You have a glob of purple stuck to the tip of your nose."

She made to wipe it off, then thought better of it. "I'll bet it makes me look adorable."

He squinted at her. "*Adorable*—you took the word right out of my mouth." Using the sleeve of his shirt, Lloyd wiped off the offending smear.

The act was so like something Ben, her dead husband would have done, it stopped Bonnie in her tracks. She studied Lloyd over the top of her cotton candy. What had this darling man done to make his wife take to the hills?

"What?" Lloyd asked.

"Nothing." She pointed with her nose toward the open-sided pavilion holding the vintage cars. "Look there."

A crowd of people—many wearing NASCAR and Pennzoil baseball caps—were gathered. In their midst stood Alf Rattlesnake Quinn holding court over a group of teenagers. At one point he slapped a tall man in a straw cowboy hat on the back. Both he and the man roared with laughter.

"Want to say hello?" Lloyd asked.

Bonnie thought only a moment before she shook her head. "I don't think so." There was something unsettling about Alf's laughter, something forced and artificial.

"You recognize the gent Rattlesnake's talking to?" Lloyd asked.

"I can't make him out from behind."

"Moses Witherspoon. The Spoonmaster himself."

Bonnie took a closer look. "Oh, my God. It *is* him. It's a wonder I don't have that young man's silhouette burned into my brain, considering all the crap he gave me over the years."

"He was a pistol, that's for sure."

Bonnie scanned the crowd, fully expecting to see

Dwight Furby in attendance. That young scalawag, who had been Witherspoon's shadow all through high school, was nowhere to be seen.

I guess the old Spoonmaster is flying solo tonight.

Bonnie checked her Mickey Mouse watch. "In about half an hour the rodeo starts. I want to catch the barrel racing."

"Since when are you a rodeo fan?" He led her toward the rodeo grounds.

Bonnie pulled herself to her full five-foot-three and adopted the indignant pose of the maligned. "I'll have you know, my skeptical friend, I am well acquainted with the various events that comprise today's modern rodeo. I can tell you the current and past professional barrel racing champions going back ten years."

Lloyd chuckled. "Very impressive. It seems Witherspoon isn't the only pistol at this fair. Bon, I got no doubt you memorized some facts about barrel racing, but that don't make you a fan. As I recall, a female math teacher in my employ once stated, *Rodeo is just an excuse for cowboys to get drunk*."

"That's all changed. Tonight, I intend to 'wahoo' with the best of them."

"Ain't you the best cowgirl at the fair?"

"You betcha. Now get a wiggle on."

At the covered stands, Lloyd and Bonnie climbed the twenty-five risers to the top tier. She plopped down and scanned the crowd below. Cowboys with numbers pinned on their western shirts walked hand in hand with girls wearing straw hats, square-dance skirts, and red bandannas. Out in the arena enclosure, rodeo clowns rolled in the barrels for the race.

"Okay, Missus Know-It-All," Lloyd said. "Tell me all about barrel racing."

Bonnie tugged at her ear, engaging the memory mechanism. She pointed at a wide gate at the far end of the arena. "Pay attention and learn something. The racers, usually quarter horses and, of course, their riders, come in at that end. When they pass the plane of the gate they trigger an electric eye, starting a timer."

Bonnie then nodded toward the trio of barrels being laid out by the clowns. "They tear ass, in a kind of cloverleaf around the barrels. When they complete the pattern, they race back to the gate, triggering the eye again, and their time stops. The racer with the fastest time wins. In the vernacular, this is known as one of the speed events."

"Very impressive. You've done your homework." A smile lifted the corners of Lloyd's mouth. "Well, lookie there." With a tilt of his chin he indicated the walkway at the bottom of the risers.

Harold T. Dobbs and his son, Jason, had halted at the steps leading into the stands. The pastor looked every inch the rodeo star he'd been as a boy—straw cowboy hat, boots, even a belt buckle the size of Rhode Island. His son, a smaller, thinner version of his father, was dressed the same.

They still hadn't seen Bonnie, and she hoped it stayed that way. Then as the pair climbed, Harold looked up and frowned.

Color rose into his already ruddy face. His meaty paw came to the brim of his hat, which he tipped maybe five degrees. "Missus Pinkwater, Lloyd."

Bonnie nodded.

"Harold," Lloyd said.

Jason caught sight of Bonnie, and his face broke into a wide grin. "Missus P, Mister Whittaker. All right!"

Jason pushed past his father who had taken a seat two rows down. The young man edged his way into the row in front of Bonnie and Lloyd, and hooked his thumbs into the loops of his jeans. "So good to see you guys. You come to see Seneca ride?"

Bonnie studied the young man. Except for a new walrus mustache, he was the same skinny point guard she remembered. "So she's going to race?"

The young man's grin went lopsided and mischief swam into his eyes. "You bet. It's driving Caleb crazy."

"Why?" Lloyd asked. "The girl's been competing since Little Britches. She's probably the best racer East Plains ever produced. I'd think her husband would be proud of her."

"Not since she got pregnant." Jason swiveled his head around and pointed with his thumb. "That's them over by the starting gate."

Bonnie rubbernecked past Jason and caught sight of Seneca. Caleb Webb had his foot propped on the first rung of the galvanized fence surrounding the arena.

"They seem to be arguing," Bonnie said.

Jason took a deep breath and let it out between his teeth. "They've been doing a lot of that lately. Caleb thinks she's being reckless, calls her selfish to anybody who'll listen. Been seeing my dad for counseling."

"Things are that bad?"

"Yeah. I think Caleb's begun thumping on Seneca, which is surprising since up until lately I would have said he worshiped her."

Bonnie gave herself a moment before she spoke. If there was one thing that made her blood boil, it was husbands who used their wives as punching bags. "You know this for sure?"

"Not for sure. But last week, Seneca came in with a swollen eye. Said she had a fall, but I don't think so."

Bonnie gave Caleb Webb a hard look. *Asshole.*

Needing to redirect her focus before she said something she'd regret, Bonnie touched Jason's hand. "How are you doing with Leo's death?"

Jason looked away, seemingly staring at something beyond the risers. For the briefest moment, Bonnie thought she saw a quiver touch the young man's face before he steeled himself. He smoothed out his mustache.

"We were close before graduation. But I haven't really been in contact with him since then."

Bonnie caught Harold, head cocked, eavesdropping on the conversation. She felt certain Jason could see him, too. Her heart went out to this young man, having to share a life, and now a vocation, with such a controlling father.

"Listen, I need to be getting back to Dad." Jason shook hands with Lloyd. "It was great seeing you guys."

"You, too, Jason." Bonnie thought Jason looked somehow diminished as he returned to his father.

Ain't my problem.

She smacked Lloyd on the knee. "Before this party gets started, I need to visit the little girls' room."

The nearest bathroom was a port-a-potty behind the midway. Bonnie had just tossed her cotton candy stem and was heading that way when, between the beer tent and the Side-o'-Beef Raffle booth, a screaming woman stumbled into view.

"Somebody help! I think he's dead."

CHAPTER 5

No sooner had Bonnie taken a step than she was caught in a press of bodies streaming into the narrow space between the beer tent and the Side-o'-Beef Raffle concession. Painfully funneled through the passage, she was barely able to breathe. Her T-shirt tore. Her back scraped against a metal pipe. A hand cupped her buttocks. Angry and anxious protests came from all sides.

"Look out for my little girl."

"Watch your elbow!"

"Do you mind?"

Just about the time she thought she might faint, she squirted like a watermelon seed into the dusty open space behind the tents. Midcrowd, she toppled onto hands and knees. Pandemonium reigned, people tripping one over another. A cowboy boot came down on her fingers.

Goddamn!

Bruised hand to her mouth, she caught sight of a mother covering the eyes of her toddler. A man in a white Stetson scooped up a crying girl and held her to his chest. A ringing in Bonnie's ears gave way to screams. Using the back of a sprawled man, Bonnie hoisted herself to her feet.

Ahead, a port-a-potty stood open. A rodeo clown sat crosswise on the commode, a spreading stain rapidly coloring his western shirt to match his red bandanna.

The idea of approaching this more-than-likely dead clown required at least an attempt at validation by her immediate peers. "Does anyone besides me think this fella might still be alive?"

"What do you got in mind?" A giant of a man in what had to be size quadruple X coveralls was fanning himself with a ruined straw cowboy hat. He offered a meaty paw. "Toby Crump."

She took the offered hand in hers. "Bonnie Pinkwater. Well, first I'd check for a pulse. Maybe see if he's breathing. I have my CPR certificate if it comes to that."

The big man considered her for a moment, then nodded slowly. "Let's do it."

"Wait." Bonnie took back her hand. She pointed at the man in the white Stetson. "Call nine-one-one please?"

When the man nodded, she caught the attention of a trio of young men with numbered rectangles pinned on their shirts. "Check if any veterinarians are still at the livestock pavilions." She didn't have time to wait to see how this last task would sort itself out. If this clown wasn't already singing in the heavenly choir, he was trying on the robe.

"All right, Toby, let's go."

As she approached, Bonnie's hopes diminished. Whoever had decided to end the life of this unfortunate young man had done a thorough job. She counted three separate holes in the clown's western shirt. The pattern formed a small equilateral triangle centered on the heart.

Why is that so familiar?

Bonnie relegated the question to the I'll-think-about-this-later portion of her brain. "Hold him so he doesn't fall over." She laid two fingers on the clown's neck. Nothing. She brought her face close to the clown's. No discernable breath. As she stepped back, she was sure she'd seen this clown somewhere before.

Another random thought I'll consider later. "We've got to get him out of there. I don't know how to do rescue breathing on a man propped on a commode."

"You're the boss." Toby crushed his tattered hat onto his head. He then lifted the clown to his feet like a rag doll, holding him at arm's length to avoid the blood. "Where to?"

"Faceup, right here in the dirt."

As Toby gently set his charge down, Bonnie steeled

herself. She knelt beside the clown. *Can't begin rescue breathing until I get the bleeding under control.*

"Lend me your hat."

The big man blinked at her. "My hat?"

Bonnie waggled her fingers at him, willing him to be quicker. "That's right. Please." As soon as the straw hat was within arm's reach, she snatched it, folded it double, and jammed it down on the clown's chest. She pressed down, one hand atop another.

"Sorry, Toby, but I couldn't think of what else to use."

"Don't you worry about it, little lady. You just do what you got to do."

Bonnie had barely begun her compression when she felt a tap on her shoulder.

"Missus P?"

She angled her head and came face to face with Deputy Byron Hickman. Behind him, standing at the ready, were two black clad EMTs and Deputy Wyatt.

"The techs'll take over now, Missus P. You did a great job."

She took a proffered arm, and she and Byron removed themselves to stand with the oversized Crump.

Bonnie pointed with her chin toward the EMTs. "How did they—"

Byron shook his head. "Emergency techs are on the scene at all rodeo events. And me and Wyatt were manning a booth for the sheriff's department when this screaming woman came running up."

Byron held up his hand. "Excuse me for a moment." He signaled for Wyatt to come over and whispered in her ear.

When he returned, he took Bonnie and Crump aside. "Tell me everything as it was before you moved the body."

Bonnie's heart sank as she realized that Byron was no doubt correct about the clown's life status. The EMTs would do their best, but this was one rodeo clown who wouldn't see the inside of a rubber barrel again. She and Crump described the original scene, ending with the trio of bullet holes tight about the clown's heart.

"Does that ring any bells with you, youngster?"

"You mean three shots to the chest probably delivered at close range?"

"You know damn well that's what I mean."

"It could just be a coincidence."

"What are you guys talking about?" Toby asked.

Byron shot her a warning glance. "Don't go off half-cocked, Missus P."

She wanted to tell this former student that she was thoroughly cocked, but she could see his point. No point in getting Crump involved in an unsubstantiated theory connecting the death of a rodeo clown at a county fair with that of a homosexual young man out on an isolated road.

"I feel like the younger brother at his big sister's

IRRATIONAL NUMBERS

slumber party," Crump said. "You two want me to leave so you can talk?"

Byron shook his head. "Nope. I've got to give Wyatt a hand with these interviews. Mister Crump, please leave a number with my deputy before you go, in case I have any more questions."

Before he could walk away, Bonnie grabbed Byron's arm. "Just one more thing, and it's bugging the hell out of me."

Byron almost succeeded in wiping a frown from his face. "Shoot."

"It's the clown. I know him from somewhere, but I can't picture the face under the greasepaint."

"He went to East Plains, probably had you for math. Used to get in a dozen different kinds of trouble with a kid who called himself Spoon."

As the realization dawned on her, Bonnie whipped around to get another look at the clown. Sure, she knew him. Even dead, she should have recognized Dwight Furby.

"Don't be silly, Bon." Lloyd grabbed Bonnie's arm to take her the medical tent. "You look like you've been through a war."

Bonnie shook her head. "No time for that. Didn't you hear what I said? Dwight Furby's dead, murdered."

"I got it, Bon. I just don't understand your hurry. Furby's not going to get any deader in the time it takes to bandage your hand—maybe look after your back."

Bonnie shrugged off Lloyd's arm. "Listen to me, boss. I forgot to tell Byron about seeing Witherspoon talking to Rattlesnake."

"And?"

"And Byron's going to want to question Witherspoon. He probably came to the fair with Furby. Hell, for all we know he could have been the one to murder him and"—she pointed to the crowds of people streaming toward the main gate—"he'll be out of here in a matter of minutes."

When Lloyd still didn't pick up the pace, she said, "We need to hurry. Witherspoon could get away, if he hasn't already."

"I don't think so."

"Oh, yeah, smarty-pants, why not?"

Lloyd pointed. "Because there he is."

Sure enough, Spoon was striding out of a livestock pavilion, beer in hand. He downed the drink, crushed the plastic cup, and dumped it in a trash barrel.

Lloyd chewed on his lower lip. "From the looks of him, that wasn't the first beer that young man put away. And you're right about him skedaddling. The old Spoonmaster's making a beeline for the gate."

"You think he's heard about the murder?"

IRRATIONAL NUMBERS

"You kidding? The only folks who ain't heard are the ones who just got here, and I wouldn't bet on them."

"Then why isn't Witherspoon heading toward the murder scene?"

"Good question. I say we follow the boy."

Bonnie stared a long moment after her friend. He'd surprised her with his renewed animation after the state she'd found him in that afternoon. She ran to catch up. "Don't let him see us, you ninny."

"So what if he does? He's hardly going to pay much attention to his old teacher and principal. Besides, that young man looks like he has other things on his mind—like he's got the hounds of hell nipping at his backside."

Bonnie had to admit Lloyd had a point, and not just on the top of his overeager head. Witherspoon took a wary look around, scanned them momentarily without a shred of recognition. He ducked into the arts and crafts pavilion.

Lloyd jammed his hands in his pockets and strolled nonchalantly to the pavilion.

"Lloyd!" Bonnie tried to whisper, but in her excitement ended up yelling loud enough to draw attention. *The hell with it.* "What are you doing?"

By way of an answer, Lloyd waved her back. His hand was on the glass door of the pavilion when he stopped. Using the exaggerated long steps of the Doo-Dah Man, Lloyd moved quickly behind a row of bushes bordering the pavilion. He turned toward her, a smile on his craggy face, his eyes wide. Using his thumb and pinkie, he made the universal telephone sign.

Bonnie joined him, crouching low in the bushes. "How'd our friend look?"

"Nervous and scared. I think the Spoonmaster's about to pee his pants. I'd give a week's pay to know who he's calling."

"The police can the get the identity later from phone records." Bonnie stared back at the pavilion and its double glass doors. "Did Spoon see you?"

Lloyd shook his head. "No way."

Ah, yes, men. Quite often wrong, but never in doubt. "I'll have to take your word for that."

Lloyd shifted from one foot to the other, obviously eager to resume the chase. "I can see why you like this sort of thing."

"What sort of thing?"

"Playing detective." Her principal thumped a fist on his chest. "It really gets your blood pumping. Beats the hell out of sitting around a dark living room drinking beer, eating stale pepperoni pizza, and feeling sorry for yourself."

"I'm glad you're having a good time, but what makes you think I enjoy these sorts of things? They just fall into my lap."

"Forgive me, Bon, if I'm more than a little skeptical." Lloyd patted her arm. "Cover me, schweetheart,

I'm going in." He quit their hiding place and made again for the doors.

Oh, no, not another man who thinks he's Humphrey Bogart.

Before Bonnie could voice a protest, her principal entered the pavilion. No more than a minute later, when Lloyd failed to return, Bonnie decided to join him. Before she reached the door, he slammed back out.

"He's gone."

Hot on Lloyd's heels, Bonnie followed him into the pavilion. Moving as fast as the crowd allowed, they elbowed and excused themselves past booth after booth selling cowboy art, patchwork quilts, Tex-Mex salsa, and beer-can men who waggled pipe-cleaner penises when you tilted their tin-can tunics. An eternity later Bonnie pushed toward the back door.

No Spoonmaster in sight.

Bonnie smacked Lloyd's arm. "The parking lot! We should have gone straight there as soon as he disappeared." She set off running.

Again, the human traffic gods conspired against them. Couples, whole families, and one rotund woman leading an army of preschoolers sprang up in Bonnie and Lloyd's path. It was all Bonnie could do not to scream at them to get out of the way.

They arrived at the parking lot just in time to see a maroon Trans Am peel away down Seventh Avenue toward Highway 84.

Panting, Lloyd leaned heavily onto his thighs. "Do we follow?"

Bonnie shook her head. Alice, The-Little-Subaru-That-Could, would have a heart attack trying to catch that muscle car. "We need to get back to Byron." She didn't relish the prospect of telling Byron that not only did they follow a potential murder suspect—and not tell the good deputy he was at the fair—but then they let the culprit get away.

Still, there's nothing for it. She pulled her cell phone from her fanny pack. Before she could punch in Byron's pager number, the phone rang.

"Bonnie Pinkwater."

"Bon, it's Armen. How soon can you come by?"

Driving away from Lloyd's, Bonnie owned a feeling of dread that had settled into her chest and felt as if it meant to sublease. Armen had sounded positively grim.

"Let it go, Pinkwater. You'll know what he wants soon enough."

Armen's carport resembled a gigantic aquarium, all pale blues and greens, even a pair of angelfish swimming overhead. The usual soothing panorama failed to do the trick this time. As soon as she shut the door of her

Subaru, the door to Armen's trailer opened. The man wore one of those grim smiles that at once declared, "I'm glad to see you," and "I'm sorry for the bad news."

He rushed down his pair of wooden steps and took her in his arms. He held her close until she really began to worry.

Whatever's on his mind must really suck.

"Come in. I made a pot of coffee."

"What the hell's going on, Armen?"

Armen nodded to the trailer the other side of the carport. Bonnie turned just in time to see a curtain slide closed.

"All right, I'll come in, but this better be good. You're scaring the bejeebers out of me."

Hand on the small of her back, Armen ushered her into the trailer. Under different circumstances, this casual show of affection would have brought a smile to her face. Now it made her brace for the sucker punch she knew was coming.

As soon as the door shut behind her, Armen asked, "How did things go at the fair?"

Strangely enough, Bonnie was grateful for the chance to ease into what promised to be an uncomfortable confrontation. She walked Armen through the murder, ending with her getting back with Byron and telling him about their snafu with Witherspoon.

"Was the deputy angry?"

Color rose into Bonnie's cheeks. "You could say

that. If memory serves, the phrases *What were you thinking?* and *Don't ever do that again!* found their place in his lengthy recrimination."

Armen whistled. "I would have loved to have seen that. Too bad you had to go it alone."

"Who said I was alone?"

Armen cocked his head and leveled a gaze at her. "You weren't?"

"Lloyd went with me."

For a long moment, Armen studied Bonnie's face. She wasn't sure what was going on in his mind, but he appeared to be trying to ascertain if she was putting him on.

"What?" she asked.

"Nothing. I was just trying to picture Lloyd Whittaker playing amateur sleuth."

"He held his own." Bonnie considered telling Armen about Marjorie and thought better of it. She was good and ready to hear whatever it was that made Armen skip their date. "Soooooo, what's your news?"

Armen inhaled deeply. "My dad fell."

"Oh, is it serious?" Bonnie inwardly cringed at the inanity of her question. It had to be pretty serious, or Armen wouldn't have made such a big deal out of it.

"Pretty bad, he broke his hip and is in the hospital, but it's not just that. Dad's been going downhill for a while. When Mom died, I invited him to move out here with me, but he wouldn't even discuss it." Armen took

Bonnie's hands into his.

"So what are you going to do?" she asked.

"I'm flying out in the morning. I don't know how long I'll be gone."

CHAPTER 6

"Emily." Bonnie pointed to the rail-thin black girl who'd been waving frantically. "With whom, my dear, shall you regale us?"

Emily popped out of her desk like she'd been sitting on a coiled spring. "Hypatia," she said breathlessly.

"Good choice. One of my favorites."

The girl picked up a stack of papers, pressed them to her chest, and stood rigid. "Before I give everyone my handout, I'd like to lodge a protest."

To Bonnie's surprise, a number of other girls grumbled their agreement.

Open rebellion?

Strangely enough, the prospect of a confrontation appealed. Bonnie was grateful for something to take her mind off the fact that at five o'clock that morning, she'd driven to the Colorado Springs airport and ushered a bleary-eyed Armen Callahan off onto his plane. They both were exhausted after she'd spent the night. Consequently, they'd hardly said coherent goodbyes before it was time for him to board. She'd left the airport feeling depressed and abandoned.

She could use a good fight and focused her full attention onto the pint-sized upstart. What Bonnie wanted—needed with some primal part of her psyche—was to say to this oh-so-smart ebony princess, "Bring it on." After a moment's consideration, what she did say was, "I'm all ears, sweetie. Lodge your protest."

The girl hiked herself up to her full height—perhaps five-foot-two. "You told us Hypatia was Greek."

"I remember saying something to that effect." Then the reality of her blunder hit Bonnie like a New York taxi. "Oh!"

To the girl's credit, she didn't play off the *Oh*. She merely nodded and looked about the room. "Hypatia wasn't Greek at all, she was African."

Bonnie felt like she stood naked in front of the class and realized her best strategy was agreement, total and unequivocal. "You're right, of course. Hypatia was born in Alexandria to parents who themselves were natives of that African city. In my defense, to me, Alexandria, like its namesake, Alexander the Great, will forever be Greek in all but geography."

Once again, the girl was gracious and didn't pounce on this lame excuse. She smiled and headed for the first row, her head high with the obvious knowledge that she had bested the teacher, on the second day of class no less. She distributed the papers to her twelve classmates.

Bonnie had to admit to a certain grudging admiration. *You win this one, munchkin.*

"Anyway," Emily began as though nothing had transpired, "after overcoming that bit of misdirection . . ." The girl stopped as if expecting Bonnie to take up the gauntlet.

She kept her face neutral. *Pick your battles, Pinkwater.*

"I found a lot of stuff on Hypatia—cool stuff."

"Math stuff?" Bonnie asked.

Emily nodded like a bobble-head doll. "Some. And a lot of stuff that made me wish I had known Hypatia. She was awesome."

"I couldn't agree more. Tell me—tell us all—one thing that impressed you about Hypatia."

"Even if it's gross?"

Bonnie knew exactly the story the girl wanted to relate. If this had been a mixed class she probably would have asked the girl to choose another, but she thought a class full of teenage girls would appreciate the tale. "Especially if it's gross." She winked at Emily.

The girl set down the remaining papers and began to wave her hands. "Okay, okay, you guys got to know she was like this really beautiful, really smart celebrity. There's a picture of her on the top of my handout. Anyway, everybody in Alexandria knew her and thought she was hot." Emily paused to take a deep breath, and it was

IRRATIONAL NUMBERS

evident this was the first since she started her monologue.

"Well, she taught this class on Neo-Platonism, which is a kind of pagan religion. In the class there was this dorky guy who was, like, in love with her."

Several of the girls in the class sighed knowingly.

Bonnie stifled a laugh, reminding herself that even if they didn't know a lot about love yet, they were probably experts on dorky guys.

"You know the type. Well, he followed Hypatia around all googly-eyed and stupid until she couldn't stand it anymore. She waited until they were alone, then she faced down the dork."

Emily paused for dramatic effect.

Nice. You've got skills, girl.

"Here's the really gross part. Hypatia was having her period, and in those days women wore this thing like a big diaper when they were . . . you know."

Several girls grunted their understanding.

"Anyway, Hypatia reached under her toga and took out her napkin."

"Eeew," said a redheaded girl named Olivia. "Was it all bloody?"

Emily nodded gravely. "Super bloody."

Several other girls chimed in with *Eeews* of their own.

"What did the dork do?" Olivia asked.

"I'll get to that, but first you got to hear what Hypatia did. She asked dorkface if he thought the rag was beautiful."

"I'll bet he did," a Chicano girl named Beatrice said. "Boys are perverts."

At that outburst, Bonnie couldn't restrain herself. She laughed out loud. The rest of the class, including Emily joined in.

Like a trained teacher, Emily waited until they settled down before she attempted to speak again. When the tumult had quieted to a small archipelago of titters, she picked up her narrative. "This pervert didn't think the rag was so pretty and backed away disgusted. When he did, Hypatia said, 'Yet you think I'm beautiful. This is part of the woman I am, part of what you think is so beautiful.' Then she said something really cool."

"What?" a number of voices chimed in at once.

Even Bonnie found herself tempted to ask.

Emily smiled broadly enough to light up a stadium. "Hypatia said, 'If you want to find real beauty, seek truth.'"

To a girl, the class nodded in admiration for this dead matriarch who had reached across sixteen hundred years to touch, if not their hearts, at least their minds.

Bonnie hated to spoil the moment, but she needed to remind everyone where they were. "Very nice, Emily. Now how about some of Hypatia's mathematics?"

For the next twenty minutes, Emily tried to impart what the Internet had taught her about Diophantine equations, one of the mathematical concerns with which Hypatia had wrestled. Although not as articulate as when she told the Sanitary Napkin Tale, Emily acquitted herself in so fine a form that Bonnie applauded when the girl finished.

Emily did an exaggerated curtsy—even going as far as placing her index finger beneath her chin—and returned to her desk beaming.

Bonnie looked at the clock and decided there wasn't enough time to do justice to any of the remaining mathematicians, at least not in a full-blown report like Emily's. Besides, the previous evening, with its mixture of murder and romance, was beginning to take its toll. She opted to expend the rest of the class giving away candy, providing these little geniuses could earn it. She went to her closet and removed a bag of Jolly Ranchers. She reached into the bag and extracted a blue prism of candy.

"The Cadillac of Jollies, blue raspberry."

An appreciative intake of breath told Bonnie she had their attention. "All right, for this azure lovely, who was the mathematician who became Voltaire's mistress?"

Beatrice's hand immediately shot into the air.

Bonnie pointed to the girl. "Go."

"Emilie Breteuil."

"Right you are." She threw the girl the candy and pulled out another.

"Okay, who was—" Before she could finish the sentence

every hand in the room was raised.

This brazen behavior reminded Bonnie of herself as a girl. She pointed to Olivia. "You know if this was Knowledge Bowl, I wouldn't finish the question, but I'll give you a break. Who was the mathematician who had her clothing taken away to force her to quit teaching herself mathematics and Latin?"

Olivia nodded knowingly. "Mary Somerville."

"Correctomundo." She tossed the candy and retrieved another. This time before she could even get the first word out, hands were raised.

"What bold young women I see before me." She pointed to a ponytailed blonde. "Georgia."

"Yes, ma'am."

"Okay, Georgia. Who was the mathematician who became labeled as a satanist because of a misunderstanding?"

"Marie Agnesi."

"Nicely done." Another candy arced across the room. While it was still in the air, hands flew skyward.

Bonnie pointed to a petite Japanese girl. "Yoki?"

The girl nodded.

"Very well, Yoki. Who was the mathematician whose father wallpapered her room with calculus notes?"

Color rose to the girl's cheeks. "That was the only one I couldn't find."

Mollified by the girl's honesty, Bonnie decided to let Yoki off the hook. "Anyone?"

Nary a hand ventured into the room's airspace. "Even you, Emily?"

The girl shook her head.

As Bonnie scanned the room, a profound silence replaced what had minutes before been raucous frivolity. Then without warning, a sound like a rifle shot sliced through the quiet.

Every head turned in the direction of Beatrice, who had dropped a copy of one of the larger Harry Potter volumes.

"Sorry, Missus Pinkwater. It just fell."

But Bonnie wasn't listening. Her mind had been rocketed back to the county fair, to the murder of a rodeo clown. She felt like smacking herself in the head. *You're so stupid, Pinkwater.*

"Class dismissed."

As soon as the last of her little geniuses cleared out, Bonnie hightailed it to Lloyd's office. She half-remembered him saying he had some admin business to see to in preparation for the first day of school. With any luck, he was still at it.

She heard his voice before she entered the office.

"Yes, sir, I think she's down in her room. Certainly, sir, I'll have her call you as soon as she's finished."

Bonnie waited in the doorway until she was sure

Lloyd was through. He looked up and smiled. "That was our mutual straw boss."

Bonnie winced, her worst fears confirmed. "And he wants to talk to me? About what?" She couldn't see how she could be in any kind of trouble. Not yet. *The doggone year hasn't even started. This has got to be a record.*

"Deputy Hickman called this morning before I got here. The phone system automatically sent the call to the Admin Building, and the superintendent picked up. I guess they had a nice little chat about rodeo clowns and math teachers."

Uh-oh. "And he's concerned about me getting involved in yet another murder?"

"Something like that."

"Did you by any chance mention to The Divine Pain—"

Lloyd shot her a warning glance. "Bon."

Bonnie continued without missing a beat. ". . . to our esteemed superintendent that you were at the fair as well?"

Lloyd reddened. "I didn't see how that would do you any good."

"Or you."

"Or me. Besides, I don't think you have anything to worry about. You couldn't help being at the fair when Furby was killed. And you can't help it if Deputy Hickman wants to talk to you now."

It was Bonnie's turn to blanch. "I haven't told you

everything, boss." She filled him in on the note found in Leo Quinn's pocket and the similarities between his death and Furby's.

Lloyd whistled. "I would say your involvement just jumped up a tad."

"There's more."

Lloyd inhaled deeply and released his breath in a tired sigh. "Might as well give me everything."

Bonnie plopped down in the red overstuffed visitor's chair. "This just occurred to me back in my room. I was finishing up with my cuties, when Beatrice Archuleta dropped a big ol' Harry Potter book onto the floor. Liked to give me a heart attack."

"Did she do it on purpose?"

Bonnie shook her head. "If I thought that, I might have had to drop that book on her head. Nah, I know the Archuletas. They wouldn't raise a kid with that much spite in her soul. It was the noise itself that got me thinking. The book reverberated like a gunshot."

Lloyd leaned forward. "Uh-huh."

"Okay, I need you to picture the murder scene. Not twenty feet in front of that clown's port-a-potty sit two major concession stands—the beer tent and the Side-o'-Beef Raffle booth. Hell, nothing separates the port-a-potties from the booths themselves but the back canvas walls of the tents."

A glimmer of understanding shone in Lloyd's eyes.

"Why didn't anyone hear the shots?"

Bonnie nodded so furiously she felt she might wrench her neck. "Damn right. There were dozens of people standing in line, not to mention the folks running the booths. Hell, I was in the vicinity. Three shots, Lloyd, and no one heard a blessed thing."

The principal shrugged. "You don't know how long Furby sat there. Could have happened while you were still at the rodeo. Or Furby could have been killed elsewhere and toted in like a sack of turnips."

"Oh, he was killed there all right." Bonnie frowned remembering the scene. "When Toby Crump moved the body, there was a trio of bullet holes in the rear of the stall."

"Okay, then Furby was murdered earlier."

"I don't think so." Bonnie tugged at her ear. "Something about that clown had seemed familiar. I just couldn't place him. Then I played it back."

Bonnie didn't need to tell Lloyd what she was talking about. Her memory was the stuff of legend. *Playing it back* meant she mentally reviewed the evening scene by scene.

"Remember looking down on the arena just before the barrel racing, when the clowns were setting up the course?"

"You think Furby was one of those clowns rolling out barrels?"

She nodded. "I'm sure of it. I can picture him when

I close my eyes."

Again, Lloyd whistled. "That means he was alive while we were talking to Jason Dobbs."

She created a centimeter space between thumb and index finger. "There's a bit more."

"Why do I always find myself bracing whenever you say those words?"

Bonnie shrugged. "Personally, I think it's a character flaw, but I'm inclined to overlook such things in a friend."

"Woman, how you do go on. What else you got?"

Again, Bonnie tugged on her ear, preparing her thoughts and her pedagogy. "How much do you know about noise suppressors?"

Lloyd scratched a callused thumb across his chin. "You mean, like silencers on pistols? A fair share. What do you know?"

"A lot more than I did just a few days ago. For instance, I know the new generation of suppressors are so quiet a murderer could reel off three shots and make less noise than the throwing of the bolt on a port-a-potty door."

"And you know this how?"

She told him of her visit to Rattlesnake's and his suppressor demonstration to the paintball kids. "And he was at the fair last night."

"Bon, Alf Quinn isn't the only one with access to and knowledge of such devices. This is East Plains after all—Survivalist Central."

"I'm not saying he is." She surprised herself at how much she wanted to defend this hypothesis she wasn't entirely invested in. "It just seems a coincidence he was there *and* was talking to Witherspoon—erstwhile friend of one murdered clown."

Lloyd stood, obviously agitated. "Okay, I'll grant you Alf had the means to kill Furby and do it quietly. What possible motive would he have?"

"How about the death of his son?" Bonnie saw that Lloyd was chomping to shoot holes in this theory, so before he could speak she hurried on. "Bear with me. On that same visit out to his shooting range, Alf went more than a little bananas. He yanked a pistol from a coatrack holster. I got to tell you, I wanted nothing more than to be out of there. The man was in full meltdown."

"Still—"

"Still, nothing! Lloyd, he was brandishing a lethal weapon, pacing around his office all the while muttering to himself. One of his ramblings included the question, *Did they really think it would be that easy?*"

"And you interpreted that to mean he intended to hunt down his son's killer. Who just so happens to be an innocuous dweeb like Dwight Furby?"

Bonnie spread wide her hands. "Okay, I'll admit I haven't got all the pieces in place just yet. Like this whole business with a nebbish like Furby shooting Leo in the chest, or Alf somehow knowing who killed his son before the police do."

Lloyd's expression changed from skeptical to pensive. He waved a cautioning hand. "Just wait a minute. You know, if you're correct, Alf doesn't really have to know for sure."

Lloyd's attitude about-face startled Bonnie. "Beg pardon?"

"Your turn to hear me out. You say Alf is bonkers, beside himself with grief. Suppose somehow he gets word—don't ask me how—that Furby was his son's murderer. Do you really think he's in a frame of mind to take the time to validate the story?"

Bonnie had to admit Lloyd was right. How many people kill friends or loved ones because of stupid misunderstandings? "And whoever murdered Furby had to be beyond caring if he was caught. Regardless of how quiet the shot may have been, even ensconced behind the concession line, the port-a-potty's a public facility. Anyone could have come along and witnessed the murder."

"Sounds like the Alf you described to me."

Bonnie studied her longtime friend wondering if he was just humoring her, or if he really believed she might be onto something. She decided to act as if the latter were true. "You know, this line of reasoning leads to another conclusion."

"I know. Moses Witherspoon has a good chance of being next on Rattlesnake's hit parade."

CHAPTER 7

"You know, I promised Xavier you would call as soon as your class let out." Lloyd opened Alice's passenger door, and Bonnie climbed in.

The act was so gallant Lloyd was ensconced behind the wheel before Bonnie realized he never asked if she wanted to drive her own car. He started the ancient Subaru and to the sound of crunching gravel pulled out of the school parking lot. *Definitely old school, Whittaker. Did you fence in your wife with a lifetime of these testosterone assumptions? Is that why she took to the hills?*

From the corner of her eye, Bonnie caught Lloyd staring at her. She roused herself, realizing, in her reverie, she had left Lloyd's declaration and its accompanying question unanswered. She waved a hand, dismissing Divine as a gnat—annoying but certainly not a problem worthy of consternation.

"Just tell him you never saw me. I scooted out the back of the school and made my exit before you could deliver the message."

Lloyd pursed his lips. "You want me to lie?"

Before she could give voice to, "Pretty much," Lloyd said, "I can do that."

This departure from her principal's normally virtuous interpretation of personal integrity caught Bonnie by surprise. She anticipated resistance. Certainly, she fully expected the man to back her up but somehow do it within the framework of the truth. This whole business with Marjorie and murder was shifting the universe's moral center. When she had a quiet moment, she'd have to assess how she felt about that.

"Well, all right then. You up for this trip?"

"Woman, I'm more than ready."

They'd called Byron with their noise suppression theory only to find the deputy out on some official business. Opting not to have him paged, Bonnie had left a message.

Lloyd had suggested they go see Rattlesnake. "Now that I'm out from under the self-pity cloud, I got no intention of falling back into that trap. This adventure is just what the ol' doctor ordered."

How do you do it, Whittaker? You spew one good-old-boy cliché after another and make them sound like personal inventions.

Bonnie studied her friend, liking what she saw. His craggy face had lost the care lines it had been carrying the day before. She just hoped recklessness hadn't replaced depression. "You're not worried this escapade might be a little dangerous? If Rattlesnake killed Furby, there's no telling what his mental state might be. And it's not likely the man will be lacking in the weapons department."

After a moment, jaw muscles working and making it look like he harbored crab apples in his cheeks, Lloyd shook his head. "Nope. Bon, it ain't like Alf's all alone, sitting around the rifle range. The man's got clients, employees. Criminy, every time I've been out there, the place was crawling with shooters."

"Or kids," Bonnie chimed in.

"Or kids," Lloyd agreed. "The way I see it, we find him, ask a few innocent questions, gauge his response, and we're out of there." Lloyd glided his flattened hand like a surfboard.

Bonnie smiled, once again impressed with this new version of Lloyd Whittaker. And truth be told, if her principal hadn't suggested they go out to the shooting range, she would have gone without him. The temptation would have been too great to resist.

Her cell phone chimed, playing her new ring tone— the opening bars of Eric Clapton's "Layla." Bonnie flipped open her phone. "City dump."

"Missus P?" Jason Dobbs's voice sounded confused.

"Guilty as charged, dear boy. What can I do for you?"

Jason cleared his throat. "I was wondering if you had a minute today to come by the church. My dad and

I want to plan the funeral."

On more than one level, Bonnie had been dreading the idea of a one-on-one with the esteemed Reverend Dobbs. She'd been hoping Rattlesnake would change his mind about the eulogy. Barring that, she was aiming to seamlessly slide into the funeral and give a short talk about Leo—all without any real face time with the odious preacher. She'd need reinforcements if she was to meet the enemy on his own turf.

"Hold on, Jason." She covered the receiver with her hand. "Boss, I need a huge favor."

"Name it."

"I need you to go with me to the Saved by the Blood Tabernacle this afternoon."

Lloyd chuckled. "Cover your back with the good reverend?"

"Something like that."

"Count me in."

Bonnie put the phone back to her ear. "We're on. What time?"

"Would two o'clock work for you?"

I do believe I'd rather have weasels rip my flesh. "Two it is."

She was just shutting down her phone when Lloyd turned Alice's nose into the long drive to Rattlesnake's shooting range. Bonnie gave her friend a sidelong glance. "You given any more thought to sharing what's going on between you and Marjorie?"

Lloyd took a long pull of air. "As a matter of fact, I have. But I'd rather show you than tell you. You still want to talk to Seneca about Leo Quinn?"

Bonnie resisted the urge to tease Lloyd about becoming almost Bonnie-Pinkwater-random in his impending senility. *Give the man a break, lady. He's got a lot on his mind.*

"More than ever." She tugged at her ear. "Plus, with the murder shutting everything down at the fair, I never did get to see Seneca race."

Lloyd nodded, evidently pleased with the direction the conversation was going. "So you mean to head out to the fair again tonight?"

"Absolutely."

"Good, we'll go together again, if that's okay?"

Bonnie felt as if she were being maneuvered, if only a little bit and albeit gently. "Want to tell me what's going on in that devious administrator mind of yours?"

"Not really, Mizz Suspicious, but I will show you tonight what's happening with Marjorie."

Now the man had gone and done it. Her curiosity was piqued. "Can I get a hint?"

"I don't think so."

She slapped him on the arm. "You're a sadist, Lloyd Whittaker."

"Takes one to know one." Lloyd pointed with his chin. "We're here."

IRRATIONAL NUMBERS

Bonnie had been so intent on imagining what could possibly be at the fair that would answer the question of the Lloyd/Marjorie breakup, she'd hadn't seen Rattlesnake's offices loom large. A pair of scarecrows, each in army fatigues and a camouflage helmet, held red-arrowed signs. One pointed left to the paintball course, the other right to the shooting range. Shouts from both directions told Bonnie each enterprise was in active and in rambunctious use.

Lloyd shut off the engine. "Shall we engage Mister Quinn in meaningful conversation?"

"I believe we should, MacDuff. Lead on."

To say Rattlesnake looked haggard would have been akin to saying a grizzly makes big potty in the greenery. From the smell of the man he'd been up to some odiferous activity and hadn't bothered to shower. His face sported an uneven patch of growth. His eyes were red-rimmed.

Lookin' good, Alf.

The big man sat behind the same refugee-from-Camp-Pendelton desk that Bonnie herself had sat behind the day before. His feet were up on the desk and a lethal-looking rifle lay on his lap. He appeared to be stroking the weapon like a pet Siamese.

"Well, if it ain't my two favorite education types." A

moment of dark storm passed over his features—eyes narrowing, forehead wrinkling—then just as quickly, it disappeared into a benign half smile. A Buddha in army fatigues.

He gingerly laid the rifle on the desk and stood. He held out a hand to Lloyd and the two men shook. "And to what do I owe the pleasure of this unexpected visitation?" With a rapid double swipe of the tip of his tongue, he licked his lips—an almost reptilian gesture.

She'd prepared an answer for just such a question, deciding that all things do indeed work together for good, even a call from Saved by the Blood Pentecostal Tabernacle. "I received a call from Jason Dobbs. I'm going over there at two this afternoon, but I wanted to talk to you before I went."

Rattlesnake narrowed his eyes but didn't ask the obvious question as to why she didn't just phone. "Talk away." He picked up the rifle, jammed the stock down on his desk blotter, and leaned on it like a staff.

"I was wondering if you've given this matter of a eulogy full consideration." She saw a look of profound disappointment creep onto Rattlesnake's face, and before he could voice his displeasure, she hurried on. "I mean, I'll be glad to do it. I was very fond of Leo. What I was questioning was using Pastor Dobbs as the minister."

"What do you mean?"

Bonnie wondered if the man was putting her on. As far as she knew, Rattlesnake had lived in East Plains forever. How could he not know about Harold T. Dobbs's rabidity when it came to matters of homosexuality?

"The man hates gays, Alf," Lloyd said. "He's crazy on the subject."

"Do tell. That's news to me." His face assumed a blank innocence that was obviously feigned.

You asshole. Why are you setting up this explosive situation?

She tried another tack. "Did you catch that piece on the Channel 5 news, about a year ago? Me and Reverend Dobbs?"

Rattlesnake shook his head. "Can't say that I did. Is that what you want to talk to me about?"

He couched the question like a challenge. Would she try to back out of her commitment? He damned well had seen the piece and for reasons of his own was pitting Bonnie against Reverend Dobbs.

And for Leo's sake, Bonnie determined to let him. She stared a long moment into his eyes before she spoke. "No, I'm good."

But you're going to answer a few questions as a fee for my services. "I saw you at the fair last night."

Bonnie could swear the man flinched at this non sequitur. Of course the reaction could just be another symptom of his deterioration.

Rattlesnake recovered and donned a blank expression. "Hell of a thing, that clown getting himself shot."

"That clown was a former student of mine—Dwight

Furby. Did you know Dwight?" She studied him, looking for any hint of guilt.

"Dwight? Hell, yes, I knew him. Him and that goofball Witherspoon came out here all the time to shoot off their pistols. One time they showed up drunk, and I had to run the idiots off." Rattlesnake tapped the side of his head. "Neither one is . . . were heavyweights in the brainpan department."

Bonnie thought it odd that Alf would be talking so callously about someone recently murdered, considering his own son was murdered in a similar fashion.

Rattlesnake must have read her mind, because he quickly added, "Don't get me wrong, that don't mean the doofus should be a candidate for three in the chest in a port-a-potty."

"I wouldn't think so. So you've got no idea who might have killed the boy."

Rattlesnake blinked at her. "Me? How the Sam Hill would I know?" He stretched and yawned.

Up until his last question, Bonnie was unsure as to whether Rattlesnake was lying. The belligerence coupled with the equally phony yawn convinced her, the man was dishing out supersized portions of bull crap. Two years ago she'd taken an afternoon class in body language. The instructor had said obvious displays of casualness—yawning, stretching, rolling of shoulders and neck—many times accompanied falsehoods. She didn't need that class to tell her Rattlesnake was full of manure.

She waved away Alf's question. "I just thought Witherspoon might have said something to you."

A moment of confusion swam across Rattlesnake's face, then he recovered. "Oh, yeah. I talked with that birdbrain."

Rattlesnake shook his head. "He didn't say anything about Furby or if anybody was after him."

He gave her a lopsided grin.

He's lying again, but this time it's as if he wants me to know he's lying. Bonnie stifled a shudder, wanting more than a little to put some distance between herself and Alf Rattlesnake Quinn.

Before she could voice this desire, Lloyd reached a hand toward the rifle Alf was holding. "Mind if I take a look at that beauty?"

Rattlesnake hesitated, then handed the gun to Lloyd, who effortlessly shouldered the weapon and sighted down its length. "An M24, isn't it?" he asked not taking the rifle down from his shoulder.

"That's right. The model developed by the Marines for 'Nam."

Lloyd nodded. "Where'd you pick it up?"

Rattlesnake licked his lips again. Something in Lloyd's manner was obviously making him nervous. "Gun show, up in Denver."

Lloyd took the rifle from his shoulder but instead

of handing it back to Rattlesnake, he walked with it to the door of the tiny room. He turned to Bonnie. "We should be going."

Bonnie stared at him for a long moment before she followed. *What are you up to, Whittaker?*

At the door of Rattlesnake's office, Lloyd leaned the rifle against the wall. "You take care of yourself, Alf."

Rattlesnake mumbled something Bonnie couldn't hear. She wanted to be out of there so badly she didn't look back. Lloyd held the outside door for her and ushered her down the trio of steps.

"What just happened in there?" she whispered.

"Tell you in the car. Let's go."

As before, he held the door for her but didn't take his eyes off Rattlesnake's offices, as if he expected the twin scarecrows to give chase. In a flash, Lloyd was around the ancient Subaru and heading Alice down the dirt drive.

By the time they reached Highway 84, Bonnie couldn't contain herself a moment longer. "Want to tell me what's going on?"

Lloyd exhaled for what seemed like half a minute. "You were right. The man's in meltdown. There was no way on God's green earth I was going to turn my back on him while he held that rifle. Especially not that particular rifle."

Bonnie pretended not to notice that Lloyd's hands were shaking on the steering wheel. "What did you call it, an M24?"

Lloyd nodded. "A sniper's rifle. In the right hands that rifle could easily pick off an enemy soldier at a thousand yards. That's definitely reaching out and touching someone."

Bonnie whistled. She didn't know much about shooting, but a thousand yards, ten football fields—she wasn't sure she could see an elephant at that distance. "You seem to know a lot about it."

"It's what I did for two years . . . in 'Nam."

CHAPTER 8

BONNIE SAT ACROSS FROM LLOYD AT GERTRUDE'S DINER and studied her friend while he sipped his beer. He'd barely touched his lunch.

"You okay, boss?"

Lloyd's eyes registered he'd been someplace far removed and was returning to the land of the living. He nodded.

"I will be." He gave her a weak smile and chuckled— a laugh two light-years away from okay. "Funny how some things'll just set you off. I hadn't seen an M24 since back in the day . . . Caught me by surprise. That's all."

"You want to talk about it?"

Lloyd took so long in answering, Bonnie considered letting him off the hook and retracting the question.

"Not much to tell," he said. "All of us did what needed doing. I'm no different from anybody else who served. I've had my share of sleepless nights, but none in years."

What went unsaid was that tonight stood a good

chance of being another. Bonnie told herself she wasn't to blame for bringing more pain into her friend's life, but that sure wasn't how it felt.

Lloyd reached across the table and squeezed her wrist. "F'gidd about it." He used his best *Sopranos* voice. "We got bigger fish to fry."

Bonnie cocked her head and smiled. "Fish?"

He returned her smile, and this time there appeared an increment more genuine humor in the grin. "Rattlesnake fish. Tastes like chicken. You catch his reference to Furby's death."

Bonnie instantly knew what Lloyd was talking about. "You mean that whole three shots in the chest business?"

Lloyd's face lost all of its melancholy. "What do you think, Bon? What's the likelihood the good deputy would share that tidbit of knowledge with the father of another murdered boy?"

"I'll go you one better. How likely is it Byron even had the opportunity to speak with Rattlesnake since the murder? Hell, we're talking Furby was rolling barrels across an arena just"—she checked her Mickey Mouse watch—"sixteen hours ago. Byron's had a bit on his plate at that time, not to mention making time for sleep."

Bonnie reached for her hummus sandwich and Lloyd for his burger. For a companionable and thoughtful time they chewed in silence. She was reminded of a quote from Kahlil Gibran's *Prophet*.

Your friend is your needs answered. Seek not your friend with hours to kill but rather with hours to live.

Bonnie was struck with how, even in a religious piece written a lifetime ago, the word *kill* reared its less than beautiful head. Before she could ruminate further, another thought drove Kahlil Gibran off center stage. "Did you get the feeling Rattlesnake chose to mention the three shots deliberately?"

"What do you mean?"

"Okay. This is going to sound far-fetched, but the whole time we were dancing around with the man, I got the impression Rattlesnake was baiting us, dropping morsels of information. Even when he was lying, I got the distinct feeling he wanted us to know he was lying."

Lloyd squinted at her. "Why would he do that?"

Bonnie shrugged, not quite sure where any of her reasoning was leading. "Beats me. But at one point I thought Alf might even wink."

"Bon, Rattlesnake is falling apart. Couldn't what you saw be just a more bit evidence he's coming unhinged?"

Before Bonnie could add more wood to her argument, her cell phone rang. She dug it out of her fanny pack. "Pinkwater."

"You wanted to talk with me, Missus P?" Byron's voice sounded weary and more than a little annoyed.

For the next few minutes Bonnie told of her first visit to Rattlesnake's and his noise suppression demonstration to the paintballers. She followed up immediately with her theory about the relative silence of the shots that killed Furby. Byron made the appropriate noises at the appropriate junctures, not interrupting until she finished.

"I'd wondered about that myself, even so far as asking ballistics if the recovered bullets showed any evidence of passing through a suppressor."

"Really?" Bonnie cringed, thinking the one-word question carried within it an implied insult to Byron's intelligence.

"Yes, really. Occasionally, we cops do have honest-to-goodness ideas of our own."

Bonnie decided the damage was done and pressed on. "So what did you find?"

"Inconclusive. All three slugs were altered when they banged through Furby and out the back side of the stall. Besides, from what I know, the newer suppressors don't leave a mark on the slug. Was there anything else?"

Bonnie debated with herself about sharing her second visit to Rattlesnake's, knowing full well Byron would read her the riot act for conducting her own inquiries into an ongoing murder investigation.

To hell with it. She told him everything, ending with a question about whether he'd let slip to Rattlesnake the exact number of shots in Dwight Furby's chest.

True to her suspicions, Byron did indeed lay into her. There were the mandatory warnings about danger, then the recriminations about fouling up the investigation, and for good measure, Byron tossed in a threat of not answering any more of her calls.

Bonnie knew if she didn't salve this open wound, she would be hard-pressed to glean any more information from her former student. "I hear you loud and clear, youngster. No more sticking my nose in where it's not needed. Sound advice, I fully intend to take to heart. Consider me a changed woman." She even crossed her heart though Byron obviously wouldn't see it.

"Missus P, you've got to be the world's worst liar."

"Now that's hardly fair. I doubt if you've listened to a very significant fraction of the world's truly terrible liars. I'll bet I don't even qualify in the top two hundred."

Bonnie held her breath, hoping this morsel of humor would grease the grooves.

Byron sighed long and heavy. "In answer to your question, I did not tell Mister Alf Rattlesnake Quinn any details of the death of Furby."

She pumped a fist into the air. "So?"

"So nothing. *I* didn't hear him say he knew the number of shots. A certain math teacher, who will go unnamed, beat me to the punch. Anything I report would be hearsay."

"Lloyd heard it, too." Even as she said it, she regretted

the tone of her voice—like a four-year-old telling her mom, "She started it."

Byron growled into the receiver. "Don't tell me you've roped poor Principal Whittaker into this."

Bonnie couldn't see how telling Byron her principal was a willing participant would help matters. While she searched for a more acceptable argument Byron broke in.

"Look, Missus P, I do know something that might put your mind at ease."

Byron sounded so condescending, Bonnie felt like telling him to take his news and put it in a safe and personal spot. Her curiosity won out. "What?"

"Witnesses place Rattlesnake all night long in the main livestock pens. He was judging hogs for the Four-H folks. No way could he have killed Dwight Furby."

Now why, on God's green earth, would you think that would ease my mind?

The Saved by the Blood Pentecostal Tabernacle sat at the edge of El Paso County's largest sod farm, affording it one of the most unique set of views in all of East Plains. A panorama connoisseur looking north would be treated to a brilliant green that rivaled any well-manicured golf course or football field. Lush acres of irrigated sod gleamed kelly green in the afternoon sun.

Conversely, south and east, the usual subdued reds and yellow-greens of sand, scrub grass, and yucca spread out as far as the eye could see. West, rising high on the horizon stood the front range of the Rockies and its regal queen, Pikes Peak. This time of year the normal crown of snow was gone, but even wearing a skullcap of reddish-brown the mountain seemed to smile down on its empire.

One would think, hanging out day after day in the midst of all this grandeur, Pastor Harold T. Dobbs would have a more expansive attitude toward the world in general and his fellow man in particular. Not so much as Bonnie could tell. Sitting behind a pricey-looking oak desk, the man positively scowled when she and Lloyd entered the pastor's office.

You invited me, you turkey.

Jason, with his back to the room, stood at a window. From the set of his shoulders and the fists balled at his side, the young master Dobbs was upset about something.

Dissension in the ranks?

Harold pointed to a pair of cushioned folding chairs facing the desk. He nodded to Lloyd.

"You look a little tight around the jowls," Lloyd leaned in and whispered to Bonnie.

"That's an improvement over how I feel." Bonnie took a deep breath, set her shoulders, and sat. She'd be damned if she was going to allow this sphincter muscle in cowboy boots to push her around.

IRRATIONAL NUMBERS

Bad enough Harold spewed his hateful monologues every Wednesday night and twice on Sunday. If it was at all within her power, she'd assure Leo was lowered into the ground with dignity and grace.

When Jason turned around, Bonnie gasped. He sported a swollen lip.

Harold must have seen her concern and tried to wave away the distraction. "My son had a bit of a mishap this morning. He'll be fine. Shall we get started?"

Bonnie ignored Harold. "What happened, Jason?"

The young man gave his father a look that spoke volumes.

My God, the two had a fistfight.

For a moment, the idea thrilled her, and she searched Harold's face for similar battle scars. A red streak beneath one eye spoke to where Jason might have clocked the old man.

And son shall rise up against father. Somehow knowing Jason gave back a little of what dear old dad tried to dish out didn't assuage Bonnie's indignation. Fathers flat-out shouldn't have knock-down-drag-outs with their grown sons.

Jason sighed and gave her an embarrassed half smile. "It's nothing, Missus P. Dad's right, we should get started."

Bonnie wanted nothing so much as to leap from her chair and smack Harold T. Dobbs in the chops. A long moment passed while she fought a losing battle with her Imp of the Perverse—the mischievous voice that urged her to recklessness and never failed to get her in trouble.

"You, sir, are a horse's ass."

Harold jumped to his feet. He sputtered, obviously trying to find a scathing yet imposing retort. In the end, he merely pointed to the door to the office. "Get out."

"Up yours, buster." Bonnie, too, rose from her chair and leaned on the oak desk until her face was only inches from Harold's. "I'm not going anywhere, until I've had my say. Or do you intend to punch me, too?"

Harold Dobbs reddened. He turned to look at his son. "I told you this was a mistake. I have no intention of working with this woman."

Jason opened his mouth to speak, but Lloyd cut him off. "All right. Everybody just settle down." He'd shifted into stern principal mode.

Without conscious effort, Bonnie bit back the insult she was preparing for Harold. Even she wasn't immune to Lloyd when he put tempered steel in his voice.

He tugged at Bonnie's sleeve. "Let's start over. C'mon, Bon, have a seat."

Bonnie did as she was told, never taking her eyes from Harold's.

"You, too, Dad." Jason put his hand on his father's shoulder and guided him down into his chair. "This isn't about you and Missus P. It's about Leo and Mister Quinn."

"Tell that to her." Harold pointed with his chin

toward Bonnie.

Eat feces and die, you slope-headed Neanderthal. "I can be civil if he can."

"Good." Jason brought a hand to his swollen lip and stroked it as if it were paining him. "Like Mister Whittaker suggested, why don't we start over? Now who wants to begin?"

Harold sat up straighter and steepled his long fingers. "Very well, I have but one reasonable condition that I must insist on in order to include Missus Pinkwater in my service. If it can't be met..." Harold spread wide his hands, letting her draw the obvious conclusion.

Uh-oh. "Spill it, Pastor. What do you have in mind?"

"I want a copy of your eulogy to see if I agree with the content and its adherence to the Scripture."

The horse's patoot isn't wasting time painting me into a corner.

Bonnie had no intention of letting Harold make changes in her eulogy—even though she hadn't written it yet—and moreover the good pastor knew it. She also knew perfectly well he'd do surgery on the piece until she couldn't bring herself to say the words, thus effectively eliminating her.

Screwed if I do and equally reamed if I don't. For her part, she couldn't sit idly by while Harold T. Dobbs bad-mouthed a fine young man. And maybe therein she had an out.

Bonnie offered the pastor the smile she reserved for individuals she wanted to irradiate. "Certainly, Harold. And would you be so kind as to provide me with an editable copy of your sermon—just in the off chance I might find portions of it objectionable?"

Harold slammed his fist down on the desk. "Of all the impertinent suggestions—God is my editor, Pinkwater. He alone will I allow to make changes in my sermons."

Bonnie waggled a finger at the pastor. "Nice speech, Harold. Pithy but unacceptable, and furthermore it leaves us kind of at an impasse. Don't you think?"

The big man appeared to be considering a response when his phone rang. Jason picked it up. "Saved by the Blood Pentecostal Tabernacle."

The room went relatively silent as each of the other three went through the ritual of pretending not to listen.

"Uh-huh. Uh-huh." Jason stroked his swollen lip. "Strange that you should suggest that. It addresses a problem at our end."

After another round of "*Uh-huh*"s and a few "*I agree*"s, Jason recradled the phone. He avoided his father's gaze, choosing instead to meet eyes with Lloyd. "That was Alf Quinn."

Lloyd nodded. "What did Rattlesnake want?"

When Jason hesitated, Harold said, "Out with it, boy!"

Once again, Jason fists balled. "With pleasure, Father. Alf said that, after much consideration, he thinks I should lead the funeral service."

Harold bent his head 'round to give his son a fatherly but condescending glance. "I hope you told him that was out of the question. You've never led a funeral."

Jason frowned. "Cut it out, Dad. You listened to every word I said, and you know that didn't happen. And contrary to your opinion, I think I would do a fine job. After all, Leo was my friend, not yours."

Harold's face went to stone, and he seemed to be swallowing and reswallowing something stuck deep in his sanctimonious craw. "This is a bad idea, son." His voice was barely above a whisper.

"I disagree."

Harold rose from his desk. "I see your mind is made up. I withdraw from the service and leave it entirely in your hands." The senior pastor's eyes locked on Bonnie's. "I half-suspect you had something to do with this."

The remark took Bonnie back to her conversation with Alf Quinn. Hadn't she suggested to the man that Harold was ill-suited for this particular funeral?

She returned Harold's stare along with an icy smile. *You might be more right than you think, you king-sized bucket of sheep dip.*

Her elation was short-lived as a sneaking suspicion elbowed out her desire to celebrate. For the second time that day, she felt as if she were being manipulated like a marionette. And once again, it felt as if Alf Rattlesnake Quinn held the strings.

CHAPTER 9

"Bon, Rattlesnake probably just took what you had to say about Reverend Dobbs to heart. You're a lot more persuasive than you think. I know from experience." Lloyd squirreled around in Alice's driver's seat, his hand diving deep into his back pocket, until he retrieved a cylindrical Copenhagen can.

"Eeew, Lloyd." Bonnie blanched. "When did you take up chew? Don't you dare get any of that nasty stuff on Alice's immaculate seat cushions."

Lloyd gave her a dubious look. He pulled a wad of black fur from the seat and let it fall airily to the floor between them. "I can tell you've gone to great pains to keep this vintage automobile in pristine condition. I'll do my best to make sure it stays unsullied."

"See that you do."

He placed a pinch of tobacco into his mouth, bulging out his lower lip. "As I was saying before I was interrupted, I think you're reading too much into this whole funeral thing. Try this on for size. Sometime after we leave, Rattlesnake decides you were making sense about Harold being maybe the world's worst fit for Leo's funeral."

"This is the same Rattlesnake you thought would shoot us in the back with a snifer riple?"

Lloyd chuckled. "If you mean sniper rifle, yes. The man had an unbalanced look in his bloodshot eyes, but that doesn't mean he couldn't make the occasional rational decision. Crazy people change their minds just like us normal folk."

Ah, yes, us normal people.

Bonnie had to admit she could find no holes in her friend's reasoning. Still, she felt like she was being played. "Humor me. Forget for the moment that my dynamic personality and charisma wowed Rattlesnake and assume the man changed his mind for unsettling reasons of his own."

"Like what?"

"I'm working on that. Maybe he wanted Jason to do the funeral all along."

Lloyd took his eyes off the road long enough to favor her with a jaundiced stare. "Then why ask Harold in the first place?"

Good question. "All right. All right. Here you go. He asks Harold and yours truly just to stir up trouble. Then when things come to a boil, he can suggest the substitution that will make everyone happy. He's a hero, and we readily agree."

Lloyd frowned. "I don't buy it for a couple of reasons. One is that I still can't see why Alf couldn't just ask the young pastor Dobbs from the get-go."

Bonnie opened her mouth to argue, but Lloyd held up a hand. "Let me finish. The second problem I have with your theory is that Alf isn't some sly conniver who wants to throw a fox among the pullets and giggle while the feathers fly. He's the grieving father of a murdered son."

Bonnie knew her theory had more holes in it than a rusty colander, but she also felt in her heart of hearts something rotten was happening. "Lloyd, this same grieving father knew how many shots killed Dwight Furby."

"I have to admit that troubles me, but Byron said the man had an alibi."

"For the murder itself. Not for having a hand in it. He could have hired someone to kill Furby."

"Because Furby killed Leo?"

"Maybe." She shook her head, feeling like it was packed tight with bubble wrap. "Damn it. I don't know."

She laid a hand on Lloyd's arm. "Boss, Rattlesnake's got his finger in a lot of dangerous pies right now, and I can't get past the feeling he wants me to know it."

"And this fits together with Jason Dobbs how?"

Bonnie shrugged and shook her head slowly. "I wish I knew."

"Well, no matter who set this particular scenario in motion, you've got to admit you're better off with Jason at the helm."

No shit.

The young master Dobbs was making nada demands on her—eulogy or otherwise. Unlike his father, Jason didn't seem to have an agenda beyond the funeral itself.

You definitely dodged a bullet with that one, Pinkwater. "Is this one of those times you're going to advise me not to look a gift equine in the mouth?"

"You could say that. Right now you got all the earmarks of someone who's searching for the dark cloud inside the silver lining."

"All right, I'll put aside my suspicions and just think about the eulogy."

Coming up on the left was the high school. Lloyd's truck sat alone in the parking lot. A lone figure leaned against the rusted Ford.

"Oh, crap," Bonnie said.

Lloyd flicked the turn signal in preparation to making a left into the lot. "What is it?"

Bonnie slid down in her seat. "Don't you dare turn! It's Superintendent Divine." She reached across Lloyd and flipped off the signal, as if this simple act would transport Alice to another quadrant of the space-time continuum.

Lloyd veered hard, going straight instead of turning.

"This is ridiculous. He's already seen us, Bon. Lord in heaven, the man is waving at us." Like it had a will of its own, Lloyd's right hand in turn lifted from the steering wheel and waved back. A frozen smile painted itself on Lloyd's craggy face.

"What are you doing?" Bonnie asked through clenched teeth.

"Just being polite," he said. "Bon, you're only forestalling the inevitable. There's no way to avoid Xavier in a school district as small as ours."

Doesn't mean I can't try. "Humor me. I will not subject myself to those beady little eyes right at this moment. And I definitely am in no mood for a lecture."

Her phone rang. She checked her call-waiting and saw the name *Xavier Divine* plastered across the screen.

Double damn. She stared at the ringing phone like it was a coiled snake ready to bite. "Should I answer it?"

"Interesting question. If it was me, I would say an immediate hello to our esteemed boss and listen to what he had to say, but we're not going to do that, are we?" Lloyd gave Bonnie a wide-eyed innocent stare. "Answering the phone would be too simple. We need to complicate matters by making Xavier angry. Isn't that how these things go?"

She turned off the phone. *Not exactly crossing the Rubicon, but the water's rising.* "You think you're so smart. Aren't you worried I'm getting you in trouble?"

"Another interesting question." Lloyd pursed his lips and sighed. "Under normal circumstances I might be, but these are hardly normal circumstances, what with Marjorie gone and folks turning up dead. Nope, I think I'm going to grab the wheel and hang on to the Pinkwater Express."

A flash of guilt immobilized Bonnie, and she considered telling Lloyd to turn the car around.

Lloyd must have read either her mind or the expression on her face. "Don't sweat it, but I will demand one concession in return for going along with this insanity."

"Name it."

Lloyd rolled down the window and spit a large goober of tobacco into the wind. "You don't give me a hard time about my chew."

The mathematician in Bonnie was already extrapolating the inadequate arc Lloyd's tobacco missile had traveled. She could picture a slimy brown streak racing the length of Alice's already filthy door.

In for a penny. "Deal."

Lloyd wiped his chin and nodded approvingly. "Where to, Holmes?"

"To the fair, Watson."

Seneca Webb, formerly Seneca Berringer, valedictorian,

not to mention prom and homecoming queen, looked beautiful even with sweat pouring down her face and strands of straw plastered to her pink, freckled cheeks. Her auburn hair positively gleamed in the half light of the stall. A checkered western shirt was tied at the waist, revealing a hint of skin. Blue jeans seemed painted on.

Damn, girl, you're not giving that baby much room to breathe.

Seneca looked up from where she had been currying her quarter horse. Her face broke into a smile. "Missus P! Mister Whittaker!" She dropped the brush and threw her arms around Bonnie. "I thought I saw the two of you in the stands last night."

She reached past Bonnie and squeezed Lloyd's hand. "You just missed Caleb."

Bonnie stepped back. Her gaze went from Seneca's eyes down to her belly and back up again. "Jason Dobbs tells me you're expecting."

"He never could keep a secret."

"Is it supposed to be a secret?" Bonnie cocked her head and squinted at her former student.

Seneca shrugged. "Not so much a secret as something I don't talk about, especially around here. Everything's easier if I don't make a big deal about being pregnant for the next few months—you know, until racing season's over."

The truth was, Bonnie mostly agreed with Seneca's

husband. Barrel racing and the gestation business hardly seemed suited for one another.

Seneca must have caught the glint in Bonnie's eyes. "Aw, come on, Missus P, not you, too? Nothing's going to happen to the baby. It ain't like I'm riding bulls." The young woman stroked the flanks of her horse. "I'm as safe as in my momma's arms on the back of Jezebel here."

There was no changing the girl's mind even if Bonnie wanted to. *Hell, admit it, Pinkwater. This is the sort of reckless stand that you would have taken for yourself in another time and an alternate universe.* She sighed. "You win."

"Of course, I do." Seneca put her hands on her hips and gave Bonnie and Lloyd a crooked smile. "Besides, you guys didn't come out to the fair on this hot and dusty day to lecture little old me on the safety of pregnant-lady barrel racing."

"How'd you ever get so smart, Seneca Berringer?"

"I had a good math teacher, and it's Webb now." She bent down and picked up her curry brush. On the way back up, she drew in a sharp breath. Her hand went to her abdomen.

"Oh, my God!" Lloyd panic-danced around the girl.

"Gotcha." Seneca threw back her head and laughed.

Bonnie wanted to slap her former student. "You're a sick young puppy, my dear."

Seneca wiped a tear from her eye. "I'm sorry, Mister Whittaker. I couldn't resist. I promise I'll be good now.

What can I do you guys for?"

Bonnie waited until she was sure her anger wouldn't show up in her voice. "I need to talk to you about Leo."

The smile ran from Seneca's face. Her cheeks flushed. "I'd rather not." She took a shuddering deep breath.

Bonnie reached out and clutched her arm. "I know this is hard."

Seneca regarded Bonnie's hand as if she were deciding whether or not to knock it away. Her eyes grew flinty.

"I need to ask you a question or two." Bonnie pulled her hand away. "It's important."

Seneca started in again to curry her horse—short, rough strokes. Without looking at Bonnie, she said, "Ask away."

The stall felt as if the temperature had dropped ten degrees. *Just get on with it, Pinkwater.* "The night Leo died, he had my phone number in his pocket."

Seneca's arm halted in midstroke. She turned to stare at Bonnie. "You don't say?"

No, I'm just making this crap up. She recognized the sarcasm as a bit of residual anger left over from Seneca's "gotcha." "I was hoping you could shed some light on why he might have wanted to get a hold of me. When was the last time you saw Leo?"

The young woman chewed on her lower lip. "Two days before he died. We went out for coffee."

"So you two were still close. How did he seem to

you?"

"Way down." Seneca resumed her brushing, timing her words to the strokes. "You know he wanted to see Rattlesnake, and the old man was still stonewalling him?"

Bonnie decided not to tell the girl she learned that bit of info from the Rattlesnake himself. What would be the point? "And did Leo mention what he wanted to talk to Alf about?"

Seneca gave Bonnie a long stare. "Isn't reconciliation with his dad enough?"

Don't try to dazzle me with self-righteous bullshit, girl. "I suppose it is, but you're dodging the question, sweetie. Did Leo tell you what he wanted to talk to his dad about?"

Seneca looked away. When her gaze returned to Bonnie, the girl's cheeks were even more flushed than before. "I promised I wouldn't tell."

Bonnie glanced at Lloyd. His sympathetic expression made her cringe inwardly, and for a heated moment, she wished she didn't have her principal in tow. This good man's first compulsion would be to honor the girl's desire to keep faith with her dead friend's wishes. That compulsion was about to get in the way of what Bonnie believed she had to do.

"It's a little late for that now, isn't it?" Bonnie asked.

Lloyd touched Bonnie's arm. "Bon?"

"Not now, Lloyd." She gave him another glance,

hoping he could see she needed him to trust her for the next few minutes and above all not to interfere.

He nodded.

Bless you.

She turned back to Seneca. "Leo's dead, honey. Someone tied him to a barbed-wire fence and put three bullets in his chest. Whoever did this stole Leo from the both of us."

The girl's entire face seemed to collapse. Angry tears welled in her eyes. "You think I don't know that? But what difference does it make what he was going to talk to Rattlesnake about?"

"Maybe none. We'll never know unless you tell us."

Seneca glared at Bonnie skeptically. "People could get real hurt."

Bonnie recognized the time had come to remain silent. Nothing would be gained by further pushing the young woman. Seneca would either tell all, or she wouldn't. Bonnie hoped her face conveyed the right mixture of empathy and trustworthiness.

"I haven't told this to anyone, not even Caleb." Seneca looked from Bonnie to Lloyd, and finally back to Bonnie. "And it definitely goes no farther than this stall."

"Count on it, honey."

Lloyd grunted his agreement.

Seneca nodded in resignation. "All right. How much do you know about Leo's decision to give that speech at graduation?"

"Just what he told me. He couldn't live the lie any longer."

The young woman noticeably grimaced. "Oh, yeah, the lie. I know something about that. I was a big part of that lie." Seneca made the pronouncement like each word burnt her tongue.

When Bonnie reached out to comfort her, Seneca raised her hands and stepped back. "Don't."

You deserved that, Pinkwater. Open up old wounds, and you're going to get some blood on your petticoat. Just shut your mouth and let the girl say her piece.

Seneca released a lungful of air. "Did he tell you he expected someone else to join him in coming out?"

When Bonnie hesitated, Seneca snorted. "I'll take that for a no. Come on, Missus P. Don't look so surprised. How does your generation put it—it takes two to tango?"

Bonnie felt like she was witnessing a car wreck. She was ashamed of herself, but she couldn't look away or, in this case, stop listening. "But you know, don't you?"

"I've known all along. Kept Leo's—both of their—secrets for all these years. But two nights before his death, Leo told me he'd made a decision."

"He planned to tell his father who his lover had been?" Bonnie asked.

Seneca nodded. "Jason Dobbs."

CHAPTER 10

Bonnie surprised herself with how little the news shocked her. In retrospect, she remembered how close the two boys had been. *Or are you just painting a new color on two good friends because it fits?*

"And Leo planned to tell his father? Why now? Why after all these years?"

Seneca fixed Bonnie with a wary stare. Evidently, the girl didn't entirely trust her old teacher. "He felt betrayed. He'd waited around East Plains for three years, hoping Jason would change his mind."

Bonnie nodded, seeing where this story was heading. "But Jason had chosen his father's path, had chosen God."

"Leo had long suspected he was just fooling himself."

"So what changed?"

"About two months ago Jason put everything to rest, told Leo in no uncertain terms he had no intention of starting back up with him. Leo was devastated."

Bonnie's heart broke for her former student. It was

one level of heartache to fan a dying spark of hope, but a deeper pain when that spark was extinguished, especially by someone you loved.

A random memory ran full-blown across Bonnie's synapses—Jason Dobbs with a fat lip after going a few rounds with his father. "Did Harold Dobbs know about Jason's . . ."

"Preferences? Damn straight, he did. A month before graduation, Pastor Dobbs arranged an"—Seneca made quotation marks with her fingers—"intervention. A cabin up in the mountains. Brought in some folks who specialize in crap like that. I don't think he ever told his congregation the truth."

"The intervention must have worked. Jason didn't come out with Leo."

"Worked well enough, although Jason kept Leo hanging on with vague promises that he was still making up his mind."

"Sounds like you're pretty angry with Jason Dobbs?"

Seneca shrugged, then shook her head. "I was for the longest time, but I got over it. Shoot, Caleb and I are members of the Tabernacle, part of Jason's young marrieds group. Pastor Dobbs is our counselor."

Bonnie felt a tug urging her to ask how the counseling was going, but she needed to keep focused. "Something still bothers me. If Leo was putting the Jason

Dobbs's portion of his life behind him, why tell Rattlesnake? Leo sure wasn't likely to get much sympathy in that quarter."

The girl shrugged again. "Good question. You're going to need to ask the old man himself."

What went unsaid and hung heavy in the air was that there was no asking Leo, now that someone had silenced him forever.

Think about that later, Pinkwater. "Have you talked to Alf lately?"

From the look on Seneca's face, she was growing tired of answering questions. Or maybe just tired in general.

"Yesterday. I drove out to the range with Caleb so he could practice with his shotgun and rifle." She held an imaginary rifle to her shoulder. "Hunting season's coming in a few months."

"How did Alf seem to you?"

"Come on, Missus P. You know as well as I do, Alf's pretty screwed up behind Leo's death. It's understandable. He wasn't speaking to his son. Now that son is dead, murdered, probably for the same reason Alf wasn't speaking to him." Seneca tossed the curry brush onto a pile of straw.

"Are we done with the inquisition?" The girl swiped angrily at her eyes and looked away.

"I'm sorry, sweetie."

When Seneca looked back, her eyes sparkled with

new tears. "No, I'm sorry. I shouldn't take it out on you. It's just that I miss that gay son of a bitch so Goddamn much."

Bonnie felt like a heel, but it couldn't be helped. "Can you handle one more question?"

Seneca chuckled. "You don't give up, do you?"

"I guess not."

"What do you want to know?"

Bonnie took a deep breath. "What was Leo doing out on Squirrel Creek Road the night he died?"

"That's where they found Leo, wasn't it? I'm sorry. I can't help you with that one, either." Seneca's eyes went wide, and an anemic whimper escaped her lips. As before, she clutched her abdomen. Only this time, she fell to her knees.

Bonnie hesitated a moment. *Fool me once, shame on me.*

Immediately, she realized the girl wasn't faking. A heartbeat later, Bonnie, too, was on her knees cradling the young woman in her arms. Blood was seeping into Seneca's too-tight blue jeans.

"What the hell is going on here?" a deep voice from the doorway demanded.

"Caleb!" Seneca screamed.

Bonnie couldn't turn, but the sound of clomping boots brought Caleb Webb into sight. A tight-muscled young man in a cowboy hat, white T-shirt, blue jeans, and an immense black handlebar mustache, he squeezed in beside Bonnie.

"Just happened a minute ago." She handed Seneca off to her husband, who scooped her into his arms and stood.

"The baby!" Bonnie felt like an idiot mentioning the obvious. "We need to get her to a hospital."

Caleb Webb—his young wife moaning and slumped against his shoulder—ran from the stall.

Lloyd and Bonnie sat on the running board of the lone East Plains fire engine. Caleb had decided to rush Seneca to East Plains' volunteer fire station rather than drive the thirty-five minutes into Colorado Springs.

Neither Bonnie nor Lloyd had spoken since arriving. She glanced across the station wishing there was something she could do.

If the girl dies or loses the baby . .

Bonnie refused to consider the prospect. In the back of her mind was the very real possibility that her insistent questions brought about the girl's miscarriage.

One thing at a time, Pinkwater. Just hope these guys know their stuff.

Lloyd took her hand. His eyes were shut.

He's praying.

She shut her eyes as well. *God, don't let my stupidity be the cause of hurt on this sweet child or her baby. If You've got to punish someone, let it be me.*

Not accustomed to praying, Bonnie found she couldn't keep her eyes closed. Not five feet away Nicky Bordeleaux, part-time EMT and full-time rancher attended to Seneca. He and another volunteer had cut off her blue jeans, and Caleb had removed the girl's panties. Thank God, there was very little blood. Seneca's collar was open, and a wet cloth had been placed across her forehead.

Maybe. Bonnie let a spark of hope illuminate her darkness.

"I'm no expert," Nicky whispered loud enough for Bonnie to hear, "but I think she's going to be all right. The bleeding stopped before you got here. Mind me; she still needs to go to the hospital."

"What about the baby?" Caleb asked.

Nicky spread wide his hands. "I got no way of knowing that with the equipment I got here. I say we haul ass into the Springs."

"Let's do it." Caleb stood and moved out of the way as a flat-board stretcher was laid alongside the girl. He stepped across the station and came back with a blanket.

With a practiced motion, the two part-time firemen slid the girl onto the stretcher and Caleb covered her. Nicky nodded to the rear door of the station wagon that served as the station's ambulance. "Open her up."

Caleb did as he was told and the stretcher was slid into the ambulance. Nicky hightailed around to the driver's side of the vehicle, while the other EMT and Caleb climbed into the back. The young husband offered a tired smile to Bonnie.

"You want to follow the ambulance to the hospital?" Lloyd asked.

Bonnie swallowed and shook her head. "Let's give this little family some space."

Lloyd helped her stand. "This isn't your fault."

"I know." And she mostly believed the words. She took hold of Lloyd's arm. "Let's go."

By the time they reached the Subaru, through sheer force of will, Bonnie convinced herself that Seneca would be okay.

Lloyd held the car door. "Never a dull moment with you, Pinkwater."

Bonnie sat and peered up at her friend, grateful for his attempt to cheer her up. "Yep, I'm a walking party."

Lloyd shut the door and was next to Bonnie before he turned to her. "Want to hear something I'm not particularly proud of?"

Bonnie drew in a deep breath and released it. "Sure, I'm not too high on one Bonnie Pinkwater at the moment. Might do me good to hear your tale of woe."

Her friend shrugged. "Don't get me wrong. I was concerned about Seneca, but for a goodly portion of time, I couldn't put what Seneca said about Jason out of my mind." Lloyd stuffed a pinch of chew in his lower lip and started up the Subaru. He pulled out of the fire station lot heading back down East Plains Highway toward the school.

Strangely enough, Lloyd's confession did cheer her up. She jumped at the chance to talk about Seneca's revelation. Still, she couldn't bring herself to take the lead.

Lloyd must have read her mind. "I can't stop wondering if Leo told Jason of his plan to out him with Rattlesnake."

Bonnie nodded. She let her mind steer her into familiar paths of logic. "What if we assume he had, or at least that Jason had reason to believe Leo would reveal their secret?"

"The young pastor has a lot invested in his new life, been working at it for three years. Leo's revelation would have been a major turd in the Jason Dobbs punch bowl."

Bonnie felt as if a weight were falling from her shoulders as she threw herself into the discussion. "You're telling me. Then there's that whole business with the fistfight between Jason and his dad."

"You don't know that for sure."

Bonnie gaped incredulously at her principal. "Don't even go there, Whittaker. I'd bet my house the two of them tussled not twenty minutes before we graced them with our presence. What's more, you know it, too."

"Okay, I'll give you this one. The question is, what did they fight about?"

"I'll give you ten guesses, but I'll bet you get it on the first one. And his initials are L.Q."

Lloyd waved his hand as if Bonnie was missing the point. "But what in particular got Harold so riled up that he felt compelled to punch his boy? I can't see him laying into Jason just because his son brings up Leo Quinn's name. Hell in a bucket, Bon, they had to speak of Leo. They were planning his funeral, for Pete's sake."

Bonnie laid a hand on Lloyd's arm. "Squeeze into this one. Jason confesses to his father that he's killed Leo to shut him up about the whole Rattlesnake thing. Jason's crazy with anxiety and grief. He plans to make a clean breast of it."

Lloyd's head performed the agreement nod. "Dad loses his cool and tries to talk Jason out of doing anything rash."

"Jason and Dad fall into harsh words, maybe *hypocrite,* maybe *asshole.*"

"You're really getting into this."

"Hell, I'm barely started. Now the words between Jason and Papa escalate into real heat. A little pushing. A little shoving. Shoot, Lloyd, Jason may even have taken the first swing, and now Daddy loses any semblance of cool. He brings it to Junior and the rest is church history."

For a long moment, Lloyd worked the lump of tobacco in his lower lip, obviously mulling over their mutual theory. "I got a problem or two."

Bonnie had to admit, she was also having her own doubts. "Hit me with your best shot."

"Let's go all the way back to Jason killing Leo."

"Barbed wire?"

Lloyd pursed his lips. "Barbed wire. And naked. I can't see Jason tying his naked friend to a fence just so he can kill him. I mean, why go to all that trouble?"

Why, indeed?

"A reason doesn't immediately come to mind. But if Jason did tie him up, then we're no longer talking a crime of passion but a premeditated killing."

Lloyd gave her a sideways glance before returning his gaze to the road. "Okay, now add this to the mix. I can't see Leo *letting* Jason hog-tie him to no barbed-wire fence."

"Another tussle, maybe Jason wins this one."

"Nope. You told me yourself there were no signs of a fight anywhere on Leo's person. No black eye. No bloody lip. Bon, you or anybody tries to truss *me* up naked to barbed wire, you better be ready for the fight of your life. Leo would be no different. He was a scrapper, if nothing else."

"All right, point taken. What about your second problem?"

"We got a dead rodeo clown. How does Jason Dobbs, youth pastor of Saved by the Blood Pentecostal Tabernacle, fit into the murder of a rodeo clown in a port-a-potty behind a beer tent at the El Paso County Fair?"

Bonnie sighed an I'll-go-you-one-better sigh. "I got two other questions for you."

"Fire away."

"First, I'm sure by now Byron's had time to compare the bullets from the Furby shooting with those taken from Leo."

Lloyd's eyes widened as he obviously considered the possibility. "And if they're from the same gun?"

Bonnie let her head rock into a slow nod. "If they are, then we have one killer, who had something against both Leo Quinn and Dwight Furby."

"Witherspoon?"

"Maybe, but consider this, as well. Didn't Jason Dobbs tell us last night that he hadn't been in contact with Leo?"

Again, Lloyd's face registered surprised understanding. "He sure as blazes did, but—"

"But Seneca said Jason got hold of Leo not two months ago and put the final kibosh on their love affair. And that makes Jason Dobbs a liar."

By the time Bonnie got back to her hacienda in Black Forest, it was close to five o'clock. She and Lloyd had driven to the school to pick up his truck, and thankfully Superintendent Xavier Divine had skedaddled for parts unknown. She said her good-byes and agreed to pick up Lloyd for the fair later that night. Truth be told, he'd volunteered to come for her, but she lived in the opposite direction from the El Paso fairgrounds. It made absolutely no sense for the man to drive to hell and gone just to assuage his knightly proclivities, sweet as they were.

Besides, he'd be providing the inadvertent entertainment soon enough. Bonnie let a minor wave of guilt wash over her. Despite the day's events, and Lloyd's sad situation, she couldn't help but view the coming evening with a supersized portion of giddiness.

Marjorie Whittaker, what the hell are you up to?

For that matter what was Lloyd planning? Would he introduce Bonnie to Marjorie's boy-toy lover? Bonnie pictured Marjorie in a skintight T-shirt that read, STRANGERS HAVE THE BEST CANDY. Was the previous Mrs. Whittaker undergoing some midlife crisis that involved tattoos and multiple body piercings?

I'd rather show than tell you, Lloyd had said. Hell's bells, what could possibly be at the fair that would explain Marjorie and her sudden escape from a marriage of thirty-plus years?

Boil me in oil, thought Bonnie, *I can't wait.*

Hypatia, the golden retriever, licked Bonnie's hand, and she scrubbed a fist across the dog's brow. "Big doings tonight, sweetie pie. Mommy is all awash in morbid anticipation."

Absentmindedly, Bonnie opened cans of dog and cat food. Euclid, the black Burmese, jumped onto the breakfast island to sneak a preview morsel. It was a testament to Bonnie's preoccupation that she didn't immediately sweep the cat airborne.

After putting out the food, Bonnie sat on the family room floor, her back to the front of the couch. She dragged a small dry erase board and a marker from under the couch and set it on her lap. The plan was to get started on the eulogy, maybe do an outline. Now that she'd finally come to grips with the fact that what happened to Seneca wasn't her fault, she fallen into a new set of worries. After all, she had less than fifteen hours until she had to deliver the damnable speech.

Bonnie wrote *Leo Quinn* across the top of the board. Immediately, she realized the problem wasn't what to say, but what to leave out. She could easily do a half hour delineating the impact Leo had on the school, the people, and the community of East Plains. The boy was an athlete, a scholar, a beloved son, a good friend, an imp capable of inventive mischief, and a brave individual who stood up for what he believed even when it cost him everything.

She also knew the temperament of the good folks of East Plains. *If I know what's good for me, I'd better limit this talk to no more than ten minutes, or I'm going have their eyeballs glazing over.*

Bonnie wrote, erased, then rewrote several beginnings to her speech before she brought the sleeve of her blouse to bear and expunged the entire mess with an exasperated swipe. Hypatia plopped down beside Bonnie and nosed at the whiteboard.

"Mommy's not having any luck, sweet girl."

Just give in, Pinkwater. You know damn well what you'd rather be analyzing.

Taking pen in hand, Bonnie wrote *Who Killed Leo Quinn?* at the top of the whiteboard and underlined it twice.

The phone in the kitchen rang.

Bonnie grunted as she hoisted herself to her feet. The phone rang again. "I'm coming, already." She fought her way through a canine obstacle course.

"Ladies, do you mind?" Bonnie reached the phone on the third ring. "Pinkwater's."

"Missus Pinkwater, this is Wilma Trotter."

The woman's voice brought a parade of images into Bonnie's mind. A thin, almost emaciated woman with one good eye and the pirate eye patch to show it off. A quick mind in almost complete camouflage hidden behind a latter-day hippie persona. The woman raised bees, ate only organic, and yet snorted down a single shot of Wild Turkey with breakfast, lunch, and dinner. Then there was the walking stick.

"What can I do for you, Wilma?"

"How 'bout stopping by for a moment this evening."

Bonnie was about to beg out of the offer, maybe even explain about going to the fair when she stopped short. A younger, slimmer Mo Witherspoon, a senior at East Plains, loomed large in her mind. The young ape had his leg propped on a split rail fence, and he was holding court with Dwight Furby and another young ne'er-do-well. The other boy was Gabriel Trotter.

"Wilma, does this have anything to do with Moses Witherspoon?"

A long moment passed before the woman at the other end of the phone line spoke. "You still can read my mind, Pinkwater. How'd you know?"

"Not important. Could I come by right now?"

CHAPTER 11

WILMA TROTTER OPENED THE ALUMINUM DOOR ON THE trailer after the first knock. She wore a tie-dyed T-shirt and a pair of coveralls resplendent with patches of Art Crumb characters—Doo-Dah Man, Mister Natural, The Fabulous Furry Freak Brothers. String-bean thin and tall, with wispy blond-gray hair, the woman myopically regarded Bonnie with one good eye, the other covered by an eye patch sporting the image of a magic mushroom. Wilma leaned heavily onto a shoulder-high walking stick whose knob was carved into the likeness of Timothy Leary.

Welcome to the twenty-first century, Wilma, my dear.

"Well, get yourself in here, Pinkwater. I made some *rooibos* tea."

Bonnie damn well knew it wouldn't do any good to explain that she hated rooibos tea. With a little under an hour before she was to pick up Lloyd, Bonnie had no time to argue with a refugee from the sixties about beverage preferences. Best to just let the woman entertain in her own eccentric fashion. Bonnie followed Wilma into her tiny kitchen and plopped down at a powder blue paisley dinette set. As a centerpiece, a Bullwinkle the Moose vase held a plastic bird-of-paradise flower and a pinwheel.

Wilma set down two steaming cups of tea and, using her walking stick, carefully lowered herself onto a dinette chair.

Bonnie adopted the receptive audience pose.

Wilma dabbed her finger into the tea, and unselfconsciously lifted the eye patch. She swabbed the rim of her sunken eye with the reddish-brown liquid. With her finger still beneath the patch, she fixed Bonnie with the good orb. "I didn't know who else to turn to. Don't know who else I could trust." She let the patch fall back into place.

Bonnie could see what the woman was hinting at and felt the need to establish some ground rules before Wilma went any further. "With all that's happened, Wilma, I can't make any promises. People have died."

"You think I don't know that?" A momentary scowl was quickly replaced by a look of resignation and remorse. "Oh, hell, do what you got to do. You've always treated Gabe fairly."

"And I always will. Now, what's going on?"

"Witherspoon's Trans Am screamed into my yard about nine o'clock last night."

The Ol' Spoonmaster wasted no time getting here from the fair. "How did he look?"

"Like the Grim Reaper had sent him picture postcards from hell. Did my heart good to see the little bastard so shook up."

Bonnie suddenly remembered why she'd always been so fond of Wilma. For a woman with a will-o'-the-wisp exterior, she could be rock solid when she put her mind to it. "And Gabe?" Bonnie asked.

Wilma splayed her fingers traffic-cop style, indicating Bonnie needed to keep quiet for a bit. "Back up, Pinkwater. I'll get to all that."

"Take your time."

"I damn well mean to. First thing, even before Witherspoon brought his ugly puss to my door, Gabe had been acting strange. Jumpy. Preoccupied."

"Uh-huh. Since when?"

"Since he went out driving with Mister Spoon and that moron Furby."

Bonnie felt the hair on the back of her neck rise up. "Are we talking Saturday night?"

Wilma nodded. "Got in late, too. I was down for the night when he got back, so I don't know what time it was, but he stayed in his room pretty much all the next day, took the newspaper in there with him." The woman took a large slurp of her tea seemingly to give herself time to organize her narrative.

Bonnie seized the opportunity to stir the cauldron a mite. "You know about Furby?"

Wilma cocked her head and gave over a quizzical one-eyed stare. "What about him?"

"Dead, murdered last night." Bonnie told Wilma an abbreviated version of the port-a-potty killing, including her suspicion that Witherspoon was somehow connected to the murder.

The color drained from Wilma Trotter's already pale face. "Oh, shit. Don't tell me that, Pinkwater. My Gabe's gone off with that numbskull."

"Did Gabe say where they were going?"

Wilma slowly shook her head. "Not for lack of me asking, but I might as well have been shouting at a birdbath."

"And he's been gone since last night?"

"Yep, and that ain't the worst of it. Before the two of them took off, I heard them talking in Gabe's room."

Bonnie resisted the urge to speak. Wilma had opened the floodgates. All Bonnie would have to do was let it all wash over her. She nodded for Wilma to continue.

"Well, the day before I had read in the paper—after I got it back from Gabe—about that homosexual getting himself killed last Saturday. The one who gave the speech at Gabe's graduation."

"Leo Quinn."

"That's the one. Like I said, I read about it in the

paper. I mean how and where he was shot, how they found him all naked, everything."

"And?"

"I couldn't hear exactly what Gabe and Witherspoon were saying, just stems and seeds, if you know what I mean."

Bonnie found herself growing impatient with the woman's roundabout approach. "But you did hear something?"

"I sure did. More than once they talked about something the three of them did out on Squirrel Creek Road."

When Bonnie arrived at Lloyd's, he was waiting outside.

He ambled up to the car and leaned onto the open window. "So did she say what they did on Squirrel Creek?"

Avoiding the stick shift, Bonnie slid across into the passenger seat, inviting Lloyd to drive. "Wilma didn't know, but damn, Lloyd, what about it? Witherspoon, Furby, and Trotter all out on Squirrel Creek at the right time, probably drinking, probably up to no good."

As he sat, Lloyd shoved a pinch of Copenhagen under his lower lip. "And you think they ran into Leo?"

"Absolutely, and I wouldn't put it past either Witherspoon or Furby to do a number on a homosexual."

Lloyd flicked the last few grains of tobacco out the window. "And now Furby's dead."

"You betcha. Somehow Rattlesnake got wind of

what those three did, and he's going after them one at a time."

Lloyd inhaled deeply and sighed. "I know I'm sounding like a broken record, but I got a few problems with this scenario. I mean beyond the fact that Rattlesnake has an alibi."

Bonnie readied herself to shoot down her friend's *few problems*. "Go for it."

"Last night when we saw Rattlesnake, he was talking to Witherspoon, the two of them laughing like long-lost amigos."

"Just for show." She pushed his arm. "If you mean to kill someone, do you tip your hand?"

"Fair enough. What about Leo's pile of folded clothes? Can you picture any of those three idiots taking the time to fold clothes, especially if they're drunk?"

Bonnie tugged at her ear. "That one crossed my mind, but hell, it could happen. They might have thought the idea of leaving their victim's clothes in a neat pile was a hoot and a holler."

"After putting three holes in his chest? Some hoot."

"They could have done it before they killed him."

"I suppose." He gave her a sidelong glance. "Tell me you informed Deputy Hickman of this newest development."

"Of course, I did. He promised he'd look into it. Include the Colorado Springs police in a search for

Spoon's Trans Am."

Lloyd scrubbed a calloused hand across his chin. "So if I understand the situation, we have no further responsibilities. We're not going on the hunt for Witherspoon and Trotter. We're going to leave police business to the police, at least for tonight?" He put the Subaru into gear and pulled out of his drive.

"I do believe that accurately describes where we stand. Soooooo, what are we going to see?" Bonnie didn't think Lloyd would really tell her, but she had to try.

Lloyd checked his wristwatch. "Won't be long now." The hint of a smile played at the corner of the man's mouth.

"I'm not going to beg, Whittaker."

"Never expected you to. How's the eulogy coming?"

Bonnie groaned. "It's not. The darned thing swims around in my brain refusing to gel. I mean to tell you, I'm not so sure I'll have anything come the funeral tomorrow."

"You'll do fine. You always land on your feet."

"From your lips to God's ear."

Lloyd slapped the steering wheel. "Speaking of God, I got a call from Xavier."

Bonnie sighed an it-had-to-happen sigh. "And?"

"Well, what do you think? He started off asking why we kept on going and ignored him."

"And why did we?"

Lloyd momentarily turned, just long enough to grin

mischievously. "You'd have been proud of me. I told him we were late to see Seneca at the fair."

"Nice, Whittaker. A nice composite of truth and fib. Watch yourself. You're getting devious in your dotage."

"It gets better. I filled him in on what happened to the girl, even launching into a spirited rendition of the scene at the fire station."

Bonnie nodded her approval. "Better, indeed. First you head him off at the pass with a right turn at truth junction, then you slather in a large helping of reality. Was the big man impressed with our activities?"

Lloyd pursed his lips, his expression changing to one of chagrin. "Not enough to forget about asking what you were up to these days."

Oh, God, tell me you didn't spill the beans entirely. "And what *is* Bonnie Pinkwater up to these days?"

"She's working with the sheriff's office because Deputy Hickman requested her assistance. I told Xavier you were just the first of Leo's teachers who were being called in."

"Bless you. For your final trick, now tell me our esteemed leader isn't privy to the fact that Leo Quinn had my phone number in his pocket—after a fashion—when he died."

"He is completely ignorant of that fact. However..."

Bonnie whipped around in her seat to give Lloyd the full brunt of her glower. "No howevers, no unfortunatelies, not even a measly uh-oh."

"However, he did say he still wanted you to call him and that he intended to give Deputy Hickman a ring."

Bonnie blew out a full lungful of air. "Things could be worse. Even though I can't do a damn thing about what Byron will tell the boss man, I can still claim I never received your message. You never saw me."

Lloyd blanched and shook his head. "Not quite. I let slip about you and me going to the fair tonight. In fact, I got the impression Superintendent Divine might make an appearance." Lloyd put on his most ingenuous half smile. "You could consider telling the big man the truth."

"We'll see." She nodded toward Seventh Street, the main drive into the fair. "I'm not going to think about any of that now. It's showtime."

Just past the fair gate, Bonnie had to quick-step around what appeared to be a trio of maybe twenty-year-old female kindergarten teachers and forty to fifty of their miniscule charges. In pairs, the children held hands, their tiny feet scuffling up a cloud of dust Bonnie absolutely had to put in her rearview mirror.

Good luck with your sanity, dearies.

As much as she had been feeling sorry for herself earlier, she felt even sorrier for these fresh-faced teachers. Sometime that evening at least one child would get sick, maybe wet himself. Certainly there would be tears, whining, and the occasional fight. Truth be told, Bonnie considered children under the age of five card-carrying members of an alien species. Cute with their grapefruit butts, oversized heads and eyes, but certainly nothing more than curiosities. If one could circumvent them, by all means one should.

So much was Bonnie in avoidance mode that she momentarily lost track of Lloyd. She was reluctantly turning back, when she felt a hand grab her at the elbow.

"In here, Bon." Lloyd held open the door of a gigantic aluminum Quonset hut. He took her arm and led her past a cloud of smoke and the pod of cowboys generating it.

As soon as Bonnie stepped into the building she was assailed by loud canned country music. Dolly Parton's disembodied voice was singing a sad farewell and promising someone she would *always love them*. Lloyd put his hand on Bonnie's back and guided her to a small beer stall.

The music was so insistent Bonnie had to lean close to Lloyd's ear. "What are we doing in here?"

"You'll see," he mouthed, then signaled for the bartender to get them three beers and a basket of popcorn. It seemed they could have any brand of beer they wanted as long as it was Coors. Lloyd handed her the popcorn and a plastic cup brimming with foam.

Dolly finished her good-bye lament, and a male

singer launched into a song that entreated everyone to *live like they were dying.*

Lloyd took a long pull on his beer and crooked a finger for her to follow him. The two of them wove through the crowd—folks toasting one another, an old couple slow dancing next to their table, teenagers tossing popcorn across the heads of their elders. Several long tables added to the obstacle course, and since some of them were at least partially empty, Bonnie wondered where Lloyd was taking her. Finally, he selected one just off the dance floor.

Curiouser and curiouser. Does he mean to ask me to dance? She set down her beer on the table and herself next to Lloyd.

Before long, a tall cowboy with an impressive beer gut and what appeared to be a brand-new straw cowboy hat waddled onto a small stage beyond the dance floor.

Bonnie elbowed Lloyd. "That's Mister Crump. The one I told you about."

When Lloyd failed to produce the appropriate expression of recognition, she said, "The one who helped me move Furby's body."

"Oh, yeah." Lloyd obviously had more on his mind than Paul Bunyan–sized cowboys.

"Ladies and gents," Crump drawled into one of two mikes. "I'm going to ask you to put your hands together and welcome onto the Appaloosa Stage, a genuine El

Paso County original. Let's hear it for Swing Town.

Four men led by a woman in a pink cowboy hat and matching bandanna and boots strode onto the stage. Two of the men picked up guitars, a bass and an acoustic, while the other two sat behind a piano and a drum set. The woman, a fiddle at her side, sashayed up to the mike recently vacated by Crump.

"Howdy, music lovers. Like the handsome man said, we're Swing Town, and I hope we can get you on your feet tonight and onto the dance floor."

Bonnie felt her back stiffen. She knew that voice. When she turned to Lloyd, he was already staring back at her.

"Say hello to the new Marjorie."

CHAPTER 12

Marjorie Whittaker jammed the fiddle into the crook of her neck and sawed out the bluesy opening licks of "Little Red Rooster." Her fingers were a blur.

Damn, the woman's good.

A cheer went up from the audience. Radiating a two-hundred-watt smile, Marjorie took a bow and blew through another quick arpeggio that ran up and down the neck of her violin.

Bonnie leaned across the table. "I knew Marjorie played—I mean I must have seen her a dozen times at parties and such—but damn, Lloyd, the woman's got game. And she knows her way around the blues. What gives, big guy?"

Lloyd tore his gaze from his erstwhile spouse, giving at least a part of his attention to Bonnie. He pointed with his chin to the piano player, a rotund aging hippie with a long gray ponytail. "When I met Marjorie at Kearney State, she was half of a duet with Chad there. The two of them worked a circuit throughout Kansas and Nebraska. Had been at it for two, almost three years, planning to get married."

Marjorie sidled up to the mike and belted, "I got me a Little Red Rooster. He won't crow for the break of day." She sounded like a smooth blend of Phoebe Snow and Bonnie Raitt.

The piano barrelhoused through an infectious boogie-woogie turn.

Again Marjorie leaned into the mike. "I got me a Little Red Rooster, people. He plum refuses to crow for the break of day."

This time when Chad's piano chimed in, Marjorie's fiddle matched it note for note.

Bonnie turned back to Lloyd. "I would imagine there's a story in how she ended up as Missus Lloyd Whittaker."

Her friend nodded. "Chad was a womanizer. Marjorie caught him with a coed and not only ended their engagement, but broke up the act as well. I just happened to be in the right place at the right time to pick up the pieces."

"Must have been hard on her."

Lloyd shrugged, but a melancholy smile played at the edges of his lips. "I suppose you could say that. But Marjorie's a tough lady. Chad came around once to try to talk her into finishing the tour, but she let him know she couldn't be with someone she didn't trust, not even in business. He found a new partner, and Marjorie stayed with me. I was about to graduate. We got married less than a year later."

"So how . . ."

"So how did she end up after all this time in Swing Town?" Lloyd shouted to be heard over the band, which had ratcheted up the noise level.

Marjorie was almost maniacal as she attacked a fiddle lead. The guitar player stood at her side, fanning Marjorie and her instrument with his black cowboy hat as though both the woman and the fiddle might catch fire. As for Missus Lloyd Whittaker herself, she wore a mixed expression of concentration and ecstasy.

Lloyd waved his now empty beer glass toward Chad. "Last May, Swing Town came through the Springs. We went to see them playing on a stage a lot like this one." Lloyd held up a finger indicating he wanted to listen to the band before he finished his tale.

A roar went up from the crowd as Chad and Marjorie swapped licks, mirroring first one melody line, then another. With each trade-off, the tempo increased. Thrown in, almost casually, were recognizable refrains from other songs, first a revved-up "Somewhere over the Rainbow" from *The Wizard of Oz*, then an equally accelerated "Wonderful World" à la Louis Armstrong. They finished their exchange and the song with a finale that modulated a series of blues riffs, building "Little Red Rooster" to a crashing crescendo. When the tune ended, Marjorie let loose a *wahoo* and everyone, including Bonnie, joined in.

Her principal sighed. "She's more than good, isn't she? It's like she was born to it."

"But she's your wife; you should be sharing all this."

Lloyd shook his head. "She's with Chad now. As I was saying, Swing Town came through last May, and Marjorie begged me to go see them."

He tipped the glass to his lips, trying to glean the last dregs. "That version of Swing Town was passable, no great shakes, but they didn't stink up the place. The lead singer, the guitar player now, could carry a tune, but he didn't really go anywhere with the songs. About halfway through the first set, Chad invited Marjorie onto the stage—seems he brought a fiddle with him."

Up on Appaloosa Stage, Marjorie launched into a sweet fiddle tune she introduced as "The Lover's Waltz." The lilting heartfelt strains of the tune stopped Lloyd speechless. He simply stared at his wife—her eyes closed in rapture. She wasn't twenty bars into it when the dance floor started to fill. Cowboys holding their ladies close—slow two-step syncopation to the melody and beat.

Lloyd blanched and set down his cup. "This was the first song she did that night. It brought down the house.

When it ended, the crowd demanded another."

"Did she know another?"

"You bet. She'd been tinkering with songs ever since the kids graduated and moved out. I chalked it up to empty-nest syndrome. She'd go down into the basement and spend hours going over tunes she and Chad had done twenty-five years before. She also added new songs, sometimes asking me to listen. Most times I was too busy." He thumped himself on the side of the head. "I should have listened more."

You think? Bonnie's heart went out to her friend. "I take it, she was a hit."

Lloyd snorted. "You should have seen her. She looked twenty again. So beautiful, her face all lit up and full of life. I think she ended up doing five more songs in that set. When she came back to the table, she absolutely gushed and informed me the band wanted her to return the next night."

Uh-oh. "What did you say?"

"I can't exactly remember. Something like, *Suit yourself*. I begged out of going with her. I had to attend some administrator thingamabob with Xavier. I think it was in Steamboat Springs. Big mistake. I should have seen how much this dealio meant to her. How much she wanted my support."

I'll say.

Bonnie felt herself reintroduced to the clueless

stupidity of the masculine portion of the human race. Somehow they had no problem demanding unconditional backing from their women but failed to see how that gate should swing in two directions. When it came to being there when they were needed most, a significant fraction of them never stepped up to the plate. Shoot, they failed to recognize a plate even existed.

"Tell me you at least asked her how it went."

Lloyd shook his head. "When I got back it was late. I was tired. She wasn't home yet, and I went to bed. I think we talked about it a little in the morning, but I didn't really listen. Instead, I went on about my conference, my boring conference and the long dull drive with Xavier."

"And she paid attention, like the good wife should."

Lloyd shot Bonnie a pained look. "You think I haven't played that morning over and over again in my mind?"

She patted his arm. "I'm sure you have."

When the waltz ended, so did the conversation. For the next forty minutes, Bonnie and her longtime friend gave their attention to a band that knew their way around a tune—tight when the song called for precision but never forgetting people were there to have fun. Marjorie even told jokes between songs.

Lloyd was right, she seemed born to it.

When Chad broke into the opening bars of the band's signature song, "Swing Town" by Steve Miller,

Lloyd stood.

Bonnie peered up at her principal. "Going somewhere, cowboy?"

Lloyd grunted. "If I'm not mistaken, this'll be the last song of this set. Going to get me some air. I can't talk to her right now." He tilted his chin ever so slightly toward the stage. Bonnie followed his gaze to see Marjorie staring first at her husband, then quizzically at her.

Bonnie could only imagine what Marjorie had to be thinking. "I'll join you."

Lloyd rested a heavy hand on her shoulder. "Nah, you stay put. I figure you're going to want to chat up Marjorie, and it'll go a lot smoother if I'm not hanging around. I won't be long, and I won't be far." Without another word, he took off through the crowded room and out the double doors.

For a long moment, Bonnie still considered following him, but inertia and a real desire to talk to Marjorie kept her rooted. She needed to hear from the woman's lips just how bad things had progressed.

Besides, this woman can play, and I need some entertainment that doesn't include sawdust and horse poop.

The Steve Miller tune ended, and true to Lloyd's word, the band announced they were going to take a break. Still holding her fiddle, Marjorie made a beeline for Bonnie.

"You look like you've been abandoned."

Bonnie signaled for Marjorie to sit. "It appears that way. How have you been, Marjorie?"

The woman shrugged and sat. "I got my good days and bad. This just so happens to be one of the really good ones."

"You look like you're having a hell of a time up there. Swing Town's got a good sound."

Marjorie turned her head and regarded the stage she recently vacated. Her head bobbed as if to a melody only she could hear. "I love the music, that's for sure." A faint smile decorated her face. "And I love the crowds, the applause, the appreciation."

Chad strode past, heading for the beer stall.

Bonnie lifted her beer glass and pointed. "And the man?"

"You get right to the heart of the matter, don't you, Bon? I've always liked and hated that about you." She shook her head. "What can I say? He makes me smile, even though I know he's a shit-bird who cares more about his hair than he does about other people."

What ho, a breach in the ranks. Cover me, boys. I'm going in. "It's none of my business, Marjorie, but if I'm hearing you right, you left Lloyd for a man you don't love."

Marjorie's face went hard, all planes and angles. "You're right. It's none of your business. Besides, Mizz

Nosy Parker, it's not as simple as that. Nothing ever is."

Bonnie wasn't in the mood to back down. "Both you and Lloyd are my friends. So when boss man tells me you're with Chad now, and then you turn around and inform me the man is a slimeball, I'm curious. Is the music that great that you're willing to chuck a marriage of thirty years?"

"Thirty-one," Marjorie corrected.

"Even more to the point, thirty-one years, for a chance to wear a pink hat and boots?"

"Don't go nasty on me, Pinkwater." Marjorie eyed her coldly. "I happen to like these boots. What did Lloyd tell you about why we split?"

Bonnie let her mind play back the events of the past few days and realized Lloyd had told her precious little in the way of reasons for the rift between himself and his wife. He had let her infer that somehow in choosing Swing Town, Marjorie had negated their marriage.

"I can't say he told me much of anything." She reached for her beer, swishing the last warm swig around in her mouth.

"And I should probably follow his lead, but I won't. Lord knows why I feel the need to be up front with you." She held up a hand, perhaps sensing Bonnie meant to interrupt. "But before I bare my soul, tell me true. Are you two sleeping together?"

Bonnie sputtered, almost choking on the beer in the

back of her throat. "Dear God, no! I just found out this week you two weren't together."

"Let me guess. Nurse Englehart, right?"

"On the money."

"The woman is uncanny. I think I hate her."

"Join the club."

They shared a rueful laugh that approached real humor but never quite got there.

Bonnie set her hand down on Marjorie's arm. "Sweetie, Lloyd's maybe the best friend I have on this screwed-up planet."

For a millisecond, she considered the blatant manipulation she was about to perform and came to peace with it. She offered up a shamelessly emotional account of how she found Lloyd dirty and unkempt amid beer cans and pizza boxes.

"He misses you."

Marjorie swallowed and blinked back tears. "You can't fix this, Bonnie."

Maybe I can't, but I'm sure as hell going to make a hard run at it. "So what's at the bottom of all this besides a woman having the time of her life?"

Mrs. Lloyd Whittaker drew in a long breath and let it out slowly. "What do you know already?"

Bonnie told her she knew about the band coming to town and Marjorie's accolades. How Swing Town asked her to come back the following night and how Lloyd didn't go with or even care to listen when she tried to explain how much it meant to her.

"He told you that? I'm surprised at his insight."

Bonnie nodded. "He knows he screwed up. He wasn't there for you."

Marjorie stared off toward the double doors Lloyd had walked through not ten minutes before. She shook her head. "I was hurting. You've got no idea how well it went. The next morning I opened up to share a major peak experience. I wanted to share everything with my man, the father of my children. Was that too much to ask?"

"Of course not, honey," Bonnie whispered.

She had butterflies beating out a rhythm in her gut and a bad feeling that refused to go away. This felt like a justification speech, and there were too few things a married woman could line up to justify—besides the big dirty. "What happened, Marjorie?"

"When I realized this man with whom I'd spent over thirty years didn't care a fig about my triumphs, and never would, I gave up. I pretended to listen when he went on about his stupid convention, but as soon as he finished, I fabricated some excuse to get out of there."

Uh-oh. "You went looking for Chad?"

Marjorie reddened. "I know I shouldn't have. I wasn't in my right mind. Certainly not in a good frame to make life-changing decisions."

"Let me guess again. Chad did listen. The man was

a fount of understanding."

"He can be very charming when he puts his devious mind to it."

"I've got no doubt about that. And you were vulnerable."

The woman nodded. "Don't get me wrong, Pinkwater. I'm not trying to excuse what I did. I screwed up, and now I'm paying the piper. My kids aren't even talking to me."

Bonnie whistled. "That's rough. I know. I went through a similar thing myself."

Marjorie cocked her head and gave Bonnie an incredulous look. "You? With whom?"

An out-of-focus image of her one-time millionaire rancher lover and their drunken indiscretion capered full-blown across Bonnie's synapses. She winced. "I'd rather not kiss and tell. Needless to say, I threw myself on the mercy of the court. Ben forgave me. I haven't looked back since."

"Good for you." Marjorie didn't try to hide sarcasm in her voice.

I'm going to let that one pass, Marjorie Lane Whittaker. But don't play on my good nature too often. Bonnie took the woman's hands in hers. "The reason I mentioned my own problem was that I think you should do the same."

Marjorie snatched her hands away. "Is that so? Well,

FYI, I did that very thing. I went home. Made a clean breast of it. Didn't even try to justify my actions with how hurt I had been."

"And?"

This time the tears came in earnest. "You know what's so messed up about all of this? The busybodies, like Nurse Englehart, probably think I walked out on Lloyd. Like I'm going through some sort of midlife crisis."

Bonnie's stomach tightened. "And that's not what happened?"

Marjorie's face went hard. "Not even a little bit. Principal Lloyd Whittaker, your best friend in the whole world and my husband of thirty-one years, threw my sorry keister out the door, telling me in no uncertain terms to never come back."

CHAPTER 13

LIKE A WOMAN IN A TRANCE, BONNIE LET HER FEET CARRY her out of the Appaloosa Club and back into the dusty night. Her head and spirit ached. Certainly, drinking beer on a school night contributed heavily to the first.

You're a real party animal, Pinkwater. One beer and you're ready for bed.

The latter strain came from being stretched thin between Lloyd and Marjorie, and realizing the soon-to-be ex-Missus Whittaker might have been right. There might be no fix for the rift between these two dear friends. The real truth—Lloyd's pride might not let him forgive Marjorie's infidelity.

Bonnie could even see the man's point. Wasn't it Marjorie herself who cut Chad loose thirty-one years earlier, saying she couldn't be with someone she didn't trust? Now Marjorie Whittaker was being hoisted on her own ethical petard.

What goes around comes around, sweetie.

Everything about the circumstances surrounding her friends seemed to have the finality of a Greek tragedy, with the same feeling of plodding inevitability.

Her mood wasn't improved as she passed through a thick cloud of cigarette smoke for the second time in one night. Her eyes stung, and her nostrils rebelled. And, damn, if it didn't seem like the very same cowboys in the exact same macho poses were causing the stink.

Give it a rest, boys. Ain't you got nothing better to do than tell each other lies and inhale partially burned hydrocarbons and thirty different kinds of poisonous gases?

One of the cowboys, a gut-over-the-belt-buckle specimen in a black Stetson and an equally ebony yoked western shirt hoisted one of his pointy-toed boots, and without a by-your-leave, let loose with a bit of flatulence that resounded admirably around the small contingent. All present thought the gesture the height of articulate humor.

I stand corrected, gentlemen. You obviously had something better to do.

Bonnie emerged from the odiferous fog of smoke and methane only to find herself staring at a sight that brought an immediate smile to her face. Superintendent Xavier Divine—The Divine Pain in the Ass to those who knew him well—was pressed close to his soon-to-be-bride, the former Angelica Devereaux. The woman towered over her massively domed and follicle-challenged swain by a good six inches.

IRRATIONAL NUMBERS

Like the dozen-plus other times Bonnie had basked in the presence of this dynamic duo, she was struck by the incongruity of the pair. Angelica was legendary for her voracious sexual appetite, voluptuous figure, kilograms of makeup, and minklike morals. Besides his ovoid-shaped bald pate, Xavier Divine's hallmarks were his lack of imagination, the enormous stick up his posterior, and a tendency to avoid scandal or personal responsibility of any kind. When Angelica had dumped her burly boyfriend, East Plains' physical education teacher Harvey Sylvester, in favor of Xavier, it was generally accepted that she would be the death of the ludicrous administrator.

No such luck.

The man not only didn't appear to be booking passage on the river Styx, he seemed to be thriving, foolish to the boundary of ridiculous looking, but thriving nonetheless. For this evening's festivities, Angelica had decided Tuesday was dress-up night. She was to be Rodeo Barbie to Xavier's rotund Cowboy Ken.

For herself she'd chosen rhinestone-studded high-heeled cowgirl boots, skintight pegged blue jeans, a pink silk western top, and a white bandanna. Her long platinum-blond hair flowed from beneath an equally white cowboy hat that had to be at least a dozen Xs.

The good superintendent had retired his usual uniform of lime green corduroy and polo shirt in favor of something with a bit more local flavor. His own blue jeans—thankfully less tight than Angelica's—were held up with a belt buckle the size of a Galapagos turtle. A fire-breathing bull stared menacingly out of the buckle, attesting, no doubt, to Xavier's virility. Divine, too, wore a western shirt, although the yoke on his appeared to be made of some sort of reptile skin, as were his boots. Tying the entire ensemble together, and to Angelica's outfit, Xavier wore a matching white cowboy hat and bandanna—his chapeau cocked on his head at a rakish angle.

Bonnie had stopped at the edge of the Appaloosa Club's walkway in the hope that neither Xavier nor his slutty fiancée would see her. Besides over-the-top outfits, another thing the pair had in common was a detestation of one Bonnie Pinkwater that was thick and viscous as tar. So far she'd remained unseen.

"Bon," a deep voice behind her yelled out.

She practically leapt from her skin.

Even as Divine and Angelica turned toward the noise, Bonnie pivoted to witness a red-faced Lloyd Whittaker coming from the direction of the arcade. He had a beer in each hand and a foamy mustache on his upper lip. He drew near Bonnie as though he wanted to take her arm but only then realized, because of his beer burden, was unable to do so. A wide and obviously shit-faced grin spread from ear to ear. He squinted past her at the fast approaching pair of Angelica and Divine.

"Well, ain't you two a sight?" he slurred.

His heavily lidded eyes settled on Angelica's ample chest. He tipped a nonexistent hat with one of his plastic beer cups. "Howdy, ma'am. You do fill out that ol' pink shirt real nice."

Bonnie was fairly certain had she been drinking milk it would have exploded from her nose.

Angelica offered a coy and knowing smile as if it was an everyday occurrence that someone should compliment her ample bosoms.

Divine's jowly face went from blotchy to bright red in the space of a heartbeat. "Principal Whittaker, you're drunk, and I might add, impertinent."

Lloyd blinked like a repentant owl, then nodded. He put an arm around Xavier, spilling a dab of beer on the man's reptilian shoulder. "Superintendent Divine, you've got every right to add. You're the boss, you son of a gun. But I mean to tell you, that don't make me wrong. No, sir! You got yourself one handsome woman there."

"Thank you, Lloyd," Angelica said in a voice so sultry it would fry an egg.

Lloyd swung his arm across Divine's Adam's apple in an attempt to glean a drink from his beer. The maneuver effectively laid a choke hold on the bald-headed administrator. Veins protruded from Divine's forehead.

"Let go of me, you imbecile," Divine croaked.

With a sense of sublime inevitability, Bonnie witnessed the ensuing debacle in seeming slow motion.

Lloyd stepped back, crushing the beer cup against Divine's chest. The entire contents erupted out of the cup, first splashing onto Divine's chin, then spilling, in a foamy river, down the front of his western shirt, reptile skin and all.

The moan-whine combination that emanated from Divine's lips was more reminiscent of a small child than a grown man. To make matters worse, his bride-to-be began to giggle.

My kingdom for a camera.

The Divine Pain in the Ass looked like his head might explode. A moment like this came along maybe once in a lifetime and certainly demanded to be immortalized for posterity.

"Look what you've done, Whittaker." Divine pulled free from Lloyd and brushed ineffectively at his sodden shirt.

Lloyd's eyes were wide, but to Bonnie's horror and delight, he also was working his way toward a simpleton's grin. Things might have gone from bad to worse if Angelica hadn't taken charge.

Divine was puffing himself up in obvious preparation for a scathing remark, when she bent low and whispered in his ear. Bonnie couldn't hear what was being said, but the effect on the superintendent was immediate. The corners of his pudgy mouth twitched. A hint of a sly smile played at those same lips. He even shuddered.

My God, did she put her tongue in his ear?

Angelica straightened and peered down at Bonnie. "You should take Mister Whittaker home. I do believe he's had enough fun for one night."

Bonnie couldn't believe it. The woman sounded positively gracious.

Almost-married life suits you, Western Barbie. "She's got a point there, Lloyd. What say you and I mosey on out of here?" She expected her friend to offer some resistance, but he merely gave her a lazy grin.

"Sure thing, Bon." He hoisted his other beer and downed it in one gulp. He crushed the cup and tossed it over his shoulder. "I'm ready."

He bowed low to Xavier and Angelica. "Sorry about the shirt, buckaroo, and good night to you, buckarette."

Divine seemed on the verge of some new indignation, but Angelica squeezed his arm.

"Good night, Lloyd," she said.

Bonnie took Lloyd's arm, thankful to be getting away from The Divine Pain in the Ass relatively unnoticed.

"Missus Pinkwater," Divine called before she could get ten steps away.

Bonnie sighed the sigh of the apprehended. She turned as little as possible to give The Divine Pain in the Ass as little of her attention as possible. "Yes, sir?"

"Please don't think a wet shirt has made me forget I need to speak with you. After your class tomorrow, come see me."

By the time Bonnie dropped Lloyd back off at home and returned to her own house, it was almost eleven. She let the animals in, set her fanny pack on her breakfast island, and plopped down bonelessly on a kitchen stool. Euclid jumped up into her lap. She ran her fingers absently through his silky fur.

"Mommy's pooped, cutie pie. You know, sometimes I envy you guys the fact that you're neutered. Sure would make getting through this veil of tears a whole lot easier."

Bonnie had wanted to speak to Lloyd about his decision to divorce. She'd seen his face as Marjorie played. He was proud of her, obviously would have liked to be a part of her new success. Certainly his decision to get drunk sprang from the hopeless mix of emotions that had to be plaguing him.

Mostly, Bonnie had wanted to tell her boss the last thing Marjorie had said. As the woman grabbed her fiddle and got up to rejoin Swing Town for their second set, Bonnie touched her sleeve.

"Sweetie, Lloyd said you were with Chad now. Is that true?"

For a long moment, Marjorie hadn't spoken. Bonnie could see her evaluating how to should interpret the question. She also gave the man in question a long hard look before she turned back to Bonnie.

"Am I with him?" She shook her head. "Not since that first night. He's just the piano player in my band."

"I'm going to tell Lloyd that, you know?"

Marjorie shrugged a fat-lot-of-good-it-will-do shrug. "Knock yourself out. I got to go. It was good to see you, Bonnie."

But Bonnie hadn't told Lloyd much of anything. The man had fallen asleep not two minutes into the trip back to his house. It had been incumbent upon Bonnie to escort him to his front door, open same, and further escort him to his bed. He'd fallen facedown into his comforter still wearing his clothes.

Maybe tomorrow, after the funeral, she'd thought at the time.

Bonnie groaned, remembering she still hadn't written the eulogy.

The phone next to the microwave rang. Bonnie set the cat on the floor and checked the digital clock on the oven.

Eleven ten. Dear God, who could be calling at this ungodly hour? Bonnie's feet felt waterlogged as she dragged herself to the phone. "This better be good."

"I'll make it as good as I can."

Armen Callahan's voice poured out of the receiver, and like a tonic, sent Bonnie's fatigue scurrying for parts unknown.

"Hello, you," she whispered.

"Hello, yourself, sweet lady. What's new on the East Plains' front?"

"You've got no idea. You flush with a spare half hour?"

"As I've told you a thousand times, I possess no moment but to await upon your sweet pleasure. Give me the lowdown, dear heart."

Bonnie began with the port-a-potty murder, walked Armen through her various misadventures with Pastor Dobbs, Seneca Webb, and Rattlesnake, and ended with the tragedy of the Whittakers.

Armen whistled. "I leave for a few days and the center comes unstuck. Tell me you've at least kept in Superintendent Divine's good graces."

"A swing and a miss there, too." Bonnie sat back on the kitchen stool. "Oh, hell, I don't want to talk about that odious man right now. Sooooo, what's going on in New Jersey?"

A long silence passed before Armen spoke. "Let me begin by stating unequivocally that I am enamored with one Bonnie Pinkwater, and if it were entirely up to me would remain ensconced in her favors the remainder of my days."

Uh-oh. "A good place to start, smooth talker, but I'm thinking I'm not going to like what comes on the heels of this charming declaration of love."

Bonnie winced. *Did I really say the L-word?*

Armen didn't seem to notice. "Probably not. I'm

sure not crazy about my untimely news. Here's the deal. My dad is a lot worse than I thought."

"I'm so sorry to hear that. How bad is he?"

"He can't take care of himself anymore. The truth is, my mom probably ran herself into the ground tending him day and night. He can barely walk, he's got memory loss, and he's having trouble breathing."

"Oh, Armen." She wanted to reach through the phone, pull this man to her. Vying with this tender emotion, a sinking feeling took residence in Bonnie's chest. More than anything she wanted to tell him to rethink whatever he was about to say. "What does all this mean?"

"I can't leave him, Bon. He needs me."

Bonnie bit back a small desperate voice that demanded she tell this wonderful man that she needed him, too. She swallowed, trying to get control of her voice. "I see. What are your plans? I mean for your job here and your trailer?"

And me?

"I'm calling Lloyd tomorrow and resigning. As for the trailer, I'm paid up through the end of August."

Bonnie took a protracted breath. She felt like screaming, but once again squeezed her desperation into a manageable package. "So that's it."

Again, a long pause. "I don't want it to be, Bon. The thing is, my dad has this huge house in Atlantic City. What do you think about living in New Jersey?"

CHAPTER 14

". . . MARRIED JOHN SOMERVILLE, WHO LIKED SMART women a lot better than her first husband did." Beatrice Archuleta made a show of inhaling deeply as if to say she was putting her all into the presentation on Mary Somerville.

Bonnie stifled a yawn and let the girl's oral report wash over her. She certainly didn't want Beatrice to think her efforts were less than stimulating. Truth was, Bonnie had been up past three writing Leo's eulogy. She felt like she'd been hosed down by an elephant and dragged feetfirst across bottle caps.

She checked her Mickey Mouse watch. *And ladies and gentleman, said eulogy will be underway in less than two hours.*

The late hour for the completion of Leo's farewell was, in part, the fault of Armen Callahan. Certainly the process wasn't made any easier by the oblique tangents her brain insisted on taking with regard to the man's

Atlantic City proposition.

New Jersey, for God's sake.

Off and on, through the wee hours of the night, flights of fancy would dredge up what meager facts she'd gleaned over the years about the Garden State.

Capitol—Trenton, the city in which George Washington attacked the Hessians on his famous No-Thanks-I'll-Stand boat trip across the Delaware River.

Home of Bon Jovi, Bruce Springsteen, and of course Old Blue Eyes himself, Frank Sinatra.

New Jersey also laid claim to the boardwalk metropolis of Atlantic City—the second most popular gambling mecca in America, one-time nexus of the Miss America Pageant, and rude model for the Parker Brothers' original game of Monopoly.

And possibly the new stomping grounds of Bonnie Pinkwater. Ye gods, what am I going to do?

"Missus Pinkwater?" Beatrice Archuleta asked, and if Bonnie's peripheral subconscious wasn't mistaken, had asked for the second time.

Bonnie blinked in the girl's direction. "I'm sorry, honey. I was woolgathering. What can I do for you?"

Beatrice peered at Bonnie as if she might be mentally challenged. "I said I was finished."

Bonnie felt her face redden. She was far too embarrassed to ask if the girl had included any of Mary Somerville's mathematics in her talk.

"That's terrific, sweetie." Bonnie stood, hearing as well as feeling several of her bones creak and pop. She needed to get up and move around before she fell into a coma. "Has anyone made any progress on our wallpaper mathematician?"

Most of the class avoided eye contact.

"That's okay. I'll give you a name to work with and a push in the right direction."

Notebooks opened and mechanical pencils clicked at the ready.

"Her name was Sophia Krukovsky Kovalevskaya." Bonnie wrote the name on the board and underlined it. "A jawbreaker of a handle, and of all the personalities bandied about in this who's who of historic females, she may possibly be the best mathematician of the bunch."

"You okay, boss?"

Bonnie whispered, but for the effect it had on Lloyd Whittaker, she may as well have dragged her fingernails down a clean blackboard.

Her principal moaned—his face in his hands. Like a tortoise emerging from its shell, he raised his head and peered at her. "Peachy."

She stepped lightly into his office. Perversely, gazing at her longtime friend and his obvious discomfort made

Bonnie feel distinctly better. She quickly discarded an unwelcome twinge of guilt that flashed across her frontal lobe.

No point in both of us suffering. Indeed, by comparison, she was beginning to feel like the rise-and-shine poster girl.

Every aspect of the man's face, from the red-rimmed and bloodshot eyes to the slack, slightly aquamarine skin and cracked lips, all bore witness to physical as well as mental agony.

"Tell me I didn't ogle Angelica Devereaux's breasts, then spill beer all over the superintendent."

"Oh, that I could, Sahib." Bonnie immediately regretted her poor attempt at humor and cast about for anything that might truly cheer up her friend. "On the bright side, I don't think Angelica was offended. In fact, I got the impression she thought you made a cute drunk."

Lloyd moaned again. "That's all I need. The superintendent's fiancée thinking I'm cute and her man, my boss, thinking I'm the village idiot. I don't suppose Xavier chalked the beer accident up to just one of those things?"

Just one of those crazy flings?

"I wouldn't go that far." Bonnie chuckled, remembering Divine's indignant expression as he demanded that Lloyd unhand him. "However, once again, Angelica came to the rescue. This time utilizing her area of true expertise."

Lloyd perked up. "Oh, yeah?"

"Indeed, I do believe Miss Thirty-Eight-D took him home and made everything all right. Truth is, I caught her sticking her tongue in Humpty Dumpty's ear."

Lloyd let loose with a dry chuckle that made him wince. "Remind me to send her some flowers."

"You do that. No doubt, flowers would go over big with our egghead boss, as well. While you're at it, why not spill some more beer on him." Bonnie checked her watch for the second time in fifteen minutes. "I don't want to be pushy and insensitive, but we need to get a wiggle on. The funeral's clear in Colorado Springs, remember?"

Lloyd blinked up at her. "Of course, I remember. I'm hungover, not senile."

"Tsk-tsk. Whose little boy got up on the wrong side of the bed?" She reached down, took his hand, and helped him to his feet. "I'll drive."

He grunted agreement, and like a grumpy trained bear, followed her to the parking lot.

They were turning off Highway 84 into Colorado Springs, when Bonnie broached the subject of Marjorie. Lloyd shook his head in a feeble attempt to refuse to even consider the topic. The effort sent a visible shudder through him.

"Spare me."

"Not this time, Mister Whittaker. You're going to listen to what I have to say because I'm shamelessly calling in the friendship chip. Got it?"

He snorted and turned his head to stare out the passenger window. "Got it."

She walked him through the conversation she'd had with Marjorie, ending with the woman's final declaration that Chad meant nothing more to her than the piano player in her band.

"She said that?" he asked, still staring out the window.

"Yep." Bonnie squeezed Lloyd's arm. "She screwed up, big guy." *Perhaps not the best choice of words, Pinkwater.*

Her friend sighed. "She screwed us both up, probably for good. Bon, this new information doesn't change anything."

Bonnie wanted to pull the car over and shake the man. She could damn well see he wanted to give Marjorie another chance. Why the hell couldn't he see it? She inhaled once to steady her voice. "Talk to her, Lloyd. That's all I'm saying."

"I'll think about it."

Bonnie spotted the wrought-iron gates of Saint Elmo's Cemetery and leaned forward to peer upward at the sky. "Looks like a good day for a graveside service."

Lloyd turned from the window and for the first time that day, he wore an expression of true amusement. "I know my alcohol-befuddled brain isn't the most trustworthy, but weren't you supposed to see Xavier before leaving the school?"

Bonnie stepped past Jason Dobbs to stand at the lectern.

At its base, lay the coffin on an aluminum miniscaffold. A breeze carried the aroma of fresh-turned soil to her nostrils, and almost involuntarily she inhaled deeply.

From her vantage point she could not only see the modest skyscrapers of downtown Colorado Springs but also peruse a surprisingly large crowd that had shown for the funeral. In a quick nervous scan, she spotted Byron Hickman and Deputy Wyatt at the outer rim of the gathering. No less than ten members of Leo's championship basketball team were represented, as were several members of the royal courts from both the prom and the homecoming dance. Completing the group was a smattering of the East Plain's High School staff.

Not surprisingly, Seneca and Caleb Webb weren't in attendance. Bonnie made a mental note to look in on the girl at Memorial Hospital later that day.

The real shocker and what had delayed the service for almost an hour was the absence of Alf Rattlesnake Quinn. When Bonnie and Lloyd first arrived, Jason was in a dither trying to reach the man. Over a half-dozen cells had been employed, trying first his office then his cell phone then anyone who might be willing to make the drive out to the shooting range to check on the man. When all avenues had been exhausted, and it became obvious Alf was nowhere to be found, Jason had made the executive decision to begin the service.

Bonnie smoothed her one page of eulogy notes.

"Leo Quinn was my student." In the uttering of those five simple words, Bonnie felt a stab of emotion that threatened to overwhelm her. It wouldn't do to go blubbering before she'd barely started. Blinking back tears, she inhaled slowly. "For those of you who are teachers, you know what that statement means. He wasn't blood, yet was more than the kid next store. He didn't deliver my paper, mow my lawn, or walk my dogs. All he did was show up in my room, for an hour and a half each day, for three years."

A random image of Leo as a sophomore laden with an enormous backpack and a weary smile on his intelligent face flitted across her brain, and once again she almost lost her emotional footing. She hurried on. "We laughed. I'm not talking jokes, although there were those. I'm talking the exquisite laughter that rears its Harpo Marx visage as a result of volumes of shared moments. That is, if you make room for it. Those of us who knew Leo, remember he always made room for laughter. We have to think no further than the night of the senior prank when he painstakingly removed the front doors of the school and drove Principal Whittaker's truck into the cafeteria."

Even as they wiped at their eyes, a number of participants chuckled. Lloyd shook his head, obviously remembering how embarrassed he'd been when he needed a ride to school and found his old Ford, framed in an octagon of lunch tables each blazing with a candelabra.

"Like many of you, I shared some tears with Leo. As a teacher, it's my privilege to share sorrow with my students. Broken hearts. Disappointment. Failure. Betrayal." She let her gaze stray to Jason Dobbs, who looked away.

"To paraphrase Kahlil Gibran, joy and sorrow are two sides of the same coin. The very tears we shed in times of sorrow deepen the cup that holds our laughter. Leo knew the value of both, and if you were lucky, as I was, he shared both with you."

The crowd had grown strangely silent. Bonnie could hear the traffic on Pikes Peak Avenue. A helicopter flying off the roof of a nearby hospital thrummed overhead. In the loose soil of the grave, not two feet from the base of the lectern, a small swarm of ground bees buzzed.

"But you want to know what I treasured most of all in Leo Quinn—more than his wit, more than his courage, more than his openness and his vulnerability?" She let her voice fall to a near-whisper. "Leo knew how to be quiet, and on occasion, permitted me the pleasure of sharing his solitude. Only a rare individual knows the true value of stillness. In one so young, it was doubly singular. Leo never found it necessary to fill his moments with clamor, but was comfortable in the beating of his own heart and the music of his own soul. I can't express how much I appreciate knowing someone whom I will miss, not just for his words, but for the things he didn't say."

Bonnie smiled a sad smile and looked out over this crowd that had given her their attention. She was grateful for the chance to not only say good-bye to one extraordinary young man, but to say it in the company of folks who would understand. In the end, Rattlesnake had done her a favor.

She sighed. "Thank you all for coming to honor the memory of Leo Quinn. Each of you has your reason for being here. For me, that reason is summed up in the proud declaration that I had the esteemed honor of being his teacher." She stepped from behind the lectern and around Jason Dobbs as he made his way back.

"Thank you, Missus Pinkwater." The young man took his black suit jacket off and draped it across the lectern. He regarded the gathering. "Please bow your heads and join with me in prayer, not for Leo, who is beyond our assistance and in the arms of Jesus, but for ourselves. In particular, let us pray for our absent brother Alf Quinn."

A moment after Bonnie knew everyone around her had lowered their heads, she lifted hers and took a peek.

Since she was a young girl, she'd been unable to resist the temptation to regard her fellow Homo sapiens as they engaged with the Almighty.

Even Jason had his peepers shut.

"Lord, be with Alf Quinn in his hour of need. Give him strength to bear up under the sorrow. Give him wisdom to seek Your face if and when that strength isn't enough." Without opening his eyes, he swatted at a bee that flew near his ear.

As the young pastor droned on, Bonnie took the opportunity to scan other people in the gathering. Several members of the championship basketball squad were holding hands and mouthing *Amen* to each of Jason Dobbs's petitions to God. A young woman, whom Bonnie had seen in the company of one of the squad, blew her nose into a tissue.

Turned completely around, Bonnie found herself staring into the open eyes of Byron Hickman. He shook his head at her reproachfully, as if she might be a five-year-old who'd been caught opening a Christmas present a day early.

That's hardly fair, Byron. Your eyes are open just as much as mine.

The next moment, those same eyes opened considerably wider. He was staring past her toward the front of the assembly, to the coffin and Jason Dobbs. A woman screamed. Bonnie turned back around. Red was blossoming alarmingly fast on the right side of Jason's cream-colored shirt. He fell forward, pitching himself and the lectern onto Leo Quinn's coffin.

CHAPTER 15

Lloyd was the first to reach Jason. Scuttling on all fours alongside the coffin, he grabbed Jason Dobbs by his shirt and unceremoniously yanked him off the overturned lectern. Bonnie winced as the bloody young man landed face-first atop Lloyd.

Bonnie crawled toward the pair, the sounds of screams and pandemonium echoing in her ears. She didn't begrudge her fellow mourners their reactions. Bonnie herself had fallen to the ground waiting for a second bullet that never came. She was still shaking.

Then there was the business of the blood. In the milliseconds before and during Jason's fall, Bonnie saw that Jason Dobbs's right arm was sodden red. Obviously, the shot had entered from the rear and exploded through the front.

"Keep your head down!" Lloyd, supine, was painstakingly dragging Jason Dobbs by his bloody collar.

Bonnie ignored the command. On her knees, she

snatched Jason's suit coat from the overturned lectern and pressed it against the ragged wound. She restrained Lloyd with a gentle touch. "Let him lie still. First and foremost, we need to stop the bleeding." From the corner of her eye, she caught sight of Byron and Deputy Wyatt, pistols drawn, racing past the fleeing crowd to a stand of cottonwoods maybe twenty-five yards distant.

"What about the shooter?" Lloyd sat up, took off his own jacket, and placed it beneath Jason Dobbs's head.

Bonnie never considered herself brave, but somehow she knew in her bones that this particular piece of mayhem was a singularity. The shooter, wherever he had been, was already gone. Moreover, she could see that Lloyd was beginning to feel the same. "I can't do anything about that. Let's just make sure young Pastor Dobbs here doesn't bleed out."

As if he recognized his name, Jason groaned.

Lloyd nodded and sheepishly offered Bonnie a weak smile. "I guess old habits die hard. For a moment there I was back in 'Nam in a firefight." He pulled a cell phone from his pocket and dialed 911.

While Lloyd was still on the phone, Byron returned, face flushed and sweating. "Couldn't find any sign of a shooter. I just can't believe someone could get away that cleanly. Deputy Wyatt is still searching."

Lloyd snapped shut the cell phone. "She won't find anything." Lloyd's voice was calm, certain.

"You're thinking maybe a distance shot?" Byron asked.

Lloyd nodded. "I heard a pop, not muffled but distant and distinct. This was no silenced pistol from close range." He squinted down at the body and then up at an angle through the trees. "If I had to guess, I'd say the shot came from over there." He pointed to a tall building about a block away.

"That's some shooting. I'd place that structure at about eight hundred yards." Byron turned a worried gaze on Jason and then on Bonnie as she compressed the jacket onto the ruined arm. "How's he doing?"

"He's losing blood like a house afire. How long before an ambulance gets here?" Bonnie gave Lloyd a searching glance.

As though in answer to her question, the siren of an emergency vehicle sounded from Pikes Peak Avenue. Moments later, the blue-red, blue-red of its lights were visible as well. The squat white vehicle was already turning into the gates of the cemetery. Not a block behind, two Colorado Springs police cars were screaming for the same intersection.

"That's fast."

"It should be." Lloyd pointed with his chin. "The hospital's right there. I'd say about eight hundred yards away."

"The same building?" Byron peered over the treetops

toward the hospital.

"It's just a guess, but there was a time when I got real good at situating an enemy shooter's position. Not a skill for which I've had a lot of use in the past thirty years. If I was the police, I'd send someone up to that rooftop pronto."

Byron pursed his lips and studied Lloyd's face as though he was estimating just how much he should trust this high school principal. "Can I borrow your cell?" he asked after a long moment.

Lloyd handed it over, and Byron strode away from the grave. Bonnie could only make out bits and snatches of the phone call, but she did hear Byron telling the police to hurry.

The emergency vehicle drove across the manicured lawn until it was alongside the grave site. The back of the truck flew open and two men with a stretcher jumped out.

At their approach Bonnie relinquished her duties and stepped away. Her back ached and she looked around as she stretched. On the main thoroughfare of the cemetery, the pair of police cars came to halt. Three uniformed officers emerged from the flashing cars. Two approached the remnant of mourners, most of which huddled together near their vehicles. The third policeman, a fellow with obscenely wide shoulders and a neatly trimmed black mustache, strode up to the grave. His nametag ID'd him as Officer Ortega.

His gaze immediately fell on Byron. "What happened here?"

Before Bonnie could answer, Byron took the officer by the elbow and drew him several feet away. Bonnie wanted to eavesdrop, but a nagging thought refused to quit thrumming in her cranium.

"Eight hundred yards is a heck of a shot, isn't it?" she asked Lloyd.

"Heck of a shot." His face took on a faraway look. "I wouldn't attempt it now even if I had the right rifle."

"You mean like the rifle we saw at Rattlesnake's?"

Lloyd brushed at his suit jacket as if a bit of fluffing might eliminate the massive bloodstain. "It's a goner."

On the way back to Alice, The-Little-Subaru-That-Could, Bonnie rubbed her friend's back. "I'm afraid so," she commiserated. "I don't think even dry-cleaning's going to get that bad boy the same again. At least your beautiful coat died for a good cause. Jason's going to make it."

Lloyd scratched at his craggy chin. "Yeah, at least there's that." He turned a troubled look her way. "Do you really think Rattlesnake had anything to do with this shooting, Bon? We're talking his own son's funeral here."

She spread wide her hands. "The police thought so. Did you see the look on Byron's face when we told him about the M24? I'll bet the sheriff's department has a car on the way to the range even as we squeak."

Bonnie's attempt at humor had little effect on Lloyd.

Tiredly, he rubbed at his eyes. "I hope you're wrong. If Alf was responsible, then all that crap about changing from Harold to Jason was just a plan to get that poor boy in the crosshairs. And why? What had Jason ever done to him?"

"There was the business of Leo and Jason . . . well, you know."

They came up on the Subaru, and Lloyd held the door for Bonnie. When she sat, Lloyd leaned in the already open window. "And for that, he tries to kill him? Besides, I'd be surprised if Rattlesnake even knew about it."

"Seneca Webb did. She could have told him. She and her husband were out to the range just the other day."

Lloyd's craggy face showed he was considering that possibility as he walked around to the Subaru's driver's side door. He was already shaking his head as he sat. "Why would she do that?"

"Good question. Want to ask her?"

When Bonnie and Lloyd entered the hospital room,

Robert Spiller

Seneca Webb lay on one elbow facing her husband, Caleb. The young man sat next to the bed with his back to the door. Dappled sunlight painted the bedspread from a partially closed set of beige louvered blinds. The smell of Pine-Sol and linen filled the air.

Seneca craned her neck to see past her husband. "Missus P," the girl exclaimed. "Principal Whittaker. How sweet. You got here just in time. They're going to release me in about an hour."

Caleb stood and shook Lloyd's hand. "Thank you for coming, sir."

What am I, chopped liver? Bonnie stepped to the window side of the bed. "Sooooo, you must be feeling better? Is everything—"

"The baby's fine." Seneca sat up and patted her tummy. "But they're not going to let me rodeo this season."

"It took a doctor to make her come around to my way of thinking."

Seneca used her chin to point at her husband as if to say, *Listen to this guy.* "In your way of thinking, I'm made of glass and might break if I walk down to the mailbox."

Caleb inhaled and blew a frustrated breath through his handlebar mustache. Obviously, this wasn't the first time this couple had had this argument.

What struck Bonnie as odd was how much vinegar Seneca had put into her criticism. This hardly seemed the kind of remark a wife might make if she was physically abused. Had Jason been wrong about Caleb?

Seneca took Bonnie's hand. "Well, tell me about the funeral."

Oh, shit, where to start? "We had a bit of excitement."

She told of the shooting and how Lloyd thought it was the work of a sniper. "Even though Jason lost a lot of blood, it looks like he'll pull through."

Visibly shaken, Seneca relinquished her hold on Bonnie and fell back onto her pillows. "I can't believe it. Someone shot him? Jason wouldn't swat a mosquito. Who could have done such a thing?"

The time has come, the walrus said. "About that, Alf Quinn never showed up at the funeral."

"What? Where was he?" The next instant Seneca's expression of confusion was replaced by a frown. "You think Alf had something to do with Jason's shooting?"

Lloyd came to the foot of the bed. "Yesterday, when we went out to the range, Alf was holding a M24, a sniper rifle."

"He has lots of rifles," Caleb said. "Doesn't mean he'd shoot anyone with them."

Lloyd nodded, in seeming agreement. "I feel the same. I can't see any reason Alf would try to kill Jason Dobbs."

"Except . . ." Bonnie said.

Seneca peered from Bonnie's face to Lloyd's and back to Bonnie's. "Except what?"

Bonnie blinked, trying to come up with a tactful way to ask her next question. *Get on with it, Pinkwater.* "Remember, what you mentioned about Jason and Leo?"

Seneca hunched her shoulders as if the question had dropped a weight on them. A shudder passed through her. She locked eyes with Caleb. "There's something I've never shared with you, babe."

Bonnie expected the young man to take his wife's hand, to tell her she had nothing to worry about, that she could tell him anything. It's what Ben or even Armen would have done had Bonnie approached them with a troubling revelation.

Caleb Webb sat back in his chair as though to distance himself from Seneca. "Uh-huh?"

Slowly at first, then in a rush, she told her husband of the love affair between Jason Dobbs and Leo Quinn. Before she'd finished, Caleb was on his feet pacing about the hospital room, a sour expression on his face.

"You should have told me. By God, Seneca, Jason's the youth pastor. He works with little kids."

Bonnie felt an overwhelming urge to defend the young pastor, but her Imp of the Perverse whispered that she should let this scene play out.

When a person's under pressure, it's what hisses out

that's most interesting, the voice suggested.

Seneca stared fearfully at her husband, and as he approached her bed she took his hand. "I'm sorry, sweetie. I should have told you."

Caleb's features softened. "Yes, you should have. We're a team, babe."

Unfortunately, Caleb's reaction made Bonnie's next question more difficult. Would the girl have told Rattlesnake something she'd withheld from her own husband?

Only one way to find out. "Honey, I know this is hard. I apologize for any trouble I've caused between you two, but I need to ask one more thing. Did you ever hint to Rattlesnake about the affair between Leo and Jason?"

Seneca paled and her hand came to her mouth. "Oh, my God."

"Enough!" Caleb gave Bonnie a dirty look as if to say she needed to stop troubling his pregnant wife.

"I understand," Bonnie said to Seneca.

There was no need to actually hear the girl say the words. Somehow, someway, maybe even innocently, Seneca had transmitted the knowledge of Jason Dobbs's homosexuality and his relationship with Leo to Rattlesnake.

From inside Bonnie's fanny pack, her cell phone rang. Automatically, she opened the pack. Fully intending to shut off the device, she looked down at the caller

ID. Byron Hickman was on the line.

"I need to take this."

She flipped open the phone and stepped into the hall. "Byron?"

"Missus P, I'm out at Rattlesnake's. No sign of him or the M24, although the one employee on duty remembers seeing it earlier in the day."

Although grateful, Bonnie wondered why Byron thought it necessary to keep her in the Rattlesnake loop. *Don't look a gift equine in the mouth, Pinkwater.* "I don't suppose this employee knows where Alf went?"

"No such luck. The guy's been working in the paintball range all morning and hasn't seen Alf since opening. When the employee finished with a screaming bunch of Boy Scouts, Alf had already taken off. The guy naturally assumed he'd gone to the funeral."

A reasonable assumption.

"Now listen carefully, Missus P. Normally, there's no way I would have clued you in to what's going on with Rattlesnake, but I'm worried about you and Principal Whittaker. The employee said that not only was the M24 missing but two boxes of ammo as well. From what you told me, Rattlesnake is bonkers and is now on the loose, if you get my drift?"

"Drift gotten and taken to heart. I'll keep a weather eye."

"You do that. Keep in touch if you hear anything."

The line went silent.

Bonnie snapped shut her phone and walked back into the room. Caleb still held Seneca's hand and whatever recriminations were in the offing had obviously blown over. The young couple seemed to be in harmony again.

"Bad news?" Lloyd asked.

Bonnie couldn't see any benefit from sharing Byron's disturbing news with Seneca and Caleb. "Nah."

She squeezed Seneca's foot beneath the covers. "I need to take off, honey. You going to be okay?"

Seneca put Caleb's hand to her lips and kissed it. "I think so."

When Bonnie and Lloyd were halfway to the elevator, he nudged her. "And are you going to tell me what that phone call was really about?"

Bonnie inhaled deeply. "It seems if we want to keep our heads, we might want to grow eyes in the back. Mister Snake has sprouted wings and flown the proverbial coop."

CHAPTER 16

Bonnie and Lloyd stopped at the hospital information desk and asked to see Jason Dobbs. A young nun wearing a smile like a halo told her Jason was still in critical condition and wouldn't be seeing any visitors. The likelihood was that he would be in surgery until late afternoon.

As Bonnie was turning to leave, Harold Dobbs strode in.

Ashen-faced, he glared at her. "I blame you for this."

"Good afternoon to you as well, Pastor Dobbs." Lloyd put an arm around Bonnie. "Have you met Missus Bonnie Pinkwater? I do believe this woman might have saved your son's life this morning."

Shaking her head, Bonnie turned away from the pair of men. "Forget it, Lloyd," she shouted over her shoulder. "He made up his mind about me a hundred years ago. He's not about to change it now. Have a good day, pastor."

She set off apace, with the idea of placing as much distance between herself and the abhorrent Pastor Harold T. Dobbs as possible. When she realized Lloyd wasn't catching up, she slowed, but refused to look back.

I'll be damned if I give that bigot, Dobbs, the satisfaction.

To make matters worse, she had to admit to a portion of guilt over Jason's shooting. After all, the idea of switching the funeral over from the old man to the son had been hers.

"Bonnie, wait," Lloyd called.

Against her better judgment, she turned back around, prepared to be lambasted by Dobbs. What she saw made her breath catch in her throat.

Harold Dobbs, undisputed leader of the Saved by the Blood Pentecostal Tabernacle, wielder of bullhorns, standard-bearer in the crusade against same-sex immorality, had his face buried in Lloyd's shoulder. The big clergyman's entire body was shuddering with sobs. He seemed to be mumbling something over and over.

Lloyd looked embarrassed, not really sure what to do with his hands. One was tentatively patting Harold on the back while the other hovered around his head.

At Bonnie's approach, Harold straightened. His cheeks were wet, and he swiped at them and a runny nose with his black coat sleeve.

"I owe you an apology, Missus Pinkwater. My behavior

was loutish and my words unkind."

Which, in my experience, is your normal modus operandi, Pastor D. Why bother changing now?

But no way in heaven or hell was Bonnie going to give voice to that thought. Here was a man broken by love for his son and for the God who had spared him. Toss in the pastor's heartfelt apology and nothing less than a hands-across-the-water gesture would suffice. Not if she intended to live with herself.

Besides, how often did one have the chance to play the generous forgiver to a repentant Harold T. Dobbs? She hushed a not-so-still voice that chided her for being opportunistic.

I'll say a mea culpa later.

"Apology accepted, Harold." Almost flinching with the effort, Bonnie took Dobbs's hand. "You know, Jason's going to be okay."

Dobbs inhaled deeply and again shuddered. The corner of his mouth twitched. "He isn't taking him. Thank You, Lord Jesus."

Bonnie resisted the urge to say, "Amen."

She peered at the pastor, trying to come to grips with this new incarnation. He seemed downright shy in his attempt at friendliness, like someone trying on a suit for the first time.

Over the years of dealing with children, who by their natural lack of power, live by their wits, Bonnie had developed a finely tuned bullshit alarm. Hers was now sounding the all-hands-on-deck. Yes, indeed, something was definitely out of whack with Harold T. Dobbs.

Give the man a break, Pinkwater. His son was almost murdered today.

The nun-receptionist reached out a hand and touched Harold on the forearm. "Forgive me for being forward, Reverend, but from your conversation, can I assume that you're the father of Jason Dobbs?"

Dobbs blinked at her and smiled. "My boy's going to be okay."

"And according to my monitor, is now out of surgery."

For an awkward moment, Dobbs seemed not to understand.

Lloyd stepped forward and peered down at her nameplate. "Sister Frances, where should he go?"

Sister Frances offered a countenance that seemed designed by the Almighty Himself to convey understanding and sympathy. She pointed down the long hall that Lloyd and Bonnie had traversed not ten minutes earlier. "If you follow the white lines you'll come to the elevators. The surgery waiting room is on the second floor. Just tell the station nurse who you are."

"Thank you." Harold inhaled and a bit of color returned to his cheeks.

Without a word of good-bye, Pastor Dobbs ambled

away. The man appeared as if he was tightrope-walking the white line, meticulously mincing his steps down the long hall. He was still keeping to the line when he disappeared around a corner toward the elevators.

Bonnie shook her fork of eggplant parmesan at her principal and friend. "You are looking at a changed woman, Whittaker."

Lloyd recoiled from the attacking vegetable. It had been a struggle to get him to agree to come to the new upscale hospital cafeteria in the first place, and Bonnie realized she shouldn't be brandishing intimidating foodstuffs in the man's direction. She lowered the offending implement.

"Sorry. It's just that if Harold T. Dobbs can join the human race, then there's hope for all of us. Yes, indeed, I'm taking a long hard look at one Bonnie Pinkwater and her cynical and some might say devious ways. As the Good Book says, I've been weighed and found wanting. I even had a moment there when I thought Harold might have more on his mind than a damaged son."

Lloyd wiped his mouth with his cloth napkin, then spread wide the yellow rectangle, seemingly studying the embroidered *M* in one corner. "Don't be so quick to discount your misgivings, Bon. Over the years, I've grown to trust your intuition. There may be more to the good pastor than just the anxious parent."

Bonnie set down her fork and studied her friend. "You know something, don't you Whittaker?"

Lloyd reddened and pursed his lips. "Don't get me wrong, I think the lion's share of what we saw with Dobbs came from the shock of hearing someone shot his son."

"But not all?"

"No, not all." For a long moment, Lloyd didn't answer, as if in doing so he would betray some agreement. "Do you remember that awkward scene when Harold dampened my shirt with his tears?"

Bonnie replayed the scene in her mind. She'd turned back to Dobbs and Lloyd to see the reverend in a clutch with her friend. Dobbs was sobbing and he was . . . Bonnie slapped the table. "He was mumbling something. I couldn't make it out, but you could."

"Yes, I could, and it set my teeth on edge." Lloyd's face went hard. "Over and over again, he hissed, *The sins of the father, the sins of the father.*"

"The sins of the father? What the hell is that supposed to mean?"

"Your guess is as good as mine."

In the space of a heartbeat, Bonnie reassumed the mantle of critical observer of one Harold T. Dobbs. Gone were any tender feelings she'd had for the man.

"I knew it! I knew something wasn't on the up-and-up with Dobbs. And what's with all this bowing, scraping, and apologizing?"

"He's a man of religion, Bon. Word on the street is that the founder of his particular creed was into forgiveness."

"Clever, Whittaker, but you know as well as I do that Harold Dobbs ascribed more to the righteous indignation slant of Christianity than to compassion. You forget I went toe to toe with the troglodyte for a few rounds. It was an experience singularly devoid of forgiveness."

"People change."

Bonnie snorted and was about to launch into another eggplant assault when she caught a wary look in Lloyd's eyes. She lowered the fork and her voice. "All right, let's put aside Harold's aberrant behavior for a moment. Where the heck has the man been all morning?"

"I don't think even you expected him to show up for a funeral he'd been practically ejected from." As if he'd just moved his knight to king's bishop three and voiced check, he took a healthy bite of his flatbread pizza and laid his hands palms down on the table, his eyes level with hers.

"I didn't until he showed up at the hospital. Did you see how he was dressed? A black frocked coat, black trousers, black shoes. Lloyd, the man was decked out for a funeral. I don't think it's a far leap to assume it was Leo's."

Take that, Mister Whittaker.

It was Bonnie's turn to feel smug. She was thoroughly enjoying the give-and-take.

Lloyd did indeed hesitate, but only for a moment. "He's a preacher, Bon. That's how they dress."

Bonnie was already shaking her head before Lloyd even finished. "Lame, buddy. It was eighty-eight degrees out there this afternoon. Even the Dobbster owns a Hawaiian shirt or two. If he wasn't coming to a funeral, why dress like it? Unless you think he changed when he got word of Jason."

Lloyd's face conveyed the message that he had his doubts. "So where do you think Harold was?"

The question caught her flat-footed, and she was about to say so, when she had a wild thought. "Okay, this is just shooting from the hip, but bear with me."

She lowered her voice and gave it her best Rod Serling. "Submitted for your approval, one Harold T. Dobbs. His son has gone off early to facilitate a funeral that Harold himself was summarily told he was unsuited to lead. The man is fit to be hog-tied."

"You do *Twilight Zone* well."

Bonnie nodded her acknowledgment of his compliment. "Thank you. Now, where do you go if you've got time on your hands and a stick up your irate self-righteous behind?"

"I figure you're going to tell me."

"And so I will. You go to see the man who orchestrated your humiliation."

Lloyd smiled, with only a hint of misgiving. "Go on."

Bonnie realized she was skating on thin ice. Any moment she expected Lloyd to let loose with a barrage of objections, and she really had no defense. Still she barreled on. "Let's assume for a moment that Harold walks in on Rattlesnake as he's preparing the sniper rifle for his little escapade with Jason."

Lloyd whistled. "This is getting a bit far-fetched, Bon. If Rattlesnake shot Jason, what would have stopped him from shooting the good pastor as well?"

Bonnie let the question percolate around her cranium before she took up her argument. "Okay, then suppose Harold somehow caught a glimpse of Rattlesnake as he was carrying out the rifle but remained unseen."

"This just gets better and better. Go on."

Bonnie knew she was blowing smoke, but she was committed. She had to finish her line of reasoning. "Later, he hears of Jason being shot, and blames himself for not stopping Rattlesnake when he had the chance."

"Do you really believe what you're saying?"

In her mind Bonnie pictured a pie chart. The portion that represented her attachment to the Rattlesnake-Dobbs theory was a slim piece of pie indeed. Still, she could sense in the marrow of her bones that something major had scrambled the pastor's brains, and now the man was carrying around a supersized portion of remorse.

"Okay, I'll admit the scenario has a few holes, but I swear, Lloyd, Dobbs is significantly traumatized."

Lloyd nodded in agreement. "Fair enough, but latch hold to what you already know about Reverend Dobbs. The man is a cold, calculating bully. If he saw Rattlesnake carrying a sniper rifle and then later heard his boy was shot, he would have notified the police, probably even before he came to the hospital. And it would have taken a lot more than what you described to knock that man off his pinions."

"So what do you think happened to make such a basket case out of Dobbs?"

Lloyd frowned, then spread wide his hands. "I don't know, but I'm sure you have every intention of finding out."

"I think this is a real bad idea, Bon." Lloyd held the elevator door for her to exit.

Bonnie had to admit, she didn't like her chances of success, but she couldn't walk away from these damn Dobbses without getting at least some of her questions answered. From where she stood, Jason Dobbs was a liar and his father had experienced something that freeze-dried his cerebrum. "You're probably right, but I've got a plan."

"Why am I afraid to ask what this plan entails?"

"I can't imagine. Probably has something to do with not being held enough as a baby. Now listen. The plan is simplicity itself. I'm going to hold back and let you quiz Harold."

"That's your plan!" Hands on hips, Lloyd shot Bonnie a frown.

"Hear me out." Bonnie turned to face her friend. "Normally, Pastor Homophobe would never put up with an inquisition featuring either himself or his son, especially considering the fact that Jason has been so recently and grievously hurt."

Lloyd sighed. "But you're thinking this ain't one of them normal times."

Bonnie smiled and nodded. "For two reasons. First, with any luck, Harold is still the chief engineer on the out-to-lunch express."

"That's just mean."

"Maybe a little, but I'm endeavoring to put unprofitable sentimentality behind me. The second reason is that Jason is probably drugged. We have an excellent chance of the boy spilling his guts because he's under the influence of benevolent painkillers."

"You're completely shameless. And now the twenty-five-thousand-dollar question. Why me?"

"Harold still trusts you. Me . . ." Bonnie bowed her

head in a self-deprecating manner. "Not so much."

Lloyd stared at her unconvinced. "And you want me to trade on that trust by blindsiding the man or his incapacitated son in the hope they'll reveal something in a moment of weakness."

"That's the idea."

Lloyd shook his head and smiled. "How can you sleep nights? You know it's likely Jason will be unconscious, if he's even out of surgery yet. That's saying nothing of the possibility he's in the critical ward and thus only family can see him."

"We'll cross that bridge of sighs when we come to it."

"Woman, you're a pistol." He reached for his door handle. "You know I'm not as devious as you. I'll more than likely blow it, and Harold or Jason will just tell me to take a flying leap."

"You're stalling." She chucked him on the arm. "I have faith in you, big guy. You can be underhanded and shifty if you put your mind to it. Now come on. Let's see what those Dobbs boys are hiding."

CHAPTER 17

BONNIE FOUND PASTOR HAROLD T. DOBBS ON HIS KNEES singing in the hospital chapel—arms upraised, head thrown back. She recognized the tune as "A Mighty Fortress Is Our God."

Composer Martin Luther, year 1529, eight years after the Edict of Worms. Inspired by Psalm 46. Translated to English in 1852 by Frederick Hedge. Theme song of the seventies cartoon show Davey and Goliath. *Sung at the funeral of ex-president Dwight D. Eisenhower.*

Get a grip, Pinkwater. There were times when the influx of unbidden factoids made Bonnie feel like Tippi Hedron, and Alfred Hitchcock's *Birds* were dive-bombing her cerebral cortex.

Mainly because Dobbs had chosen the front of the chapel, Bonnie nodded toward a back pew, letting Lloyd go in first. As they sat, she knew they'd crossed the Rubicon. When Dobbs turned round he couldn't miss them.

The die is cast.

"You okay?" Lloyd whispered. He obviously mistook the excitement on her face for anxiety.

"Couldn't be better."

Seemingly oblivious to his surroundings, Dobbs's surprisingly sweet tenor rose as he marched through the rhythmic punctuations of Luther's opus magnum. When the pastor reached the end—"His kingdom is forever"—his head fell to his chest, a marionette whose strings had been cut.

"Is he crying?" Lloyd asked.

Before she could answer, Dobbs stood.

Hands still raised, he began to furiously nod in great swooping arcs. "I understand, my Lord. Your way is hard, Your path steep, but Your voice is honey to my soul. Show me Your mind." He lowered his hands, and bending over, scrubbed his palms on his thighs.

Lloyd leaned in. "We shouldn't be here; this feels like voyeurism."

"Hush."

Unfortunately, the small chapel was blessed with outstanding acoustics.

Like a feline on alert, Harold Dobbs's shoulders hunched and his back arched. Slowly, he turned round. When he caught sight of Bonnie and Lloyd, his eyes went wide, but surprise was only the first emotion displayed. On the heels of shock came a definite wrinkling of the forehead and a pronounced glare. This expression, in turn, was supplanted by a look of abject resignation and a marked drooping of shoulders.

Bonnie elbowed Lloyd. "Showtime."

"Howdy, Harold." Lloyd manufactured an open-fingered wave to accompany his brief and alliterative greeting.

"Smooth, Whittaker." Bonnie felt an overwhelming urge to skedaddle.

A sullen Harold T. Dobbs listlessly ambled the half-dozen steps to where they sat. Bending down, he embraced Bonnie, then held her at arm's length as if inspecting her for warts. "God hath made a table for me in the company of mine enemy."

That would be me. Bonnie squirmed beneath this unexpected show of affection. "Good to see you, too, Harold." *So much for taking a backseat while Lloyd interrogates the pastor.*

With a wave of his hand, Dobbs indicated Bonnie and Lloyd should slide into the pew and make room for him. As he sat, he patted Bonnie's knee. "Before we talk, you need to know you might possibly be the last person on earth I would choose to hear my confession of shame. But God has taken that choice out of my hands. Since I seek forgiveness, it seems I must open my heart to my adversary. You, Missus Pinkwater, for better or worse, are God's elected."

Bonnie's Imp of the Perverse desperately wanted to announce, *I've long suspected that.* With an effort of will, she resisted the urging. She merely nodded and presented what she hoped was a sympathetic expression. "I'm honored, Harold."

Dobbs turned in the pew so he could face both Lloyd and Bonnie. "First, let me say that Jason came through the surgery successfully and is in recovery. He is no longer considered in critical condition, and they'll be taking him to his room within the hour. I assume you'll want to visit."

"That would be great, Harold," Lloyd said.

Bonnie regarded this man of the cloth, who decided to leave his wounded son to seek out a solitary audience with God. Whatever was troubling Dobbs must have weighed heavily on his mind and had demanded immediate atonement.

"My aim is alacrity, because from here we must contact Deputy Hickman." Dobbs exhaled and held Bonnie's gaze. "I woke this morning with anger in my heart. Anger directed at you, my son, and an overwhelming anger directed toward Alf Quinn."

I knew it. "So you went to see him."

Dobbs reddened. "I did, indeed. I hoped to catch him before he left for the funeral."

"And did you?"

"Yes. He was alone in his office. Alf had deteriorated since I last saw him. He looked, for lack of a better word, unbalanced. Almost immediately, I lost all desire to take the man to task. I offered to pray with him, but it had been a long drive. I had to go to the bathroom. You know that tiny room in back?"

Bonnie could, indeed, picture the small bathroom hidden in the rear of Rattlesnake's office. The door was constructed of old ammo box lids and blended in so completely with the martial theme of Alf's décor that unless a person knew it was there, they could easily miss seeing the darn thing.

She nodded for Dobbs to continue.

"While I was in there, someone came."

"Who?" Lloyd asked.

The pastor shrugged an I-wish-I knew shrug. "Although, from a crack in the door, I could see an arm or a leg now and then, I never could make out a face and the party never spoke much or loud enough for me to recognize a voice. Truth be told, Alf did most of the talking."

Bonnie resisted the urge to ask the obvious questions like, *What did Rattlesnake say?* or *Didn't you poke your head out once?* What was needful at the moment was to keep quiet and let the man tell his story in his own way.

"After an initial interchange, Alf got upset. His voice grew louder, more insistent, more heated. The first clear words from Alf made the breath catch in my chest."

Bonnie was about to break in when Lloyd piped up. "What did he say?"

"*No more killing. And then, I'm having second thoughts.*"

Synapses started firing in Bonnie's brain like Roman candles. Alf *had* hired someone to kill Furby. She wanted to turn straight around and tell Lloyd her theory had been right.

"Once again, the other speaker didn't say much but whatever little there was, it incensed Rattlesnake further. He told his visitor to vamoose and hinted he meant to call the police."

Uh-oh. Not a wise move with a murderer, Rattlesnake. "I'm going to go out on a limb and guess this last bit didn't sit well with Alf's guest."

Dobbs shook his head. "Not at all. He pulled a gun. The next thing I knew, he had pistol-whipped Mister Quinn."

"How much of this pistol could you see?" Lloyd asked.

"Enough to ascertain it was a nine millimeter."

Bonnie and Lloyd exchanged glances.

"What?" demanded Dobbs.

"That's the type of pistol that killed Leo," Lloyd said. "Go on, please. I didn't mean to interrupt."

Dobbs waved away the apology. "I'm grateful for the chance to gather my courage." He licked his lips, obviously ill at ease over the prospect of telling the next portion of his story.

"And herein my tale is one of vanity and cowardice.

It is this sin and this shame I will bear the remainder of my days. Understandably, you will despise me after."

Dear God, pastor, does everything that comes out of your mouth have to resonate like a sermon? "I don't want to be a noodge, Harold, but didn't you say something about having to contact Deputy Hickman."

Dobbs's face reddened and his eyes went flinty.

Now you've done it, Pinkwater. Your Imp of the Perverse resurrected the old Harold T. Dobbs.

However, Dobbs quickly recovered. Through gritted teeth, he said, "You're right, of course." For a moment, Harold looked lost in his narrative.

"Vanity," Lloyd offered.

Bless you, Lloyd.

"Yes. Well at this juncture, the unwanted guest fired his pistol. The bullet pierced the bathroom door, narrowly missing me." Dobbs licked his lips again. "I'm afraid I soiled myself."

Bonnie permitted the tiniest of smiles before she extinguished it. More than anything she wanted to ask if the good pastor had done a number one or a number two. Even her Imp of the Perverse recognized the impertinent question as stupidly unproductive.

"Go on."

"My legs turned to water. Quite truthfully, I felt light-headed and thought I might pass out. I sat on the commode. To my shame when the intruder got what he came for and finally took Alf with him, I stayed hidden. I made no attempt to even see in which direction they left."

A nagging feeling took hold of Bonnie. Something felt out of kilter with the good pastor's story. She couldn't lay a logical finger on where her difficulty lay, but it buzzed round her psyche like a hornet.

Lloyd reached across Bonnie and tapped Dobbs on the wrist. "I need to know something, Harold." Lloyd made the request sound like a command and not a friendly one. "The killer came for a rifle, am I correct?"

"Yes. I caught a fleeting glimpse of it."

"The M24."

From what Dobbs said about contacting Byron, Bonnie was fairly sure they were the first to hear this story. *Not good for Rattlesnake. I wouldn't give a fig for his chances.*

Bonnie checked her Mickey Mouse watch. "It's past three, Harold. What time did you go to Rattlesnake's?"

"Some time before ten."

Bonnie wanted to smack the man. Over five hours had elapsed and the police still hadn't been notified about Rattlesnake's abduction. She inhaled a long breath and held it in an effort to gain equilibrium.

When she felt sufficiently calm, she asked, "Harold, why did you wait so long before telling anyone?"

Red climbed from Dobbs's neck into his face. He

shut his eyes. His lips moved in a silent prayer. When he opened his eyes again, he said, "Please forgive me. This is proving harder than I thought."

He held Bonnie's gaze for a long moment. "My vanity was my undoing. First, I convinced myself that Alf would emerge from this encounter relatively unscathed."

When Bonnie opened her mouth to disagree, Dobbs raised a silencing hand. "I know I deceived myself, but such was my self-deception and fear that I believed it. From there I reasoned that no purpose would be served if I was seen in a state of filth."

Bonnie could hold her tongue no longer. "Do you mean to tell me that you went home and changed?"

For a fleeting moment, Pastor Harold T. Dobbs went rigid. Again his eyes grew hard and a dark storm raced over his features.

The moment passed and in the next, the spiritual leader of the Saved by the Blood Pentecostal Tabernacle seemed to diminish. He nodded. "My shame goes further than that. By the time I'd reached home, I'd determined to tell no one of my visit to Alf Quinn's. I even went so far as to change into my funeral coat to give the impression I planned to attend."

This final admission purchased a grudging respect from Bonnie. *If our positions were reversed, could I have told this man the lousy things he's confessing to me?* "Then you heard about Jason."

Once more, the big man nodded. "I can't even remember who called . . . someone from the funeral no doubt. Even then, I refused to believe I had an obligation to publicly embarrass myself. You see by then, I would have to explain why I didn't immediately report the abduction."

"Didn't you realize the rifle was more than likely used to shoot your own son?" Lloyd asked.

From years in her principal's company, Bonnie could tell Lloyd's temper was on the rise. He had, no doubt, moved into a mental state where he had little use for the Reverend Harold T. Dobbs.

Dobbs grimaced. "When a man is running from God, sometimes he's afraid of his own mind lest he find his Savior there. And by then, I was running as fast as I could. Only later, after I encountered the two of you at the information desk, did I . . ." Dobbs shuddered and his face collapsed into a mask of sorrow.

You poor schmuck.

Bonnie reached into her fanny pack and pulled out her cell phone. She dialed Byron Hickman's office. Her former student picked up on the second ring.

"Youngster, there's someone here you need to talk to." She handed the phone to Dobbs.

For the next few minutes the man looked positively cowed. As he related his tale to the deputy, Bonnie was struck once again that something was missing. Events simply could not have transpired the way Harold was delineating them. The fact that she couldn't pin down the problem was driving her batty.

"Deputy Hickman is coming here immediately. He'll meet us in Jason's room." Dobbs handed the phone back to Bonnie, who snapped it shut. "I can't say I'm looking forward to repeating my disgraceful story in front of my son."

"I don't blame you." Lloyd didn't appear as if he was ready to cut Dobbs any slack. His face was tight with disapproval, all planes and angles. "You don't come off looking so good in all this, pastor."

The remark and Lloyd's stern appraisal obviously stung Harold. His cheeks colored. "I don't deserve to."

Unlike Lloyd, Bonnie found herself surprised with how willing she was to forgive this man, who just twenty-four hours before was prepared to toss her from his office. Despite her misgivings about his tale of woe and shame, Bonnie definitely preferred this incarnation of Harold T. Dobbs over the preacher she'd grown to detest.

Face it, Pinkwater. You're a sucker for folks who are up to their armpits in the deeper caca.

She was about to reach out and comfort Dobbs when the solution to her mental dilemma sprang fully formed in her mind. "How the hell did he get there?"

Both Lloyd and Dobbs turned to stare at her.

"Beg pardon?" Dobbs asked.

"You say the man abducted Rattlesnake at gunpoint. And Rattlesnake's employee said Alf's truck was missing. A reasonable assumption is that both the abductor and Alf left in that truck."

Lloyd's face registered understanding. "But how in God's name did the kidnapper get to the shooting range in the first place? That range sits in the middle of nowhere, at least three miles off Highway 84."

"Byron needs to check out all the cars that were present when he and his deputies talked to that lone paintball employee." Bonnie reached for her fanny pack and her cell phone. "For all we know, the abductor's vehicle is still parked there and the lunatic will return for it."

Even as she said this last, Bonnie felt certain the sheriff's department would come up empty-handed. If she were kidnapping someone at gunpoint, she certainly wouldn't leave her own car behind at the scene of the crime. It would make more sense to force Alf into Alice and drive off in that.

From the look on Lloyd's face, he was having similar doubts.

"This just isn't playing out, boss." Bonnie set her fanny pack on her lap, not sure what she could tell Byron if she called. "Certainly, you don't kidnap someone and then take separate vehicles. And, like you, I don't think the man walked the three miles from Highway 84."

Lloyd nodded. "No way. That would mean planning

to depart Rattlesnake's on foot carrying a sniper rifle. Besides, we can be reasonably sure two hours later our killer plans to be positioned on the roof of Memorial Hospital. Going for a stroll in the desert doesn't figure into this scenario."

From the corner of her eye, Bonnie saw Harold Dobbs tentatively raise his hand. The act was so child-like, it brought a smile to her lips. "Yes, Harold?"

"I probably should have told this to Deputy Hickman, but before the intruder showed, I heard the sound of a motorcycle."

CHAPTER 18

His eyes heavily lidded and unfocused, Jason Dobbs slowly turned toward Harold, Bonnie, and Lloyd as they filed into the hospital room. A sliver of diagonal sunlight sliced across his pillow and chalky face, revealing a hint of a smile. The light gave the young man a beatific aura.

A clear oxygen tube pinched at Jason's nostrils like a translucent mustache, while an IV tube ran from the crook of his left arm up to a rotund plastic bag. Completing the young man's connections to medical technology, a flesh-colored vise capped the index finger of his right hand. A similarly hued wire ran to an oscilloscope, which regularly blipped, displaying evidence that Jason Dobbs remained among the living. The entire upper left side of his body was swaddled in bandages.

"Father." Jason's voice rasped as if every molecule of moisture had been surgically removed.

Harold strode across the room and gently laid a hand

on his son's chest. "I've brought visitors."

Jason licked his lips. His eyes seemed to move independently, then hone in on Bonnie. "Missus Pinkwater." The two words came out in a breathless rush.

"How you doing, Jason?" Bonnie felt in the throes of a pair of simultaneous and contradictory impulses. One part of her wanted nothing more than to wrap her arms around this damaged young man. She grappled with an equally strong urge to run from the room rather than inflict on Jason the questions she needed to ask.

"Pretty good." He tilted his head to see past Bonnie. "Principal Whittaker, come on in."

Lloyd stepped around Bonnie and nodded. "Looks like you should have ducked, buddy."

A dry chuckle escaped Jason Dobbs's lips. "No fair. I'm so doped up, I'll giggle at anything."

Bonnie inwardly winced as the young man's comment brought to mind her own callous suggestion that Jason would be easy prey because of painkillers. *Serves you right, Pinkwater. A guilty conscience is the least price you should pay for being such a sphincter.*

As she was readying herself to speak, she heard Lloyd clear his throat. She turned her head just enough to catch his eye. His conspiratorial expression told her he hadn't forgotten their agreement. He would play the inquisitor.

Bless you, Lloyd Whittaker.

"You gave us quite a scare there, hoss." Lloyd took a step toward the bed. "You got any idea who might have wanted to take a potshot at you?"

Jason looked puzzled by the question, his mouth open and his eyes darting from Lloyd to his father.

"Give it some thought, my boy," Harold said.

Jason shook his head. "I've been doing nothing else since I woke up. I got no idea who'd want to kill me."

Lloyd placed a hand on Harold's arm. "I need to ask some hard questions, Harold, and I want your permission to ask them."

An eternity passed before the preacher responded. "I think I know the nature of your questions, but my son has to be the one to decide." He patted the boy's hand.

In that moment, Jason's vision apparently cleared. He stared levelly at Lloyd. "I think I know, too, Principal Whittaker. Fire away."

"Fair enough. Remember that night in the grandstands, when we were talking about Leo Quinn?"

A faint hint of pink crept into Jason's pale cheeks. "I remember."

"You said you hadn't seen Leo in quite a while. I think the implication was that it had been more than a year, maybe a couple of years." Lloyd knitted his fingers behind his neck as though asking this leading question was making him ache.

You're doing great, boss. Keep it up.

Jason Dobbs's face went hard. "We might as well cut to the chase, Principal Whittaker. I lied."

Lloyd seemed taken aback by the sudden admission, but he quickly recovered. "I know." He delivered this brief response as though he was giving absolution. "You saw Leo just two months before his death, didn't you?"

Jason nodded. "Since you know a lot about my comings and goings—and I believe I know how—you probably also know what Leo and I talked about." The young man glanced nervously at his father.

Harold Dobbs gave his son a reassuring smile. "The Lord abhors the darkness, my boy. Bring everything into the light and rest easy in the knowledge that I and Jesus will love you no matter what."

Nicely said, preacher. I hope this new Harold T. Dobbs sticks around for a while.

Lloyd scratched at his craggy face, obviously trying to find a tactful way of completing Jason's thought. "You told Leo that you'd made up your mind to follow in your father's footsteps. That you and Leo were through."

Jason pursed his lips and turned toward the window. "Leo took it badly. Called me a coward and worse. Said I was denying who I really was, was living a lie. I tried to tell him I still loved him, but he wouldn't listen. He insisted I take him back home."

"And that was the last time you saw him?"

Jason Dobbs's head made a slow pivot on the pillow

as if he was reentering the world of the present. "What are you suggesting?"

Lloyd, his brow furrowed and his hands clenching and unclenching, clearly wasn't enjoying his role as inquisitor. "Leo Quinn's body was found on a remote stretch of Squirrel Creek Road. Do you have any idea what he was doing out there?"

Now Jason's eyes bore straight into Lloyd's. "No, Mister Whittaker, I have no idea whatsoever. I did not meet Leo again as his lover or his killer. Leo Quinn was the best friend I've ever had and probably the best I ever will have. I wanted nothing for him but his happiness, and you see how that turned out."

Lloyd shook his head. "Sad business, this."

"You have no idea, Mister Whittaker."

A rattle at the door made Bonnie start. She turned to see the unhappy countenance of Deputy Byron Hickman.

Lloyd moved a three-year-old copy of *Newsweek* from the plastic seat next to Bonnie's and sat. They had the hospital waiting room to themselves.

Bonnie slapped Lloyd's knee. "How are you holding up, big guy?"

"I'll live." He stretched and, lacing his fingers in front of him, cracked his knuckles. "What do you think of Jason's story?"

Bonnie shrugged a your-guess-is-as-good-as-mine shrug. "It's basically the same story we got from Seneca. And still, I don't know what to think. If Jason *was* out there on Squirrel Creek Road, then what we got is one odd bundle of sticks."

Lloyd grunted and gazed unhappily toward the waiting room door. He obviously didn't want to be cooling his heels in some hospital waiting room, but Byron had said he needed to speak with them after he was finished with Harold.

Bonnie had to admit she felt the same as her friend and principal. It had been a long day, and she was anxious to get home and soak in a hot tub. "Let it go, Lloyd. Staring at the door won't make Byron show up one minute quicker."

"It's not just the waiting. I'm worried about Rattlesnake, Bon." Lloyd shook his head, anger reappearing on his face. "Dobbs should have done something, dammit. The least of which was to report the kidnapping the minute it happened."

"I agree with you, boss, but be reasonable." Bonnie shifted in her chair so she could force eye contact with Lloyd. "If Harold would have come barging out of that stall, he most likely would have been killed. I admit, the man didn't acquit himself in an admirable fashion—"

"You can say that again."

"If you insist. The man didn't acquit himself admirably, but he made a clean breast of it, and I, for one, think we should forget Dobbs and concentrate on Rattlesnake. Now that Byron knows what we know, he'll be on the lookout for Alf's truck."

Lloyd's knuckles were white as they gripped his knees. "Now it's your turn to be reasonable. The shooter certainly didn't bring Alf with him to the roof, and he damn well couldn't let the man go. Not with what the killer was about to do."

Bonnie sighed, feeling Lloyd's despair. There was no denying the logic of her principal's argument. Still, a nagging voice impelled her to consider another possibility. "What if Rattlesnake wasn't abducted?"

"What do you mean?"

"Just that. What if everything Dobbs saw was staged." Bonnie could feel a full head of steam building. "Stay with me. Remember Dobbs saying he couldn't make out anything the intruder was saying and initially couldn't even hear Rattlesnake? Why not?"

Lloyd gave her a perplexed look. "Because they didn't talk loud enough?"

She slapped his arm. "Duh! But why did they talk quietly? Picture this. The intruder walks in. Rattlesnake signals to him that Dobbs is in the bathroom. They talk in hushed tones until Rattlesnake says, *No more killing*. By that time, both men have come to the conclusion that since Dobbs had failed to emerge, he had no intention of doing so. They intensify their conflict, even to the point of faking a pistol-whipping and firing a gun toward the tiny stall."

"That shot could have killed Harold."

It was Bonnie's turn to give Lloyd a jaundiced stare. "These are men who have murdered at least once and plan to kill the son of the man in the bathroom. I think the welfare of one Pastor Harold T. Dobbs wasn't high on their list of priorities. Besides, I'll bet the shot wasn't as close as Harold makes it out to be." *Although it was close enough to make Harold wish he'd worn a diaper.*

"All right. All right. You're saying Rattlesnake and our killer finish up by traipsing off together. So, where is Rattlesnake now?"

Bonnie shrugged. "Where is the intruder now? Why couldn't they be together?"

Lloyd scratched at his stubble of beard. "Okay, what about the motorcycle that Dobbs heard?"

Bonnie sat back in her chair. She'd been thinking of this angle ever since Harold had mentioned it. "I admit this one bothered me for a while. If the intruder rode in on a motorcycle, then he'd no more want to leave it behind than leave a car. There's only one possibility. Somehow, the bike was loaded into the back of Rattlesnake's truck."

Looking decidedly unconvinced, Lloyd pursed his

lips. "I'm having trouble picturing the logistics of this one. Either Rattlesnake loaded the bike all by his lonesome, with our killer looking on..."

"Which isn't beyond the realm of possibility. Alf is a big man."

"Or they loaded the bike together. In which case—"

Bonnie slapped Lloyd's knee. "Now you're getting it. In which case, they were probably working together."

"Not necessarily."

Bonnie shook her head, disappointed in her friend. "You know, there a fine line between playing devil's advocate and just being contrary. Alf Quinn is six-foot-six, all marine muscle. Are you telling me our intruder sidles up—within arm's reach of Alf—and makes himself vulnerable by lending a hand?"

Lloyd reddened. "He could have kept one hand on the pistol and—"

"Now we're just talking silly, not to mention awkward." Bonnie shook her head, definitely negating the last possibility. "If we accept Harold's assumption that our intruder rode in on a motorcycle, then we have two cases. Either Alf was truly abducted at gunpoint..."

"In which case he more than likely loaded the bike alone."

Bonnie nodded and smiled sheepishly. She'd already begun to regret how surly she'd acted toward her friend.

"Indeed. Or if he was in cahoots, he and the killer worked in tandem."

"I'm not saying I buy into this trumped-up abduction fantasy, but it certainly has a boatload of symmetry."

"Doesn't it, though?" She nodded enthusiastically. "If I'm right, we need to stop calling Rattlesnake's partner the intruder. From Alf Rattlesnake Quinn's perspective, Dobbs was the unexpected intruder and"—she waved her hand—"whosits was actually expected."

A half smile crept onto Lloyd's face. "And that's the problem with your theory. Harold *wasn't* expected. And we don't know if a motorcycle isn't still out there."

"There's no motorcycle at the range." A weary-looking Byron Hickman leaned against the waiting room doorway. "I was there this afternoon and know that much."

Bonnie pounded her fist onto the arm of her chair. "Then the motorcycle is in the back of Alf's truck."

Lloyd laid a sympathetic hand on her arm. "Bon, it's possible Harold was mistaken about what he heard. Maybe there was no motorcycle."

Of course, that's true. "Then we're back to our original problem. How did Whosits get to the range?"

Byron took a chair across from Bonnie and put his feet up on a long glass coffee table. He dug the heels of his hands into his eyes and yawned. The face that emerged from behind the hands looked like it belonged to an unfortunate who hadn't slept in a week. "I'm going to assume Whositz is the unknown assailant who ran off with Rattlesnake and most likely shot Jason Dobbs. I need to speak with both of you about that."

Bonnie mirrored Byron's yawn. *Ye gods. Just looking at the man is draining.* "Fire away, Kemosabe."

"First of all, Missus P, I personally believe Harold's account of what happened at the range. It jives with what we've discovered in the last few hours."

"Which is?" Lloyd asked.

Byron blinked, studying Lloyd's open, honest face. Finally, as if a wall had broken down, he sighed. "The Colorado Springs police found Alf Quinn's truck parked in a remote corner of this hospital's parking lot."

CHAPTER 19

"And Alf?" Bonnie was sure she already knew the answer, but had to ask anyway.

"No sign of the man anywhere." A yawning Deputy Byron Hickman pushed his hat far back on his head, folded his arms across his chest, and hunkered down in his chair. "No sign of violence, either, which supports that harebrained theory of yours that Rattlesnake faked his own abduction."

Bonnie could feel heat creep up the back of her neck. "You heard that, did you?"

Her former student sighed, then offered a weary smile. "Every word. You weren't exactly whispering, Missus P. However, if you don't mind, I went ahead and called it in as a kidnapping."

Bonnie tried to ignore the additional heat that had moved from her neck onto her face. She waved her hand as if she were giving her blessing to Byron's decision. "That's probably for the best."

"I'm glad you approve." The deputy checked his watch, then with what appeared a Herculean effort, pushed himself upright. "If I don't get moving, I'm going to fall asleep right here in this chair."

He stood. "What say we finish our talk on the way out?"

"Amen to that, youngster." Bonnie sprang to her feet. She felt like someone whose cage door had miraculously opened. *Hot bath, here I come.*

She offered a hand to Lloyd, who declined and stiffly hoisted himself out of his chair.

Bonnie shook her head in mock disgust. "You two make a fine pair. I was going to offer to race you both to the parking lot, but from the looks of you, I'd win. Then I'd have to contend with the bother of wounded male egos."

"Thank you, Bon," Lloyd said. "You've always been the considerate one."

"True, all too true." Bonnie led the way from the waiting room to the elevator. While she was walking ahead she caught bits and pieces of conversation between the two men—"Nine millimeter" from one sentence and "M24" from another.

When the elevator doors closed, Bonnie wheeled on Byron. "I've been thinking."

"Uh-oh." The deputy shook his head as if he didn't approve of uncontrolled cognition. "I'll bet you have a theory."

"Not so much a theory as I want to propose a *what if*." She hurried on before Byron could interrupt. "Harold told you about the black nine-millimeter Glock?"

The elevator door opened, and Byron held the door while they all filed out into the white-lined hall. "And you're thinking that's the same weapon that killed Leo Quinn?"

Byron's leapfrogging to her next supposition rendered her momentarily speechless. She could see it amused the deputy even as it annoyed her. She stuck her tongue out at him.

"Very mature."

Bonnie threw back her head in mock defiance and led the way along the white-lined corridor. "I don't have to be mature, youngster. I'm an educator. I'll be fifteen forever. Now as to that pistol, I'm not saying there couldn't be more than one nine millimeter in all of East Plains, but just suppose it *is* the same weapon."

"I can't believe I'm about to tell you this, but here goes. If all your speculations are true, then Rattlesnake's abductor is in possession of the gun that also killed Dwight Furby. We already know the same weapon killed both Leo and Dwight."

Again, her former student succeeded in catching her flat-footed. She had been prepared to ask about the Furby-Quinn connection but not immediately.

Lloyd whistled between his teeth. "How long has the sheriff's department known about that little tidbit?"

"Since yesterday morning. And don't give me that look, Missus P. I don't have an obligation to keep you informed about all the comings and goings of this investigation."

Busted.

Bonnie adopted a wide-eyed, innocent expression. "The look, Deputy Hickman, that you are so unjustly maligning, is merely that of contemplation. And unlike you and your department, I am more than happy to share all the fruits of my musings."

Byron chuckled. "That's true enough. You are likely to share your thoughts even when they're not asked for."

"I'm going to ignore that unkind remark in favor of a cogent question. Has anyone considered how weird it is that two people who were out on Squirrel Creek Road last Saturday night are now both dead by the same killer?"

Byron shook his head. "We don't know that. All we know for sure is that it was the same gun."

Bonnie frowned what she hoped was her I'm-disappointed-in-you frown. "Come off it, youngster. What about the tight triangular pattern of shots on both victims? And what about Moses Witherspoon and Gabe Trotter?"

Byron rewarded her question with a perplexed stare.

"What about them?"

"They were out on Squirrel Creek Road Saturday night, probably in the company of Dwight Furby." Even as she made the statement, Bonnie wished she could rewind. Since she had spoken with Wilma Trotter, Bonnie hadn't found the right opportunity to fill Byron in on what the woman had told her. She shared an oh-my-God-I'm-in-deep-feces look with Lloyd.

Byron's tired face became like stone, looking for all the world like he might burst through his skin. "And how do you know Spoon and Gabe were out on Squirrel Creek last Saturday?"

He asked the question in the kind of soft, long-suffering voice that made Bonnie wish for shouted recriminations, the way a child wishes for a spanking just to get his parent's anger out in the open and over with.

For a long moment, Bonnie kept a smile plastered on her face while she gathered excuses for not telling the sheriff's office about her visit with Wilma. One by one, Bonnie sorted through them. A class to teach. A eulogy to write and deliver. The funeral. Jason's shooting. The passion play with Harold Dobbs. In the end, she discarded them all.

"I went to see Wilma Trotter." As she delineated her entire conversation with the eccentric woman, Bonnie utilized all her powers of recollection to make sure she left out nothing. She owed Byron at least that much.

The telling hadn't been made easier by Byron interrupting repeatedly, asking for a detail or having a point reiterated.

How did Wilma look?

When was the last time the woman saw her son?

With each interruption Bonnie had to bite back her annoyance. She kept reminding herself that patience was a virtue and whereas she hadn't been naturally blessed with an abundance of the stuff, nothing would be served by both she and Byron getting out of sorts.

When she finished, Byron, lips pursed and brow furrowed, merely nodded. Hands clasped behind his back, he paced. Each time he passed where Bonnie stood leaning on Alice's trunk, he gave her a thorny look.

On his fourth pass, she reached out a hand and stopped him. "I get it. You're angry with me."

Byron shook his head savagely. "You know what really torques me? Not five minutes ago, you got your bloomers in a twist because I didn't share some ballistic information with you. All the while, you were withholding something this crucial."

Bonnie offered an apologetic smile. "Ironic, isn't it?"

Her former student blinked at her like she might be mentally challenged. "Irony?" He laughed a mirthless laugh. "In what upside-down universe is any of this ironic?"

Even though Byron still was angry, Bonnie drew courage from his laughter. "It depends on how you look at it. What we're talking about here is a half-full versus half-empty glass sort of situation."

From behind Byron's back she could see Lloyd signaling she should quit while she was ahead, but she ignored the man and barreled on.

"We can either view this dual and untimely release of information as an awful mistake or believe that all things work together for good. That's from the Bible, you know?"

Byron nodded morosely, like a man condemned to listen to bad music. "I know that. Just as I know you have a point to make."

"Indeed I do." Bonnie linked her hands together like a chain. "I choose to believe that the business about the pistol and the Saturday whereabouts of Gabe Trotter and Moses Witherspoon came to light at this nexus in time so that we could consider them in tandem."

Deputy Byron Hickman squinted at Bonnie, giving evidence he was at least partially interested. "Go on."

"The black nine millimeter was used initially out on Squirrel Creek Road on Saturday night. Put that fact together with the new information that we can place at least two living individuals in proximity to this same gun."

Lloyd joined Bonnie and Byron at the rear of the Subaru. "And when the pistol was used at the fair, Witherspoon was there again."

"Another country heard from and right again. Now

here comes the complicated bit. Add all of this together with what Harold overheard at Rattlesnake's."

"*No more killing,*" Byron quoted.

It was Bonnie's turn to nod. "Precisely. Which brings up a pertinent question. Considering the same gun was used to kill both Leo and Dwight Furby, why was Alf Quinn supplying weapons to the man who killed his son?"

Bonnie held up her hand for silence.

Her baker's dozen of students scaled back their enthusiasm to a reasonable buzz.

"This situation presents a unique dilemma," Bonnie said.

It seems that once they had a name to glom on to, no one had trouble clueing into facts about Sophia Kovalevskaya. Now they were all vying for the right to present their findings.

"Did anyone have a partner? That way, two people can get credit for presenting?" Yoki, the oriental student who'd earlier that week had missed out on a Jolly Rancher, and Georgia, a gangly, freckled-faced blonde, raised their hands.

Bonnie nodded in their direction. "Go for it." She took up residence at her desk in the back of the room.

Robert Spiller

The two girls exchanged nervous glances and then stood. While Georgia appeared as if she might burst into anxious giggles, Yoki adopted the demeanor of a lawyer about to give her summation. Her jet-black hair pulled back into a severe ponytail, she smoothed down her flowered dress. She strode to the front of the room and her dark eyes took in her classmates and finally Bonnie.

Child, you have a presence. Way to work it.

"Georgia, will you pass out Sophia's picture?" Yoki asked solemnly.

The blonde nodded and snatched up the stack of papers on Yoki's desk and distributed them to her classmates. When she was finished, she handed the remaining papers to Bonnie.

The photo showed a young girl, in her midtwenties maybe. The face wasn't classically beautiful, but possessed strength in the set of the jaw and the intensity of the eyes. Her hair was short, almost mannish. She wore a high-necked blouse clasped under the chin with a scrimshaw cameo. Beneath the photo was the quote, *It is impossible to be a mathematician without being a poet in the soul.*

Although Bonnie had read the quote a legion of times, she found herself nodding approval at the sentiment. She herself considered mathematics an artform as well as a science.

Yoki cleared her throat. While Bonnie had been

perusing Sophia Kovalevskaya's picture, the young oriental girl had ensconced herself behind Bonnie lectern. She extracted an index card from a pocket of her dress and set it in front of her.

"*Say what you know, do what you must, come what may.* I think this quote, more than any other, tells what Sophia Kovalevskaya was like. She fought for what she believed in a world where women could do hardly anything except have babies and be wives."

Yoki stepped from behind the podium. Once again Bonnie was impressed with the young girl's charisma.

Sophia would like your style, cutie.

Bonnie expected the girl to return to the lectern to check her notes, but she moved to the blackboard. She wrote *1850–1891* on the board.

"Sophia only lived forty-one years, but in that time she was a lot of things. She was considered one of the leading mathematicians of her time, although she had trouble finding a college to let her in to study. Eventually she would become the first European woman since the Renaissance to receive a doctorate in mathematics. I thought about that fact, and it made me sad and happy at the same time."

Yoki inhaled deeply and for a moment Bonnie thought the girl was tearing up. If she was, the moment passed. "I was happy because here was this really passionate, brilliant woman kicking butt in a man's world. I was sad because I thought of all the other women in almost two hundred years who never got the chance to show what they could do just because they weren't men."

From across the room, Bonnie noted the grumblings of her charges.

That's right, ladies. Get pissed off. And don't for a moment think this crap is completely done away with yet. The glass ceiling still exists, and women still get paid less than 80 percent of their counterparts for the same work.

"But Sophia wasn't just a mathematician. She was a scientist. She wrote a paper on the rings of Saturn. The paper got awards."

Yoki returned to the podium and checked her notes. "She was a novelist. Her autobiography, *Recollections of a Childhood*, was like a best seller. It told about growing up in the country with her father, who was a general in the czarist army. She was scared of him, but he saw that she was really, really smart." Yoki glanced back to where Bonnie sat. "He's the one who wallpapered her room with mathematical notes."

The girl reddened slightly. "Although, Missus Pinkwater, they weren't Newton's notes. They were notes about Newton and Leibniz on calculus and analysis. Actually, the notes belonged to a Russian mathematician named"—again, she checked her index card—"Mikhail Ostrogradsky."

Bonnie didn't mind this particular correction. She

had known she was stretching the truth when she said Isaac Newton's notes papered Sophia's bedroom. Everybody knew Isaac Newton, but who the hell was Mikhail Ostragradsky?

In a toss-up between the legend and the truth, ladies, always opt for the legend? It makes better press.

Yoki walked back to the blackboard. She wrote *The Nihilist Girl* on the board and put it in quotes. "This novel, which was published after Sophia's death and translated into seven languages, showed another one of her passions. She was a revolutionary. She fought for women's rights in Russia, and when she moved to other European countries she fought against oppression there, too. She had to marry someone she didn't love just so that she could travel to Germany to study math. Unmarried women weren't allowed to travel in those days. Can you believe that?"

Bonnie smiled at Yoki's indignation. *Honey, that particular stricture is still practiced on three continents.*

Yoki leaned heavily on the podium, her unlined face rigid with anger. "The crummy part was that when she got to Germany, the University of Heidelberg wouldn't accept her as a student. No women allowed. If it wasn't for some guy named Weierstrass tutoring her on the sly— I think he was secretly in love with her—she wouldn't have gotten any degree at all and would have had to return to Russia, the wife of a paleontologist whom she didn't love."

Once again, Yoki inhaled deeply. From what Bonnie could tell, the girl delivered her last monologue in one long breath.

"A lot of folks thought her husband might have been gay, but he must have liked girls a little. In 1878 Sophia had a baby."

A few of the girls giggled at this.

Nice work, Yoki. You got them now. Bring it on home.

"Anyway," Yoki continued, "even with a doctorate, Sophia couldn't find work in Russia, Germany, or even England. Same old story—no women allowed. She ended up taking a job teaching in Sweden. Her husband asked her not to go. He was a gambler and really bad at business and lost a lot of money, so they needed the money this job would pay. She took their child and went to Stockholm. Not long after, he committed suicide. For the rest of her life, which was only three more years, she blamed herself for his death."

Yoki looked back to where Bonnie sat. "I won't be much longer. Anyway, over the next three years, although Sophia did a lot of important math and science, her heart just wasn't in it. Even as she got more and more famous, her health got worse. Finally, on a trip to Paris, she exhausted herself carrying her luggage. She passed out at the railroad station and within a couple of days she died. Like I said, she was only forty-one years old. My dad's older than that now."

Again, Yoki looked back to Bonnie. "That's all I have to say about Sophia Kovalevskaya." The girl pointed with her chin toward her partner. "Georgia's going do some of Sophia's math."

Bonnie stood. "Hold off for a moment, Georgia." Stretching as she went, Bonnie walked to the front of the classroom. She dipped into the Jolly Rancher bag, came out with a blue raspberry jolly, and handed it to the girl. "Nice job, Yoki."

"Thank you, Missus Pinkwater."

Her classmates, including her partner, Georgia, applauded.

Bonnie waited until the applause died before she spoke. "I'll let Georgia get up here in a minute, but before she does, I'd like to say a bit more about Sophia Kovalevskaya. Actually, I have quite a bit more to say, so I'm going to save most of my talk for the next class. What I'd like to leave you with now is more in the way of a teaser. Many people, Yoki included, say that Kovalevskaya died of exhaustion. I like to offer an alternative explanation for her death at such an early age."

Bonnie paused, letting the drama of her words fill the silence. "I'd like to suggest that Sophia Kovalevskaya, mathematician, scientist, novelist, and revolutionary, died not of exhaustion, but of something a lot more common and infinitely more tragic."

CHAPTER 20

There's something about a school bus, a rumble and hum that differs from every other form of mass conveyance. Bonnie hated them as a rule, but this time the ride was smoother, the seats softer, the normally stifling air, cooler. Outside was another story altogether. Beyond the sliding glass windows, a blizzard was scouring the landscape. Ice clung to the windows. Visibility couldn't have been more than ten feet.

"You okay, Missus P?"

Bonnie shifted her line of sight from the storm to whoever had inquired into her well-being. "Leo?"

"In the flesh." The freckle-faced boy—he appeared to be about fifteen or sixteen—reddened. "So to speak."

"You're dead, my boy."

"That's the rumor." He flashed her the patented Quinn smile, all two hundred watts of it. Dimples punctuated both cheeks. "I have to tell you, death doesn't make long bus rides any better."

She wanted to reach out, pull the gangly miscreant into a tight embrace, tell him she was sorry she hadn't called. The look on Leo's face made it all unnecessary.

He shrugged. "Ain't no biggie."

Bonnie took a quick scan of the interior of the bus. Behind her sat the Kettle twins, Mike and Sean, tall, spindly, with shocks of hair so shiny black, the stuff looked plastic. The twins were playing some game where the object was to punch the other person's arm as often and hard as possible. Any other time, Bonnie would have felt obliged to put a halt to the proceedings with an admonition to settle down or suffer dire consequences. Now, she just let the pandemonium wash over her. Truth be told, she couldn't really make out what the boys were saying, even though they sat no more than three feet away. The same held true for Randy Welsh and Lisa Yerber in the seat across the aisle. Both were obviously holding forth on some matter of great import.

Bonnie turned back to Leo. "Where are we?"

Leo gave her an admonishing frown. "Don't you recognize the group? We're your Knowledge Bowl team from my sophomore year—on our way back from Durango. We took third in state out of the double A schools."

Of course.

She did know these children—although a part of her also knew they were children no longer. Lisa and Randy had gone on to get married, and divorced. God knows what happened to the Kettle twins once they escaped from East Plains.

"I remember that—this—trip. I was worried we would never get over Wolf Creek Pass."

"But we did."

She regarded Leo, feeling the old warmth and kinship return. "You kept me sane by talking to me until we reached the other side of the pass."

"Do you remember what we talked about?"

Bonnie didn't hesitate. "Oscar Wilde. Your language arts class had just gone to see *The Importance of Being Earnest*." She nodded to him, and winked—their signal to start their favorite interchange between Jack and Algernon, two of the characters in Wilde's play.

Leo didn't disappoint her. He sat up rigid, his chin tucked, his eyes fixed on hers. "Oh, that's nonsense, Algy. You never talk *anything* but nonsense."

"Nobody ever does." Bonnie licked her lips, hoping she'd achieved the right tone of aristocratic carelessness. "It looks like you followed in Mister Bunbury's footsteps, doing the sensible thing and dying at your doctor's advice."

"What choice did I have?" A wistful look came over Leo's countenance, and he laid the back of his hand against his forehead as if he might swoon. "Alas, my moment to fret upon the stage of life has passed. No point in regrets. Well, maybe one."

"Tell me."

Leo waved away the request. "Another time, maybe."

His face brightened. "Do you remember when we talked about Oscar himself?"

Bonnie nodded slowly as the memory of the conversation played frame by frame across her mental View-Master. "I remember you loved the man, his work, the stand he took when he went to prison."

"And you told me it was hard to be a homosexual in Victorian England." Leo patted her hand. "I think you had already begun to suspect, even before I was ready to admit it to myself."

Bonnie had to swallow before she could speak. "Not really. It was what you said next, that made me wonder. *Missus P, it's hard at any time.*"

"Hard at any time," Leo whispered as if hearing his own words for the first time. He raised his eyes to meet hers. "We're over Wolf Creek Pass, coming down the other side."

She looked out the window. Sure enough, the snow had nearly stopped—just a scattering of flakes, swirling each in their individual dance.

Bonnie took Leo's hand in hers. It felt warm the way she hoped it would. "You have to go, don't you?"

He looked down at their hands, refusing to meet her eyes. "Wasn't it Thomas Wolfe who said you can't go across the pass again?"

She chuckled. "I think there was something about home in there. Besides, here we are crossing the pass for the second time."

"Maybe with mountain passes you get two times before you're done."

"Maybe. Before you go, I have to ask you something." She let go his hand and lifted his chin until they were eye to eye. "Why was my name in your pocket?"

The boy sighed and no longer looked like a child of fifteen. Here was a man staring back at life from the other side. "I wanted to talk to you, get your advice about something"—Leo hesitated, evidently searching for just the right word—"significant."

"Well, I'm right here. What was it?"

Leo shook his head. "It's not important now. What is important is that you stop the killing before it's too late. Before it reaches Timothy."

"I don't understand. I don't know any Timothy."

"You will."

"Bon?"

A gentle hand shook Bonnie, rousing her. She blinked awake, and stared up at the smiling face of Lloyd Whittaker. The final frames of her bus ride with Leo Quinn began to fade.

Timothy? "What time is it?"

Lloyd directed her gaze to the clock, which she would have noticed had she not been so out of it. "Just past eleven."

Over an hour, ye gods. Truth be told, she didn't remember falling asleep. Last she recalled, her thirteen charges had filed from her classroom, leaving her sitting alone at her desk.

"I dreamed I was with Leo Quinn." She rubbed her eyes and delineated the Wolf Creek bus ride, ending with Leo's reference to the mysterious Timothy.

"Do we know any student connected with Leo Quinn named Timothy?" With a grunt, Lloyd hoisted himself onto the top of a student desk.

"I was hoping you could tell me."

"Fat chance. If you can't remember, what hope does a mere mortal like yours truly have?" With a sound like sandpaper, he scratched at his chin. "It was just a dream after all. I didn't think you put much stock in such things."

"Normally, I don't, but this felt different, like something Ben would splatter on me." She hoped the reference to her dead husband didn't make her sound too loopy.

"You still carry that hawk stone?" Lloyd asked.

She nodded, reached across the desk, and dragged her fanny pack to her. The smallish stone she retrieved from the pack's innards was no more than four inches long, pointed at each end. To say it resembled a hawk's head might be stretching the truth, but that's exactly what the darn thing looked like to Bonnie. A red-tailed hawk to be precise—the totem of Ben Pinkwater, her dead husband.

Only two people on the planet, Armen Callahan and Lloyd, knew the story of how she came to own the stone and how it more than likely saved her life. She didn't trust anyone else with that bit of metaphysical nonsense.

Lloyd took the rock from her hand. "Looks more like a banana."

She was about to gift her friend with a frown when the door opened. Superintendent Xavier Divine poked his egg-shaped cranium into the room.

Bonnie snatched the stone from Lloyd and tucked it in the fanny pack. She spent a moment indulging the irrational hope that the rotund visage of The Divine Pain in the Ass would fade along with her dream of Leo Quinn.

No such luck. The man has a perverse staying power.

Divine maneuvered his ample rear end into the room and smiled his I've-got-you-cornered-now smile. "Ah, just the two I want to see. If I didn't know better, I'd say, except for that ridiculous debacle two nights ago, the pair of you has been avoiding me."

The Divine Pain in the Ass appeared to jealously regard Lloyd's position on the student desk, obviously thought better of it, and remained standing. He inhaled a barrel of air. "I won't waste time asking questions I already know the answers to."

He fixed his gaze on Bonnie. "Word on the back roads of East Plains is that you've insinuated yourself into still another murder investigation. And now you've included one of my principals in your nefarious activities."

Lloyd leaned forward, evidently trying to interject a comment.

Divine silenced him with an upraised hand. "Your time to speak will come. For now, you've lost that privilege. I bought and paid for it with the indignities you've both heaped upon me." He peered from Bonnie to Lloyd, daring them to dispute him.

The man has a point. Which is surprising for a head so profoundly ovoid.

"Good," Divine said. "Now, here is how we will proceed. First, let me dispense with some minor business. Principal Whittaker . . ."

Lloyd, still tilted forward, brought his reluctant gaze up to meet Divine's.

The superintendent, for his part, gave Lloyd his full and enthusiastic attention. "In the future, you will refrain from unwelcome familiarities. These include assaults upon my person in the form of embraces, good-ol'-boy salutations, and anything involving beer."

Once again, Lloyd seemed on the verge of a reply

Robert Spiller

and once again, Divine silenced him. "In addition, you will henceforth cease, whether in my presence or not, making mention of Miss Devereaux's bosom. On this matter I am most adamant."

"You have my word, superintendent."

"I knew I could count on you. And now, Missus Pinkwater."

Even though Bonnie had been preparing herself for when Divine would draw a bead on her, she still felt herself flushing. A wave of annoyance washed over her.

Damn it. How do I get myself into stupid situations like this? "You want me to stop my connection to the Quinn investigation?"

Divine shook his egg-shaped dome. "Au contraire. I want you to continue."

What the hell?

A hint of a mischievous smile played across Divine's moon face at Bonnie's obvious consternation. "Indeed. I wouldn't dream of hindering you in your self-destructive proclivities. Truth is, neither Leo Quinn, Dwight Furby, nor Jason Dobbs are students at EPHS. And aside from the fact you are teaching a voluntary gifted and talented class, you are on vacation. Your time is your own."

Bonnie eyed the man suspiciously. "Forgive me for my cynical nature, but what's the catch, superintendent?"

Divine adopted the look of the innocent babe. "Why must there be a catch?" He cocked his enormous head.

"However, I have taken the liberty of informing the community at large as to your involvement. In the past few days, a number of East Plains' citizens have contacted me with a myriad of questions concerning the case."

Uh-oh.

Divine seemed gratified at the understanding he found in Bonnie's expression. "You see my dilemma. I tried to gain audience with you to ascertain the answers these good people sought. Without definitive direction from you, I was merely guessing. So, I hinted that they should go to the source for their inquiries."

Lloyd stood, his face hard, his eyes flinty. "You gave them her phone number?"

Divine feigned shock. "That would have been unethical as well as an invitation to a lawsuit. I merely mentioned your name to a few select members of our community as someone in the know."

You son of a bitch. "And since my phone number is listed, they could look it up."

"I suppose that's a possibility." Divine licked his lips. "Well, I should be going."

He waddled to the door, opened it, then halted without looking back. "There is one more reason I'd like you to continue. Alf Quinn is an especially good friend of Angelica's."

Lloyd held the school's front door as Bonnie, who was checking her cell phone, passed through.

She snapped shut the phone and chuckled. "Twelve messages—eight on my home phone, four on the cell. I've got to admit. Divine played that hand well. He's completely divorced himself from the murders while dropping me squarely in the middle, and in the public eye as far as East Plains is concerned. As long as this investigation goes on, the Nosy Parkers of our little community will feel they've got the right to call me and find out what I know. Hell, they've been directed to do so by the superintendent of schools."

"You could always stop answering your phone."

"Good solution, Whittaker." A sheriff's cruiser, parked down the road on East Plains Highway caught Bonnie's eye. "Check it out. Isn't that at the bus barn?"

Lloyd nodded and picked up his pace. "Come on." He set off at a jog and Bonnie followed.

Outside the sprawling powder blue cinderblock structure, not one but two sheriff cruisers, lights blazing, sat at an obtuse angle to one another. Practically bisecting the angle, squatted a silver and black motor scooter, a pizza box bungeed to its rear fender.

What the hell? Wilma Trotter's scooter?

Hanging back, Bonnie located Wilma, who evidently rode over from her house bearing Italian cuisine. She was weeping, her head on Byron Hickman's shoulder.

Bonnie eased forward.

The rolling metal door of the barn was raised. At first, all Bonnie could spy was Witherspoon's maroon Trans Am, but as she drew close she saw a pair of boots. In increments, she bore witness to the sprawled form of the Spoonmaster himself. His straw cowboy hat was tilted on his head, partially obscuring his face. The front of his shirt was soaked in blood. Deputy Wyatt was kneeling by the body.

My God, when will it end?

A wave of guilt passed through Bonnie. She had never particularly liked Moses Witherspoon—in fact, if asked, she would have placed the young man squarely in the *dislike* column. Yet here he was, all his tomorrows, every shred of his potential, stolen by some maniac. Maybe if she had taken the time, she would have found something worthwhile in the boy.

Now, she would never have the opportunity.

Byron lifted his gaze. For a long moment, the deputy regarded her over the top of Wilma's head, then, with a crook of his finger, indicated she and Lloyd come over.

"Missus Pinkwater's here," Byron whispered.

Wilma Trotter turned a tear-streaked face toward Bonnie. Her eye patch was askew, partially revealing the shriveled socket beneath. "He's gone, Pinkwater. The bastard took him."

Bonnie had been prepared for the worst. With Wilma

on the scene, it seemed a foregone conclusion that the corpse of Gabe Trotter would be found somewhere in the interior of the bus barn. Now several other possibilities presented themselves—even the off chance that Gabe had murdered his friend and fled.

Bonnie didn't think so. "Who took Gabe, Wilma?"

"I recognized him on his motorbike, no helmet. There wasn't another vehicle for miles. I thought the other rider looked like Gabe, but he was wearing a helmet. Dammit, I should have . . ." Wilma's hands went into her hair. Wild-eyed, she yanked first one then another tendril from her scalp.

Bonnie stepped forward and took Wilma's hands into hers. "Who took Gabe, Wilma?"

Wilma Trotter squinted at Bonnie—the understood question—*Why couldn't Bonnie understand?* "That cowboy. The one married to Rodeo Girl."

She jerked her fists free from Bonnie's grasp. "Why isn't anyone listening to me? Caleb, Caleb Webb, Goddammit!"

CHAPTER 21

"GET THIS CRATE MOVING, PINKWATER." WILMA Trotter leaned forward from Alice's backseat. She checked her watch. "God damn. Almost a half hour. That maniac's had my boy for half an hour."

Bonnie had willed herself not to dwell on that aspect of their quest. Why had Caleb taken Gabe when he had summarily executed both Furby and Witherspoon? "Lloyd's driving as fast as he can, Wilma. We'll be there in less than five minutes."

Missus Trotter, breathing in quick shallow gasps, looked like she might hyperventilate.

Bonnie did her best to keep her voice steady. "Losing your mind won't make the car go faster. Try to relax."

Wilma shot Bonnie a frown but did as she was told. She leaned back in her seat, shut her eyes, and inhaled through her nose, then exhaled long and deliberately through her mouth. With each increment of respiration, Wilma calmed noticeably.

A throwback skill from your Haight-Ashbury days, Wilma? Still, Bonnie envied the woman. There were times she certainly could use something to take the edge off. Right now wouldn't hurt, as they headed for a murderer's house.

Before he'd left, Byron hadn't minced any words as to their staying clear of the place. Deputy Wyatt, left behind with Witherspoon's body, echoed her boss's sentiments, even adding the kicker that they would just be in the way and could endanger Gabe by their presence.

Wilma Trotter had suggested the young deputy blow her advice out her uniformed rear end.

A considerably calmer Wilma Trotter leaned forward again. "The bastard probably followed me, just like Hickman did today."

Bonnie figured as much. From the number of pizza boxes scattered about the bus barn floor, Wilma had been providing the fugitives sustenance for at least a couple of days. She must have learned where Gabe was holed up not long after talking to Bonnie.

Was that only two days ago? And how the hell did Witherspoon and Gabe get access to the bus barn? Bonnie supposed she could ask Wilma, but the answer seemed inconsequential right at the moment.

"We had a secret knock," Wilma said absently.

A probable scenario played across Bonnie's synapses. Somehow, Caleb had witnessed the knock and replicated it. A new idea grabbed Bonnie in its jaws.

"Did you always arrive on your scooter?"

Wilma gave Bonnie a what's-this-got-to-do-with-the-price-of-tea-in-China frown. "Yeah?"

Lloyd turned to Bonnie, the light of understanding in his eyes. "And Caleb Webb was riding on a motorcycle."

"Damn, damn, damn." From the sound of her voice, Wilma understood as well.

Caleb more than likely arrived on his bike, the same one on which he visited Rattlesnake—it wouldn't sound exactly like a scooter but close enough. No wonder Witherspoon had opened the bus barn door.

Bonnie's attention was jerked back into the present. Not two hundred yards down the narrow dirt road, red and blue flashing lights heralded the Webb ranch.

"Now what?" Lloyd slowed Alice down to a crawl.

"Get a little closer." Bonnie tried to sound decisive, but now that she was here she hadn't the faintest idea what to do. Hightailing it after Byron had just sounded like a good idea at the time. And she certainly couldn't have let Wilma—who, no doubt, would have gone regardless—take off alone. No telling what the woman would have done on her little scooter.

A hedgerow growing along the shoulder shielded Alice from Webb's house. Lloyd parked the Subaru next to the tallest section, and opened his door.

Byron's voice boomed across the landscape. "Nothing good can come out of this, Caleb. Let the boy go?"

"I'm getting closer." Wilma was out her door and three steps down the hedge before Bonnie thought of the first of her dozen reasons why that little stroll was a real bad idea.

Shit, shit, shit. She ran to catch the woman.

Ten feet this side of Webb's driveway, the hedge ended. A state police vehicle was parked half on the drive and halfway sticking out into the dirt road. It was only a matter of seconds before some member of some police organization caught sight of Wilma and all hell would break loose.

At the end of the hedge, Bonnie could see the Webbs' front porch. Caleb Webb held Gabe by the back of the neck, a long-barreled pistol against his Tabernacle.

". . . don't think so, deputy." Caleb smiled as if he didn't have three guns trained on him. "I let go of this bozo, and I'm hamburger."

"Not true, Caleb. We can work something out. Think about your wife, your unborn baby."

Webb shook Gabe Trotter like a rag doll. "My wife!" he shouted over his shoulder, evidently speaking to someone in the house. "How's that old joke go? Take my wife please. That's the ticket, deputy, take my wife, please."

Wilma's fist came to her mouth. Her boy was in the

hands of a certifiable nut job.

"Did you hear me, Seneca? I'm coming for you, babe. First, I'm going to take care of business here, then it's your turn, bitch. I'll finish what I started."

The curtain behind the front window stirred. From her vantage point by the hedge, Bonnie couldn't see within the house. She assumed it was Seneca moving the curtain, but whomever it was stood far enough back to remain hidden.

Didn't this place have a back door? Why wasn't Seneca making tracks?

"Don't do this, Caleb," Seneca's disembodied voice shouted from inside the house. "Please, no more killing."

"Shut up!" Caleb screamed. He threw Gabe to the porch floor and swung the barrel of his pistol toward the window.

Like thunder, both of the state patrol officers fired their weapons. Again and again, Caleb Webb absorbed the shots, jerking like he was being subjected to repeated electric shocks. Stubbornly, he held on to his pistol, even managing to fire into the ceiling of the porch.

Horrified, Bonnie found herself unable to look away.

Finally, still holding the gun, Caleb sank to his knees, then fell face-first onto the porch. Two state patrol officers advanced in tandem. While one kept his service revolver trained on Caleb, the other removed the pistol from the young man's still fingers.

Wilma Trotter sprinted to her son, who had scurried

out of the way of the shooting. Beyond the end of the porch, the two of them held tightly to one another.

Byron Hickman caught sight of Bonnie, shook his head, and frowned. He returned his attention to the bloody scene. "In the house," he screamed out of the bullhorn, "please stay where you are. We will come and lead you out."

Whoever was inside either didn't hear or was in no mood to obey orders. The front door to the little house opened. Like a wraith, Seneca Webb appeared in the shadowed doorway. She wavered on shaky legs, clinging to the frame. A trooper moved to assist her, and she slapped his hand away.

At first, Bonnie thought the shadows were playing tricks. Even though the girl emerged from the doorway, the entire left side of her face was still dark. Then Bonnie's breath caught in her chest. What she had assumed had been shadow was blood. It stained not only the girl's long blond hair but the right side of her face and the shoulder of her blouse. Seneca took one more faltering step and collapsed into the arms of the trooper.

Bonnie was moving before she realized her brain had given the command. She gave a cursory glance at Caleb. A part of her knew the young man had to be dead, but that part was submerged in her anxiety for Seneca. The damaged girl seemed so small in the arms of the trooper.

He gave Bonnie a surprised glance, then seemed to reconcile himself to her presence. "There's a large gash in the crown of her head. No telling how much blood she's lost."

Byron Hickman appeared at Bonnie's elbow. "I've called for the East Plains' ambulance. In the meantime, bring her in the house."

The other trooper looked up from his ministrations with Caleb. He shook his head.

Byron exhaled as if this final death had stolen the last fragment of his soul. "Fair enough. We're going to need to move your cruiser before the ambulance gets here."

He turned a hard stare on Gabe. "I want you in the house. You come, too, Missus Trotter. The two of you have some explaining to do. Mister Whittaker, would you stay outside and help Officer Haley?"

Bonnie didn't wait for an invitation. She followed the big trooper, who had scooped up Seneca. "Set her down here." Bonnie pointed to a large throw rug in the center of the kitchen. She gathered up a pair of hand towels from a hook next to the sink and knelt by the unconscious girl.

Bonnie peered up at the trooper. "Unless you have an objection, I do have first aid certification."

The big man didn't challenge her.

The wound was a jagged slice atop a nasty bump. Caleb had obviously clocked Seneca with something heavy that had an edge or at least a corner. Bonnie folded one of the towels and pressed it onto the bump. She handed the other to the trooper. "Could you wet this with cold water? And then bring me a pillow and a blanket."

Bonnie was worried that Seneca, who was lying so still, might be going into shock. Or worse, the injury had done brain damage. Was she, even now, in the initial stages of a coma?

Settle down, Pinkwater. Just do what you can. Stop the bleeding. Keep her warm and comfortable. The ambulance will be here any minute.

The trooper handed off the wet towel and left the room.

Bonnie cleaned the blood from around the laceration, then reapplied pressure. From the next room, she heard the voice of Byron Hickman.

"You need to know, young man, that unconscious girl in there more than likely saved your hide."

"I know. Her husband would have killed me. I get it."

Bad time to cop an attitude, Gabe.

Byron cleared his throat. "I'm glad to see we have an understanding. Now you're going to tell me everything that happened last Saturday on Squirrel Creek Road. Begin with when you and your friends ran into Leo Quinn."

Seneca stirred beneath Bonnie's hand. Bonnie looked down to see the young girl's eyelids fluttering. A moan escaped her lips.

You hang in there, sweetie. You didn't survive this

IRRATIONAL NUMBERS

nightmare to give up now.

In the next room, Gabe related how he, Spoon, and Furby had come upon Quinn walking along Squirrel Creek carrying a gas can.

"Hold on," Byron said, "did you take the gas can with you when you left?"

"No. It was still there when we took off."

Bonnie was so engrossed in her dual tasks of tending to Seneca and eavesdropping on the interrogation she didn't see the trooper return until he was right up on her. She gave a yelp.

The trooper allowed a hint of smile to appear on his chiseled face before he extinguished it. "Sorry, ma'am, didn't mean to startle you."

Bonnie snatched a blanket from his hand. "I'm fine." The voices in the next room had quit and Bonnie was certain that Byron, Wilma, and Gabe were staring at her. She felt heat creep up into her face.

Stop being such a baby, Pinkwater. This isn't about you. She situated the blanket over the girl. "I'm going to lift her head. Put the pillow under."

The big man did as he was told.

The front door opened and Lloyd appeared. The sound of a distant siren crept into the room. "The trooper wanted you to know the ambulance will be here in about two minutes. He's going to send them for Seneca first." Lloyd gave Bonnie a half smile and disappeared back outside.

"How's she doing, Missus P?" Byron asked.

"I don't know. She's awful pale, and her skin feels clammy. I just wish that ambulance would hurry." Bonnie's hands were shaking.

"Take some deep breaths," Wilma Trotter offered.

The advice brought a smile to Bonnie's face. *Touché, Wilma.* After a few repetitions, she did indeed feel calmer.

"Finish your story, Mister Trotter," Byron said.

Gabe told how Leo had refused Spoon's help and how Spoon got insulted. Then they ran down Leo, stripped him, and bound him to the barbed-wire fence. "We just wanted to have a little fun with him."

Bonnie desperately needed to throw something at the hapless idiot. What kind of person finds someone walking along a road and leaves them naked tied to barbed wire?

"I believe you, Gabe," Byron said. "So, did Witherspoon shoot Leo?"

Bonnie held her breath. She knew darn well that Byron didn't believe the idiot trio killed Leo. So what was he playing at?

"No way!" Gabe shouted. "None of us killed Quinn. You got to believe me."

"Do I?" Byron's voice carried just the right mixture of sympathy and incredulity. "Here's what I do believe. You admit you were out on Squirrel Creek Road. You accosted Leo Quinn. You tied him naked to a fence.

And that's where we found his lifeless body seven hours later. Have I left anything out?"

"You tricked my boy, deputy," Wilma Trotter said. "He's answered all your questions, and now you're going to use his honest story against him."

Bonnie didn't think that was Byron's intention. First of all, he never read Gabe his Miranda rights. Second, she was certain they'd find that the gun they'd pulled from Caleb's dead fingers was the gun that killed not only Witherspoon, but Leo and Furby as well. Byron knew all this as well as she did. He was just frightening the boy to glean every scrap of information.

An idea lit up her psyche like a Roman candle. "Who folded the clothes?" she shouted over her shoulder.

"What?" Gabe sounded as though this question coming out of left field—or at least the kitchen—might send him spinning out of orbit.

"Leo Quinn's clothes." Byron picked up the inquiry. "Are you the one who folded them?"

"I don't know what you're talking about. No one folded his clothes."

"But you see, that's where you're wrong. Someone did fold Leo's clothes and stuffed his socks into his shoes. Made a neat little pile of it. So I'm going to repeat Missus Pinkwater's question. Who folded Leo Quinn's clothes?"

"For the last time, we didn't kill Leo, and we didn't fold any clothes. When we left him he was alive."

CHAPTER 22

As the ambulance carrying Seneca and Caleb Webb sped off, Byron Hickman wheeled on Bonnie. "Missus P, was I unclear when I told you to not show up here today?"

Damn, another few seconds, and I'd have made a clean break. She, Gabe, Wilma, and Lloyd were gathered by Alice, The-Little-Subaru-That-Could. "I wouldn't beat myself up over it, youngster. You did your best."

The muscles in Byron's jaw tightened. "Let me rephrase. I specifically told you not to be here, and you recklessly endangered the lives of your friends."

"It's my fault, deputy," Wilma Trotter offered. "I was bound and determined to chase down my boy. Missus Pinkwater was just trying to keep me out of trouble."

Byron wearily shook his head. "Well, she didn't succeed. If I didn't have ten million things on my plate right now, I'd arrest you and your son."

Wilma drew herself up, and Bonnie was afraid the

woman intended to give Byron a New Age ration of grief. To Bonnie's relief, Gabe laid a hand on his mother's arm, and she deflated.

"I've got no time for any of this nonsense." Byron checked his watch. "I need to follow that ambulance to the hospital." He turned to Bonnie. "I don't suppose Seneca came to long enough to tell you what Caleb did with Rattlesnake."

"She never regained consciousness." Not for the first time, Bonnie wondered just how much Seneca knew of Caleb's murderous activities. Hot on the heels of that thought came the realization that if Seneca died, and Rattlesnake was stashed somewhere, maybe tied up, they might not find him before he died of thirst or exposure.

The larger of the two state troopers strode around the hedgerow. "No sign of anyone else in the residence or that Mister Quinn has ever been held there."

Byron nodded gravely. "I didn't think that little house would tell us anything. Maybe the crime scene people will find something." He smiled ruefully. "Although I'm sure they're going to have my liver for breakfast for having so many people traipsing around the place."

The trooper shrugged noncommittally. "If you don't need anything more, Alvin and I are going to head back and make our report."

"No, we're good here. Thanks for everything, Teddy."

With a wave, the state trooper made for his cruiser and his waiting partner.

Once the trooper had ensconced himself in his vehicle, Bonnie said, "Alvin and Theodore?" She made no attempt to keep a goofy smile from her face.

At first, Byron's features seemed at war between a frown and a reciprocal grin. After a long moment, the smile won. "Believe it or not, their supervisor's name is Simon."

He threw up his hands. "You're something, Missus P, you know that? I can't believe I'm making chipmunk jokes with you. Get out of here, the lot of you." He turned on his heel and walked back into the Webb compound.

"You heard the man." Bonnie climbed into Alice's passenger seat.

They were less than a mile from the Webbs when Lloyd spoke. "I'm not going to ask you how you got into the bus barn, young man, but you be in my office in the morning. I think a little work around the school will compensate for breaking and entering."

When Gabe sputtered like he meant to be difficult, Wilma said, "He'll be there, bright and early."

Bonnie turned in her seat so she could see both Wilma and Gabe. She was surprised how little the young goofus had changed since graduation. Most students, because of work, family responsibility, or even the experience of college, alter drastically in three years. Often when they returned, sometimes in the company of a toddler, she didn't recognize them. Besides the fact that he still seemed physically the same—long, curly brown hair; baby fat; and a bad complexion—he also carried himself with the same sullen immaturity he sported during the days of his high school captivity. Not a glowing recommendation for staying at home with momma and spending your time playing video games.

"So Gabe, did Caleb say anything to you on the way?" Bonnie asked.

The young man eyed her suspiciously. "What do you mean?"

Wilma slapped her son in the back of the head. "Boy, you are getting on my last nerve. Stop acting like you've got a rectal-cranial inversion. Two of your friends are dead. You could have easily joined them today. Now, answer Missus Pinkwater's question."

Way to go, Wilma. Slap him again for me.

Gabe slid away from his irate mother. "Okay! Okay!" He did his best to erase the poor-me look from his face and almost succeeded. "What do you want to know?"

It's a start. "What did he say when he took you from the bus barn?"

Gabe inflated his cheeks, evidently engaging his limited memory mechanism. After a moment's cognition, he put his index finger in the center of his forehead.

"He stuck his gun right here and told me get moving."

"He put you on the back of his bike?"

Gabe nodded. "Gave me his helmet, told me to climb on. If I made any trouble, he promised to blow me away."

"Anything else?"

Once again, Gabe imitated a blowfish. "When we passed my mom's scooter, he started cursing like his head was about to explode. Banged his fists on the handlebars. Scared the shit out of me. I thought for sure he was going to stop the bike and kill me."

Bonnie considered the timing and choreography in this passion play. If Wilma had been just five minutes sooner, she would have interrupted Caleb Webb, caught him in the act of shooting Witherspoon and abducting Gabe. More than likely, Caleb would have shot her as well. Then again, she said Byron had tailed her to the bus barn. If she was right about that, Byron and Deputy Wyatt would have been added to the mix. Who knows what Caleb would have done then, but she didn't think surrendering would have been an option.

"What about when you reached the house?"

Gabe twirled his right index finger about his ear. "That's when Cowboy Caleb went really Strangelove. He made me sit on the porch. Tied me to a post. Told me he'd be right back, and if I moved even an inch he'd kill me. He went in the house. About a minute later, the screaming started."

"Seneca?" Lloyd asked.

"Uh-huh. Sounded like he was killing her. Tell you true, that's what I thought happened. Surprised the crap out of me when she later shouted through the window."

Bonnie sighed, picturing the scene inside that nightmare home—Caleb Webb returning with his latest prize, heated words passing between husband and wife, and Caleb in a rage clubbing his young wife over the head.

You son of a bitch, I hope they have an especially hot section of hell waiting for you.

Bonnie tugged at her ear. "You never went in?"

Gabe shook his head. "A good five minutes later, he comes back out, unties me, tells me to sit, then sits down next to me. There were tears in his eyes. I figured he felt bad about killing his wife—like maybe he might let me go."

Really? thought Bonnie. "And he just waited there on the porch until the police arrived?"

"Never said a word. Just sat there tapping the gun against his knee. When the cops came, he made me stand, like he'd been waiting for them. The rest you know."

Indeed, like he was waiting for them. Like he was waiting to die.

Bonnie dropped Wilma and Gabe off at the front of the school, where Wilma had left her scooter. As the pair made a wobbly exodus down East Plains Highway, Bonnie checked her Mickey Mouse watch.

Two o'clock, straight up.

"I'm embarrassed to say this, but I'm starving. You up for some lunch?"

Lloyd shook his head. "I'm going home." He reddened. "I promised Marjorie I'd call this afternoon."

Bonnie turned a smiling face her friend's way. "That's wonderful. Why didn't you say anything, you sly dog?"

"There was never a good time—what with the superintendent then Gabe Trotter and Caleb Webb."

Bonnie slapped Lloyd in the belly. "So what's going on, big guy?"

Lloyd didn't seem ready to share Bonnie's elation. His mouth was a tight line. "So far, nothing. She left a message, asked if I would give her a ring."

"And?"

Lloyd gave her a puzzled look. "And what?"

"How do you feel about talking to her, listening to what she has to say?"

Her friend seemed genuinely lost. Bonnie could actually see the two warring elements of his dilemma tugging at him. Certainly, Marjorie had betrayed his trust, but he'd failed to be there when she needed him.

Grown-up problems are a bitch. That's for sure.

After a long moment, Lloyd blew out a long breath. "I honestly don't know. I'm mad at her. Hell, I'm mad at me. And I'm tired of all of it. I guess I'm just ready to hear her voice again, sometime when she's not singing."

On impulse, Bonnie threw her arms around her friend and gave him a hug. "It's a start," she whispered in his ear.

She pretended not to notice the glisten in her friend's eyes when she broke the embrace. Lloyd was a lot of things, but he hadn't yet evolved into a SNAG, or a Sensitive New Age Guy. Maybe never would. He'd be embarrassed by any mention of tears.

"Well, good luck, cowboy. I'll be rooting for you."

"Thanks, Bon. I'll let you know how it all turns out."

She left him standing by his truck, still looking a little lost. *He's a big boy. Hopefully, he can figure out what's best for Lloyd Whittaker without his ego getting in the way.*

At the moment, Bonnie had other things on her mind. She also had a phone call to make. To New Jersey.

"Callahan's Roadkill Diner."

Bonnie pulled her kitchen phone away from her ear and chuckled. "How's the possum look for tonight?" she said when she reinserted the device to her head.

"Flat and juicy, ma'am. Just scooped up on Interstate 95 this morning." Armen sighed. "You got any idea how good it is to hear your sultry tones, Mizz Pinkwater?"

"I had no idea I *had* sultry tones. But the feeling's mutual, Mister Mouse."

Now that she'd connected to Armen, albeit electronically and across a couple of thousand miles, Bonnie felt the day's tension draining. God, she missed this man.

"Bon?"

"Right here, lover. Just thanking my lucky stars your Armenian mother gave birth to you."

"Does that mean you're giving serious consideration to my proposal?"

Proposal?

The question jerked Bonnie out of her euphoria back into reality. Did she really want to leave Colorado forever, even if it meant being with Armen? "I'm definitively up to my elbows in a serious consideration mindset. Can you give me a little more time? I need to finish my gifted and talented class before I can even consider leaving."

Bonnie winced. Even coming from her own lips, the excuse sounded lame. From the protracted silence at the other end of the line, Armen thought the same.

"Look, Bon, I'm not trying to pressure you in any way. It's just that I'm committed to staying here with my dad."

A spike of annoyance washed over Bonnie.

No pressure? In two days, you've already put down roots in New Jersey. If I want to be with you, that's where it has to be. But hell, no pressure.

Before she could put her confused thoughts into even more confused verbiage, Armen broke in.

"I have a surprise for you. Although, maybe I shouldn't have done it."

In the space of ten seconds, Bonnie's befuddled mind ran the gamut of things Armen damn well shouldn't have done. By the end of that brief space of time, she had him running naked and drunk on the beaches of Atlantic City in the company of bimbos. For good measure, he was sporting a tattoo of Foghorn Leghorn across his right butt cheek.

Snap out of it, Pinkwater. She took an additional ten seconds to steady her vocal cords. "Oh? And what is this surprise?"

"I bought you a plane ticket for Atlantic City."

The nine words rendered Bonnie momentarily speechless. She knew Armen was only streamlining the possibility of her visiting New Jersey, but she was having trouble wrapping her mind around the presumption of the man. He hadn't even waited until she gave him her answer before he made this monumental decision on her behalf. Once again, Bonnie's cerebral cortex went into hyperdrive. She pictured a life where Armen swaggered into restaurants and ordered the wine at meals.

How about my hair, Callahan, or my clothes? Do you approve of those? What next? Are you going to tell me who my friends can be?

"Uh-oh." The voice that squeaked out of the phone was shaky. "Would it help to mention it's a round trip ticket?"

Bonnie wasn't sure she should trust herself to talk to him. Her Imp of the Perverse was screaming, demanding she cut loose with something she damn well knew she'd regret. Swallowing down every scathing remark she'd seen capering across her psyche, she settled for the mundane. "What's the date of the flight?"

"Bon, I'm sorry. I—"

"What's the date, Mister Mouse?"

"Sunday. Out of Colorado Springs at one fifty."

Bonnie inhaled a long deep breath and let it out slowly. "I've got to go. I'll talk to you tomorrow." She hung up the phone and stared at the receiver.

A small, not-so-still voice sounded in her brain. *What the hell was that all about? The man was just trying to do you a favor.*

Bonnie knew nine-tenths of her reaction stemmed from how stressed she'd been in the last few hours. She bore witness to two dead young men and if things didn't go well, Seneca Webb might not survive the day.

Even with this excuse for letting Armen off the hook, she held on to a bit of residual anger. *Goddamn, the man didn't even ask me.* Bonnie pulled a stool over and sat at the breakfast island. Her head ached and more than a little she wanted to call Armen back and just hash out this problem.

She knew she wouldn't. She didn't trust herself and her Imp of the Perverse not to flare up again. *You are some piece of work, Bonnie Pinkwater.*

Hypatia sidled up to Bonnie's leg and rubbed against it. Absently, she stroked the dog's soft fur. "Mommy's all screwed up, sweetie."

A low growl emanated from the dog. Evidently, the golden retriever disagreed.

"I love you, too. What say you and I go for a walk?"

Bonnie gathered up her fanny pack and by the time she reached the front door had collected two additional dogs: Hopper, the black lab, and Lovelace, the border collie.

Euclid, the black Burmese, merely looked up from his repose on the sofa, as if to say, *Knock yourselves out. I'm too comfortable to move.*

Without what seemed like conscious thought, Bonnie's feet aimed for the Bluffs, the high mesa about a half mile behind her home. The dogs, so familiar with the path, scampered ahead.

By the time she'd reached the rim of the mesa, her head was clearing.

One of your better decisions, Pinkwater.

The afternoon had developed into one of those that made people in the rest of the country wish they lived in Colorado. Small clouds punctuated a sky so blue it seemed unreal. A hint of a breeze played in Bonnie's hair. In the distance, beyond Colorado Springs, Pikes Peak held reign on a horizon to die for.

Purple mountain majesty, indeed, Mizz Bates.

Bonnie hoisted her posterior onto a flat rock overlooking the valley at the base of the Bluffs. The faint discordant cry of a blue jay wafted up from below. On the valley floor, a gray ovoid shape, probably a rabbit, darted between the sprays of yucca.

Despite the picture-perfect setting, Bonnie felt unsettled. She tried to dismiss the butterflies in her belly, telling herself it was just the remnant of how she'd left things with Armen.

She knew better.

Her innards had been trying to tell her something since she'd left Lloyd. The events of the day and the previous days just didn't mesh.

She had no doubt that the gun Caleb wielded, and more than likely used to kill Moses Witherspoon, was the same pistol that had killed Leo Quinn and Dwight Furby. She wasn't sure where this certainty came from, but she was certain nonetheless. But therein lay the problem.

What the hell was Caleb doing out on Squirrel Creek

Road with a damn nine millimeter?

And that wasn't the only thing bothering Bonnie.

Logically, assuming Gabe Trotter was telling the truth, when Caleb came upon Leo Quinn, he was already trussed up to a barbed-wire fence, compliments of the idiot trio of Furby, Witherspoon, and Gabe.

Why did Caleb then proceed to kill Leo Quinn?

The immediate answer was that Caleb Webb was a homophobe. Bonnie remembered the young man's reaction to finding out Jason Dobbs was a homosexual. Webb had just about split a seam. It had been all Seneca could do to settle him down.

"Okay, Caleb killed Leo because he was gay," Bonnie voiced aloud. "A hate crime. Violence dealt out because of bigotry." Even as she said it, Bonnie knew there was something she was missing.

Even more troubling, knowing, as Caleb did, that the idiot trio was innocent of the murder, why then did he set out to assassinate Furby and Witherspoon?

Bonnie tugged at her earlobe, her mind in a swirl.

And why in God's name did Caleb think it important to fold Leo Quinn's clothes?

CHAPTER 23

Gabe Trotter was standing outside the main office when Bonnie stepped through the doors of the school.

Her estimation of the young man went up considerably at this evidence of integrity. She gifted him with a smile. "Ah, the prodigal son has returned. Waiting for Principal Whittaker?"

Gabe shook his head. "Already seen him. He's got me working with the custodians for a couple of days. I'll be stripping the floors until noon today."

Bonnie was surprised Lloyd had started the boy off with only a half day's penance. "Not too bad. I might have put you to work until five. Mister Whittaker's growing soft in his old age."

"He meant to, but I talked him into letting me off early so I could go visit Seneca. It's the least I could do after she saved my life."

Even visiting the sick. What next, Master Trotter, do

you plan to give alms to the poor?

"Good for you." Bonnie checked her Mickey Mouse watch. "Well, listen, I have to go. Got a class to teach."

Gabe stepped aside to let her pass. "Missus P, I want to thank you for all you've done for me and my mom. She told me how you were worried about me."

Your mom was stretching the truth a little bit, dear boy. But what the hell. "You're welcome. It was all worth it if you get a wiggle on with your life."

"Funny you should mention that. There's a part-time custodian job opening up here at the school. I'm thinking of applying."

Bonnie felt like hugging the boy, but held herself in check. *Let's see how he does with stripping the floors.*

She offered her hand for a high five. "Go for it. Make a good impression on Principal Whittaker, and who knows? Now, I really got to go."

"Settle down, ladies. I thought since this is the last class, we'd do something a little different this time. Give me a hand here."

Bonnie and her class of thirteen arranged the desks in a circle and sat themselves on top. A circus atmosphere permeated the classroom. Jolly Ranchers all around. Even the usually severe Yoki was giggling.

Admit it, Pinkwater, you love this let's-have-fun crappola as much as these cuties, maybe more.

"All right, listen up. You decide how much or how little of what I'm about to tell you want to keep as notes, seeing as a portion of my lecture is simply my opinion."

Normally, this advice would sound a death knell for note taking, but Bonnie felt pretty certain these type-A girls wouldn't be able to resist saving information. The need for organization was hardwired into their DNA.

Bonnie pointed with her chin at Yoki. "Our resident Kovalevskaya expert has done an excellent job of laying the groundwork for Sophia's short and impressive life. Revolutionary, mathematician, novelist, Sophia Kovalevskaya crammed a lot of living into her forty-one years. However, I won't be speaking so much of Sophia's life as of her untimely death."

Bonnie leaned forward and fixed her gaze on first one, then another of her charges. By the time she was finished with this exercise, the silence in the room was so dense you could slice it like cheesecake.

"In order to understand Sophia's undoing we need to understand her personality. She was Russian through and through. By that I don't mean she was stolid and stoic, not Sophia." Bonnie made a fist and shook it. "Sophia Kovalevskaya was passionate, in every sense of the word—her beliefs, her work, both mathematical and literary, and most especially in her love life."

Several girls whispered, and Bonnie adopted the pose of the patient narrator. Other, supposedly more mature girls policed the room back into quiet.

"As you remember, Sophia married not for love, but for a passport away from her father and into the life she desperately wanted. A life of the mind. A life of the spirit. It needs to be said that although Sophia may not have been in love with Vladimir Kovalevsky, she did appreciate his friendship. For most of their lives together, she would hold that friendship as precious. Once again, for the most part, she stood by him when the things went tragically wrong. Keep in mind she did have a child by Vladimir, her beloved Foufie."

This time Bonnie fully expected the giggles, which came on cue.

How could you not laugh at a name like Foufie?

Fortunately, her thirteen's need to hear more outweighed their natural desire to be goofball teenagers. Bonnie hadn't long to wait.

"Sophia Kovalevskaya was considered, by all who met her, an attractive young woman. Yoki mentioned that Sophia's mentor, Weierstrass, might have been in love with her. There may have been some truth in that. A friend of Weierstrass, the chemist R. W. Bunsen—"

Hands shot up in the air. Once again, Bonnie expected to be interrupted at this juncture. In fact, she would have been disappointed had she not been. She pointed at Beatrice. "Yes?"

"Is that the guy who—"

"You would think so, but the Bunsen burner was actually perfected by Bunsen's assistant."

"Weird."

Weird, indeed. "Now where was I?"

"Sophia's love life," Beatrice offered.

"Oh, yeah. Bunsen, who was worried that Weierstrass might be overly fond of the young woman, warned him that Sophia was dangerous. Although it needs to be said that Bunsen was a renowned woman hater."

From the looks on the faces of several of her charges, she was sure that had Bunsen been present he would have gotten an earful from these feisty young women. They had the makings of dangerous women themselves.

"I'd like to tell you that Sophia Kovalevskaya was a saint who remained faithful to her husband all through her days. Such is simply not the case. History tells us that Sophia had at least two extramarital affairs."

If anything, the silence in the room grew more pronounced.

Bonnie wondered how many of these young women thought less of Sophia because of this character flaw. Bonnie knew most of their families and many were religious.

Would you guys be shocked to learn your gray-haired teacher had an affair in her impetuous youth?

"Of the first affair, I will only say this. It happened

while Sophia was in Paris and away from her husband, Vladimir. It ended when Vladimir committed suicide in 1883."

If the girls hadn't been incensed at this long dead mathematician's behavior before, their openly angry faces showed they were at this juncture. One of the things Bonnie admired about teenagers was their sense of justice. To most of them, right and wrong were acutely defined concepts. Black and white. Only later in life did the majority of the human race get lost in the vast gray areas of morality.

How did Bobby Dylan put it? I was older then; I'm younger than that now.

Bonnie considered defending Sophia Kovalevskaya's choices, telling them about the strain Vladimir put on their relationship by squandering not only his own money but Sophia's inheritance as well. She decided against it.

Anger is good for the soul.

"It's the second affair that we'll focus on. Less than two years before her death, Sophia had been altered in almost every conceivable way from the firebrand of her youth. This version of Sophia was superstitious—she spoke constantly of the meaning of her dreams. She'd fretted obsessively about how history would remember her. And she had never really recovered from the breakdown she'd suffered when Vladimir died. Into this atmosphere came Maxim."

Bonnie paused to catch her breath and to gauge the attentiveness of her audience. Although they were slouched on their desktop perches, no one's eyes seemed to have glazed over. And no one was yawning.

Don't push your luck, Pinkwater. Run to the end while you still got them.

"Very little is known about this mystery man except that Sophia loved him as she had loved no one else in her entire life. And for a while, he returned that devotion. He was generous, kind, understanding, solicitous as to her well-being, and made compromise after compromise in order to accommodate the necessities of her mathematical career. Unfortunately, for this new version of Sophia, it wasn't enough."

Bonnie leaned forward and presented her hands as upturned avaricious talons. "She needed to be in control. As he became more devoted, Sophia became increasingly tyrannical. No aspect of their relationship was immune because she viewed all of it in the service of her ambition, her destiny. In the end, her impossible demands drove him away."

"That's so sad," Beatrice said.

"I believe Sophia would agree with you. I can't help feeling there came a moment when she realized what she had done. How she had, after a lifetime of searching, found someone to love, then threw it all away. From all accounts, after Maxim left, her health deteriorated to the extent that one cold night at a railway station in Stockholm, she simply didn't have the energy to go on living. Many folks say she died of exhaustion. Others say influenza. But I say Sophia Kovalevskaya, arguably the finest female mathematician of all time, died of a broken heart."

When Bonnie stopped into the office, Lloyd was on the phone, his feet propped up on his desk, his left hand behind his head. He saw Bonnie and waved her in. She plopped down in the big red plush chair, her notes from her morning lecture on her lap.

He covered the receiver. "It's Marjorie. I'll be right with you." He handed her a sticky note.

It contained a short message from Byron Hickman. Seneca Webb had regained consciousness and seemed to be on the mend.

Bonnie considered beating a retreat to the hall and calling Byron, but her curiosity about Marjorie wouldn't permit it. Lloyd was actually grinning like a schoolboy.

Good for you, boss.

"It's Bonnie," Lloyd said. "Sure, why not?"

He extended the receiver to Bonnie. "She wants to say hi."

Bonnie took the phone. "What's going on in the

world of big-time music, girlfriend?"

"Same old, same old. But Lloyd and I are having dinner tonight. Keep your fingers crossed."

"I'll do that. My toes, too." Bonnie wasn't sure how much she should quiz Marjorie with Lloyd sitting just a few feet away. She decided she'd have more to talk about after the dinner date. "I'll yak at you in a day or two."

"Thanks for everything, Bon."

"Shut up. I didn't do anything. You take care of yourself, honey." Bonnie handed the phone back to Lloyd.

Her principal chatted for another minute and hung up. He inhaled deeply and regarded Bonnie across the expanse of his desk.

When after a full minute he still hadn't said anything, Bonnie rolled her Kovalevskaya notes and slapped them on the desk. "Well?"

"We talked yesterday."

The infuriating man seemed to believe that short sentence would suffice. "You're going to have to do better than that, Whittaker."

A smile sliced across her friend's craggy face. "Okay, we talked a long time, maybe two hours. Talked about everything. Us. The kids. What happened with what's-his-name."

No way on God's green earth was Bonnie going to call Marjorie's erstwhile lover by his Christian name if

Lloyd wasn't prepared to. She merely nodded. "You worked some things out?"

"You could say that. I'm not saying everything's perfect. But it's a start. We're having dinner tonight."

Bonnie reached across the desk and squeezed Lloyd's hand. "That's what I heard. Some place romantic, with wine and soft music?"

"The rib place in Limon."

Fair enough. She waved the sticky note. "What's the skinny on Seneca?"

Lloyd scratched at his chin. "A severe concussion. A dozen stitches. She'll probably hang out at the hospital for a day or two."

Bonnie considered going to see the girl and decided not to. She'd let Gabe Trotter be a visiting angel without competition from Bonnie Pinkwater. "Did Byron say anything about Rattlesnake?"

Lloyd shook his head. "I asked. The good deputy said the girl claims to know nothing about the abduction of Rattlesnake or the shooting of Jason Dobbs."

Bonnie stood, unable to contain her frustration. She brandished her notes like a war club. "Well, Seneca damn well knows about something. Am I the only one who remembers her shouting, *No more killing*? Boss, I'm not saying she's guilty of anything, but come on!"

Lloyd chuckled. "Don't hold your feelings in so much, Pinkwater. You'll hurt yourself."

Bonnie stuck her tongue out at her friend. "Well? Did Byron mention anything about Furby or Leo?"

"First of all, you're not the only one who remembered the girl's words. But when I asked about that, Byron clammed up, wouldn't say a thing one way or the other."

Don't send a man to do a woman's work. Clam up, my saggy rear end. I damn well would have gotten the youngster to spill the beans.

Bonnie eased herself back into the stuffed chair. Weariness settled over her that demanded a definitely reduced expenditure of energy. She'd let Byron do his job without pushing and prying.

At least not from one Bonnie Pinkwater. "I'm going home."

Lloyd rapped his knuckles on his desk. "A capital idea. I've got a few things to finish up here, then I'm going to quit this place as well. Got a rendezvous to attend."

Bonnie remembered how she'd left things with Armen and blanched.

"Anything wrong?" Lloyd asked.

She considered telling him her tale of woe then thought better of it. "Another time, big guy." She pushed herself to her feet. "Let's just say I've got a rendezvous of my own, and I'm not looking forward to it." Without another word, Bonnie left Lloyd's office.

Bonnie climbed into Alice, tossed her class notes onto the passenger seat, and started up the Subaru.

Pinkwater, you've got a good forty-minute drive to consider what you'll say, and not say, to Armen.

As she pulled onto East Plains Highway, Bonnie prepared her battle plan. First, she needed to shake off her lethargy before phoning Armen. It wouldn't do to lose her cool—and give rein to her Imp of the Perverse—merely because she was brain weary. Right at the moment, she had no idea what she meant to say to the man, but she had an almost geometrical image of how it needed to be said. She would inhabit the midpoint between indignation and graciousness.

Bonnie intended to listen patiently while Armen made his case for purchasing the tickets without consulting her. The man had had almost twenty hours to construct a logical argument in defense of his position. Bonnie was well acquainted with the inner working of Armen Callahan's excellent mind and a part of her was looking forward to his verbal machinations.

On the flip side, she needed to establish some ground rules and parameters for future negotiations. Armen going off and making decisions that affected Bonnie intimately without a by-your-leave would henceforth be unacceptable. If they were to be together—and God knew how that would be defined—they would have to be a team.

This last thought literally stopped Bonnie in her tracks. Only partially aware she was doing it, she guided the Subaru onto the shoulder of the road.

A team?

Where had she last heard those words? Just recently, she was sure. She tugged on her earlobe and engaged her View-Master memory for playback. Immediately, a not-so-still voice sounded in her head declaiming the idea of searching for this abstract tidbit of information, at least at this moment, as a ridiculous waste of precious time. She damn well needed to get ready for what might prove to be one of the most important phone calls of her life.

For once in your life, Pinkwater, don't let yourself get sidetracked.

Bonnie forced herself to resume her homeward trek. Over the next thirty minutes she auditioned, rejected, revised, and polished what felt like a cogent set of reasonable guidelines for a possible future with Armen Callahan. She felt comfortable in her skin and ready to compromise if Armen was reasonable.

Absently, she had unrolled and smoothed her classroom notes. From the corner of her eye, she caught bits and snatches of her Sophia Kovalevskaya lecture. She had underlined key sections of the talk, and the final piece where Sophia's romance with Maxim had begun to unravel seemed to leap off the page.

"Oh, my God," she exclaimed. "Of course."

CHAPTER 24

"How did you get through, Missus P?" Byron sounded like he wanted to yank Bonnie through her kitchen phone line and toss her to a pack of wolves. "I left Deputy Fishbach with explicit instructions that I didn't want to speak with anyone until I finished my lunch. I may have to kill him after I hang up on you."

I would imagine my name came up once or twice in that set of explicit instructions. "Don't be too hard on the poor man. I can be pretty persuasive when I put my mind to it."

"Tell me about it." Byron sighed a let's-get-this-over-with sigh. "So, what earth-shattering news couldn't wait another twenty minutes?"

Bonnie had expended all her energy in getting access to her former student, even to the point of hinting she would give preferential treatment to Deputy Fishbach's daughter Mindy in the coming school year. Now that she had Byron on the hook, she was at a momentary loss. She didn't want to come off sounding like a loon by informing him she was inspired by the tragic life of a lady mathematician who died almost two centuries ago.

"Before I get into it, I need you to send someone over to Memorial Hospital. If I'm right, Gabe Trotter is in grave danger."

"What are you talking about, Missus P?"

"I'm talking Seneca Webb, Byron." Bonnie inhaled once and released it slowly in order to stay calm. *Take your time, Pinkwater. Make your words count.* "The murder of Leo Quinn was no hate crime. We're talking love here, or at least the heartbreak that comes from love lost."

The sound of Byron's breathing came back on the line as if he'd had his hand over the receiver. "Missus P, Seneca Webb is one of the victims in this tragedy. Her husband almost killed her yesterday afternoon."

"I know but—"

"No buts. That young woman is in no shape to be a threat to anyone. Hell, I postponed most of my interrogation because I thought she might slip into unconsciousness if I stressed her too much."

"Are you through?" Bonnie knew she was treading a very fine line in being terse with Byron, but she couldn't hold the reins on her Imp of the Perverse. "That young woman, as you put it, has manipulated every man she's ever met, and now she's working her magic on you."

"I'm going to give you a bye on that one, Missus P,

because of our past relationship. But I need to tell you, I don't appreciate being told I'm someone's puppet. You got about two minutes to make your case."

Two minutes it is, then. Time to play Scheherazade.

"There's a photograph in Rattlesnake's office of Leo Quinn and Seneca, prom night I suspect. Rattlesnake keeps that photo around because he loved Seneca like a daughter. It was his fondest wish that she and Leo would give him grandbabies."

"I've seen that photo. They looked real good together."

"That photograph represented not only Alf Quinn's plans, but Seneca Webb's hopes and dreams. Hell, youngster, she and Leo had been inseparable since early childhood. They were sweethearts all through junior and senior high—prom, homecoming, hayrides, bonfires. There must be a dozen snapshots of the pair in yearbooks and the school newspaper."

"I get it, Missus P. Seneca Webb loved Leo Quinn." Byron exhaled loudly across the receiver. "But things and people change. Truth is, she and Leo broke up. Seneca moved on and married Caleb Webb."

Bonnie shook her head, even though she knew Byron couldn't see it. "Yes, she married Caleb, but she never got over Leo." Bonnie checked her Mickey Mouse watch. Her two minutes were almost up.

Time to try for the long kick. "Or hating Jason

Dobbs."

"For stealing Leo from her?" The barest hint of cynicism peeked out of Byron's question.

You're coming round, Deputy Hickman. "You bet. Then two months ago, Seneca's world did an about-turn. Jason Dobbs officially made a clean break with Leo. Her one-time soul mate needed a shoulder to cry on."

"I think I know where you're going with this."

"Then you also know the math gets a little coincidental here. I have no way of divining the particulars, but I believe Seneca Webb tricked a devastated Leo Quinn into making love to her. Byron, Seneca is two months pregnant."

Bonnie braced herself for a battery of objections. What she got was silence. Once again, the sound of Byron's breathing was absent from the receiver. It returned a few moments later. "I got to go, Missus P."

"What's happening, youngster?"

"It appears you may have been right. When you first suggested I send someone out to the hospital, I had Vern Fishbach call. Gabe Trotter came to visit Seneca at twelve thirty. The nurses checked the room a few minutes ago. Both Gabe and Seneca are gone."

Bonnie hung up her kitchen phone. She sat down

hard at her breakfast island and settled her head onto her arms.

Seneca has Gabriel Trotter.

Bonnie had no doubt the murderous heartsick girl would kill Gabe before the day was through. Never mind that the goofball was guilty of nothing that warranted such extremes. A similar truth hadn't saved either Witherspoon or Furby.

Or Rattlesnake.

The faces of the dead crowded into Bonnie's brain. Furby, with his clown makeup and dirty Pennzoil cap. The Spoonmaster sitting behind the wheel of his muscle car. Alf Quinn, staring out of a photo, his arm around his unfortunate extraordinary son. And these didn't take into account the suicidal stand of Caleb Webb.

So many.

Bonnie had successfully kept the specters in the wings thus far by compartmentalizing her psyche. So many things clamored for her attention since she'd gotten that phone call Sunday morning. Lloyd and Marjorie. Armen's abrupt exodus to the Garden State. Her class. Each time the knocking of the dead became insistent, she could forestall them with the rationalization that she was busy, had other things to think about. Up until now they seemed to understand.

Now they were demanding front row center.

What can I tell you guys? I'm all tapped out. I

did everything I could to stop the insanity, but it wasn't enough.

Gabriel Trotter's melancholy countenance swam into focus, baby fat, zits, and all. Soon he would join the troop of the dead. Soon Bonnie would have one more specter rapping at her door.

"Screw this."

Bonnie sat up on her stool. If she was to be of any use to Gabe Trotter, she needed to clear the decks—lay out all the facts and analyze them.

Bonnie considered calling Lloyd and rejected the idea. Her friend was in no shape to help her sift through details. He had all he could handle with saving his marriage. She reached for the phone and dialed a number in Atlantic City.

"Callahan's."

Armen seemed so close she could reach out and touch him.

"Mister Mouse?" Bonnie made no effort to hide how glad she was to reconnect with this man she'd hung up on the previous day. She was also in no mood to play relationship games. "Before you say a word, I need to tell you something."

"I love you, too."

Bonnie chuckled dryly. "That was my line. Mister Mouse, I need a favor."

"I have no moment but to await upon your pleasure."

"You sweet talker. I'll take you at your word. Fasten your seat belt." For the next fifteen minutes she delineated the chronology of death and destruction that had strode across East Plains.

Armen listened with only the barest of comments until she finished. "I'm not sure what you need here, Bon."

"I need you to help me save a boy's life."

A long moment passed before Armen responded. "That's a tall order. I'll do what I can."

"I know you will." Bonnie took a moment to let her thoughts arrange themselves into a semblance of order. "It all begins with Sophia Kovalevskaya."

"The Russian mathematician?"

"Uh-huh." She gave Armen the short course on Sophia, emphasizing the final months of her tragic life.

"That's sad."

"That's what Beatrice Archuleta said."

"Who?"

"Never mind. The thing is that on my way home from class, I let my attention drift to my lecture notes."

"While you were driving?"

"Now is not the perfect time for the safety sermon, Callahan. If it helps, picture me stopped at a traffic light."

"Strangely enough, it does. Please continue."

"How Sophia came to her heartbreaking end at that

railway station in Stockholm opened my eyes as to what had really happened that night on Squirrel Creek Road. Both Sophia and Seneca were strong women, used to getting their way, and not averse to manipulating the men in their lives when they felt it would serve their purpose. Each lost the great love of their life because of unreasonable demands placed upon the relationship."

"Hold on. I thought Leo broke it off when he came out of the closet."

"I don't think so. Leo's homosexuality redefined their relationship. No longer was this shining knight her destined soul mate, her timeless lover. As far as Seneca was concerned, Leo was lost to her. I'm sure she blamed Leo and certainly she blamed Jason Dobbs, but in the end I would wager Seneca Webb couldn't accept her new role as trusted friend and severed the tie."

"I'll have to take your word for that."

Fair enough. "Fast forward to two months ago. Two events changed the status quo. First, Jason Dobbs cuts Leo loose." She ran down the skinny on the youth pastor and his decision to follow in his father's footsteps.

Armen whistled. "Three years seems a long time to wait for anybody. If you ask me, Leo should have moved on."

Bonnie shrugged. "Love makes fools of us all. Regardless, following on the heels of this revelation, Leo contacts Seneca."

"Who's now married to Caleb Webb."

"Whom I'm certain she loved only nominally. And here's where our story heats up. Like I told Byron, I believe Seneca saw this happenstance as a fortuitous opportunity to set things right. I'm betting liquor was involved, but in any event, Seneca gets a mixed-up Leo Quinn to play heterosexual, at least for five minutes."

"And now she's pregnant."

"And now she's *two months* pregnant."

"I've got to say, Bon. I see a problem with this theory. The Caleb Webb you painted for me wouldn't take kindly to being made into a cuckold."

Bonnie tugged at her ear. This aspect of her theory had troubled her as well. "If you don't mind, I'd like to put off discussing Mister Webb until later. He's a study in perversity all by his lonesome."

"We can do that. Lead on, MacDuff."

More than anything, Bonnie wished she could reach out and squeeze this sweet man's hand. "Now, move our tale to Saturday night. Not only were Furby, Witherspoon, and Trotter out on Squirrel Creek Road, but I claim so were Seneca and Leo—the latter to discuss the miracle of gestation."

"And what Leo's response should be to the news he was an impending father?"

"You betcha. Now, according to Trotter, they spotted Leo walking along Squirrel Creek carrying a gas can. If we believe him, the simplest explanation is that whatever vehicle Leo or perhaps Seneca was driving ran out of gas."

"Makes sense. And that's when Leo was accosted by Witherspoon and company, stripped naked and tied to the fence." Ten seconds stretched into twenty before Armen spoke again. "Why wasn't Seneca with Leo?"

Good question. "For some reason, she must have opted to remain with the vehicle. She was close but not so close that Witherspoon and the boys knew she was there. Whatever the particulars, she became aware of Leo's situation."

"And came running in time to see the Trans Am take off."

"Not exactly. She must have skinned it a little nearer than that. For the rest of this passion play to work, she needed to arrive in time to identify exactly who Leo's assailants were. This information would be crucial when she returned home to Caleb."

"But they couldn't have seen her. Otherwise, when the killing started, Witherspoon would have dropped a dime on her."

"Wow, Callahan. Four days on the East Coast and you're already sounding like a Soprano. But you're right, until my phone call with Byron, her name has never been linked with the incidents on Squirrel Creek Road."

"Now we have a pissed-off Seneca Webb and a naked homosexual tied to a barbed-wire fence."

"Don't forget she is in possession of a nine-millimeter pistol. At first glance this seems strange until you realize that a significant fraction of East Plains travel about armed, either with a loaded rifle hung on the racks of their truck or with a concealed weapon on their person. In any event, armed and angry, she comes upon a trussed-up Leo Quinn."

"And shoots him?"

"Not immediately. What I see happening is that, for some reason or another, she revisited their discussion, and Leo tried to tell her he could never be the husband she wants. Angry words ensue, and she loses control."

"Seneca must have regretted her actions. She folded Leo's clothes."

Bonnie didn't like the sympathetic undertone in Armen's assertion. "Not so repentant. I see her drying her tears quick enough to concoct a story to tell first Caleb then Rattlesnake. Once she'd set that homicidal machine in motion, she had no qualms about letting an increasingly unbalanced Rattlesnake and an already-screwy hubby take out Furby and Witherspoon."

"But why try to kill Jason Dobbs?"

"I think it has a lot to do with why dogs lick themselves."

Armen chuckled. "Because they can?"

"Uh-huh. Seneca had already been part of the murder of one innocent, although I'm sure in her mind, if

Furby hadn't accosted Leo she wouldn't have found it necessary to shoot her lover. Regardless, she had created in her hubby an ideal killing machine. Why not use him to eliminate the man who had stolen her Leo?"

"But Rattlesnake wasn't entirely on board for this killing."

"Not entirely. I'm sure he was no big fan of the young pastor once Seneca slyly let slip that Jason had been Leo's erstwhile love interest. Still, that's hardly a sufficient reason to take a sniper rifle and blow him away."

"So Rattlesnake had to go."

Bonnie felt something catch in the back of her throat. She pictured the man patiently introducing round-headed children to a visiting math teacher.

Ladies and gents, this here is Missus Bonnie Pinkwater. She's one of the teachers at East Plains, and if you ask me, the best of the bunch.

"Bon?"

Armen's voice snapped her back to the present. "I'm okay. Just woolgathering. You're right, of course. Rattlesnake became a liability when he developed a conscience. Caleb couldn't let him live."

Now you've said it out loud. Move on. "Which brings us to today."

Armen cleared his throat, evidently uneasy about what he had to say. "Bon, I don't need to tell you that the dynamic has changed. Up until now, Seneca worked assiduously to shift blame away from herself, to use others to do her dirty work."

Bonnie heart sank. "But now that she's abducted Gabe Trotter, she may be beyond caring." *In other words, Gabe Trotter is probably already dead.*

"Truth is, Seneca may have crossed that line yesterday," Armen said. "You stated Caleb Webb killed Dwight Furby and Moses Witherspoon outright, no finesse, no hesitation."

Of course! "But Caleb had no intention of killing Gabe. Caleb was bringing Gabe home for the little woman."

Across Bonnie's synapses, a scene from *Dracula* played out in Technicolor. The king of the vampires in the spirit of gift-giving extracted an infant, chubby with blood, from a carpetbag. Then, with smiles all around, he presented this tasty morsel to his three vampire brides. The scene ended with the ravenous fanged beauties descending on the wailing child.

Except in Bonnie's conception, all three brides wore the hungry visage of Seneca Webb. "If Wilma hadn't caught sight of Caleb and Gabe on that motorcycle—"

"More than likely we wouldn't be having this conversation, and Gabe Trotter would be singing tenor in the heavenly choir."

Bonnie shook herself free from a descending cloud of despair. "I can't think any of that right now, Mister

Mouse. To keep my sanity, I need to believe Gabe is still alive."

"So, the circle brings us back to the million-dollar question. Where has Seneca Webb taken him?"

The circle! The words hadn't left Armen's lips before Bonnie knew the answer.

CHAPTER 25

AN ORANGE AND MOLTEN SUN WAS SINKING ONTO PIKES Peak by the time Bonnie drew up the courage to drive out to Squirrel Creek Road. She crested a shallow hill and spied the diminutive form of Seneca Webb standing in the shoulder. No doubt the girl had already spotted Bonnie's Subaru, or at least the cloud of dust that accompanied it.

That's right, dear girl. It's just your old math teacher. No need to go postal.

This particular stretch of Squirrel Creek Road wasn't familiar to Bonnie, but she had no trouble finding it. Hell, the location of Leo's murder had been burned into her psyche over the last six days. She could have told a blind man how to get there.

Or a deputy sheriff.

Bonnie had debated whether or not to even call Byron. If the police came screaming to the scene, lights flashing, sirens wailing, the outcome would be a foregone conclusion. Seneca would dispatch Gabe without a second thought. And then likely die in a summer shower of bullets.

Along with Leo Quinn's baby.

The flip side of the argument was that to not clue Byron in to her intentions was a foolishness that would qualify her for *The Guinness Book of World Records*. She'd gone that route more than once and had no desire to repeat the high-wire-without-a-net experience.

Even lab rats learn from their mistakes.

In the end, she'd opted for a compromise. En route she'd phoned Byron only to discover that he and his limited staff were occupied. Deputy Wyatt, playing receptionist, had informed Bonnie that the East Plains sheriff's contingent were either heading down to Memorial Hospital or were at the Webb residence hoping to find Seneca there. Wyatt promised to relay Bonnie's information to Byron, and let him decide what to do with it. The unspoken implication was that he might do nothing.

What Bonnie should have done was to wait. That would have been the wise thing to do.

One of these days, Pinkwater, you're going to have to purchase a little of that wisdom stuff. Time for the high wire.

As she approached Seneca, Bonnie could see the girl had been busy. A naked Gabe Trotter was spread-eagled and secured nicely, both arms and legs, to a section of barbed-wire fence. The scientist in Bonnie was perversely curious as to how Seneca had accomplished this feat and just how much Gabe himself had cooperated. After all, Seneca Webb was an attractive female even with her head bandaged. Perhaps the young man thought nude bondage was a prelude to even more kinkiness.

Imagine his surprise when Seneca pulled out a pistol.

Once again, Bonnie's curiosity kicked in. This weapon certainly couldn't be the infamous nine millimeter that had wreaked havoc over the last six days. That gun had been confiscated from Caleb's dead fingers on Friday. And yet, here was a duplicate, albeit no noise suppressor affixed to the barrel. No doubt, also compliments of Alf Rattlesnake Quinn.

Bonnie was forced to admire Seneca's adherence to detail.

"That's far enough," the girl shouted when Alice was about five meters away.

A wide-eyed Gabe Trotter looked on the verge of apoplexy. "She's crazy, Missus P. She means to kill me."

You think, Einstein?

"Shut up." Seneca waved her pistol, indicating Bonnie should exit her car. "Real slow, Missus P. I don't need to tell you, no surprises."

Hands raised, Bonnie emerged from her car. "It would have been more dramatic if you'd waited until dark to set the scene."

Seneca looked west to the setting sun, as if she was

considering Bonnie's suggestion. Her eyes had an almost unfocused look to them. "Close enough." She pointed airily with her gun toward Gabe Trotter. "You can't have everything perfect."

The girl shuddered and momentarily squeezed her eyes shut.

You should have stayed in the hospital, my dear.

Bonnie, her hands still raised, took a step forward. "Sure would have been a whole lot more convenient, if Caleb hadn't been spotted delivering the goods yesterday. The two of you could have driven Gabe here and waited until midnight."

A dreamy look came over Seneca's countenance. "That would have been sweet." She sent an admiring half smile Bonnie's way. "You figured the whole thing out, didn't you? You *are* as clever as they say."

To her shame, Bonnie felt a flush of pride at the girl's compliment. "Thank you. Can I lower my hands?"

Seneca nodded in acknowledgment. "I have to admit, I was a bit panicked when Caleb told me he'd blown it. But he knew what he had to do. We'd planned a dual exit strategy since the beginning. He just made his escape first." She pointed with her gun to Gabe. "I'll follow along when I finish up here."

A macabre portion of Bonnie's brain objectively regarded this young woman who could talk so cavalierly about her husband's choice to die.

Seneca stroked the barrel of the pistol against the side of her bandaged head. "The toughest thing was to convince him he needed to brain me so I wouldn't immediately go down the crapper with him." She chuckled and winced again. "In the end the moron damn near killed me."

Bonnie felt like smacking the smug girl. A man had died trying to save her, and she was making light of his sacrifice. Moreover, when she murdered Gabe, Seneca would render that sacrifice meaningless.

Swallow your indignation, Pinkwater. It won't help anyone right now. "So what was yesterday's plan after doing Gabe? Were you going to go after Jason Dobbs again?" The surprised look on Seneca's face almost made the stupid risk Bonnie was taking worth it.

"Oh, my, clairvoyant as well as clever." Seneca leaned in as if she and Bonnie were coconspirators. "If Caleb would have been a little more careful, no one would have suspected us. Finally nailing Jason would have been a breeze. Hell, we still had the sniper rifle, and this time I'd be the one taking the shot."

"Rattlesnake taught you well, didn't he?"

The look of amusement on Seneca's face evaporated. She chewed at her lip. "Yeah, both me and Leo growing up, but I was always the better shot." Her lips became a tight line. "I'll miss that old man."

Bonnie could feel her Imp of the Perverse pushing

the unwise question out of her mouth, and she was powerless to reel it in. "So why did you kill him?" Bonnie held her breath expecting Seneca to explode.

Instead the girl spread wide her hands as if she needed Bonnie to see she was a reasonable person. "We had to. It was only a matter of time before he started bragging about the killings. He was growing more and more unstable."

Unlike you and Cowboy Caleb who were rock solid citizens. "Then there was the business of Rattlesnake not completely copasetic with killing Jason Dobbs."

This time Seneca did get angry—her face grew stormy, her eyes dark slits. "And how the hell do you know that?"

Bonnie told about Pastor Dobbs hiding in the bathroom.

"I'll be damned."

Very likely.

Seneca made an exaggerated show of scanning Squirrel Creek Road in both directions. "You know, Missus P, it wasn't very smart, coming here alone. Did you really think you could talk me out of killing what's-his face here?"

Bonnie reddened. "That was the plan."

Seneca waggled a finger as if to indicate Bonnie should have come up with a better plan. "What's to stop me from shooting you, then blowing away angel boy for an encore?"

Two-handed, she sighted down the long barrel at Gabe Trotter's exposed testicles. "Ker-pow."

"Oh, shit. Oh, shit. Oh, shit," Gabe whimpered.

Bonnie reached for the first thing she could think of to distract the girl. "Did Caleb know the baby was Leo's?"

Seneca turned a smiling countenance back to Bonnie. "It's none of your business, but Caleb did not know of"—she hesitated, then cleared her throat—"the baby's paternity. Let's just say he wouldn't have taken the news with grace."

"Do you mind my asking why you married him?" Bonnie had no desire to revisit the topic of Seneca blowing anyone away.

The young woman cocked her head and regarded Bonnie. "Stalling for time isn't going to change anything. But since nothing you or the cops can do will stop me from sending this loser to hell, I'll answer your question. I'm not sure you'll understand."

"Try me."

Seneca drew in a long breath. "Leo's big announcement did a number on me, screwed me up good. I didn't eat. I got sick. I should have talked to Leo, but I hated him."

"I can understand that. It's not a far jump from love to hate."

The young woman frowned at Bonnie.

Can the platitudes, Pinkwater.

"Anyway, the only thing that seemed to help was rodeoing. I wasn't competing, but it felt good to hear the crowds, taste the dust, see my old friends."

Of course, Caleb was a bull rider!

"Caleb was there." Seneca shuddered again and this time seemed unsteady on her feet. She took a wider stance. "I'd seen him around the circuit before. Rode a pretty good bull."

Bonnie long suspected that bull riders might be a little crazy, but she was certain none as much so as Caleb Webb.

"I knew he was screwed up, but when he started coming around—" She shrugged. "There's something very sexy about being worshiped. He was sweet in a nut job sort of way. Plus he let me know there was nothing he wouldn't do for me. And I have to admit he was as good as his word."

Seneca pointed with her chin, and Bonnie turned around. A cloud of dust was approaching from the west. "I'm thinking the cavalry has arrived. I got a one-time offer for you. Get back into your car and drive the hell out of here."

Bonnie shook her head. "I'm not going anywhere unless you come with me."

Seneca stretched out her arm and pointed the nine millimeter at Gabe. "I can't do that."

"He ... didn't ... kill ... Leo ... Seneca ... you ... did." Bonnie emphasized each word in the ragged hope she might get through to the girl.

Seneca fired. The gun whistled and a tiny dust devil appeared a meter below Gabe's crotch. The young man screamed. A trickle of urine sprayed onto the sand.

Nostrils flaring, Seneca turned a stony countenance Bonnie's way. "Leo Quinn was an angel sent by God to this earth—the best person I ever knew. Oh, God, how I loved him." Once again she pointed the nine millimeter at Gabe. "This one and his friends humiliated him, treated him like he was nothing, then hopped into their souped-up car and drove away laughing."

Behind her, Bonnie could hear the crunch of vehicles coming to a stop. She was grateful whomever it was had not turned on their sirens. "He's not laughing now, sweetie. Don't do this."

Seneca blinked away tears, but her arm was steady. "I have to."

Car doors opened. "Missus P, get out of there!"

Even though she expected to hear his voice, Byron's tenor startled Bonnie. Arms trembling, she held them out in a gesture she hoped would forestall any precipitous action. "Everybody cool it!" she shouted.

She locked eyes with Seneca. "If you fire that pistol even once, they're going to kill you."

"I know." Seneca's finger tightened on the trigger.

In the remaining heartbeat, Bonnie fumbled about for anything to stop the madness. Her Imp of the Perverse stepped forward. "You selfish little bitch."

Seneca's hand wavered. She gaped openly at Bonnie.

She had no intention of letting the girl speak. "*Leo's an angel. Leo's the best person I ever knew.*" Bonnie squeezed as much sarcasm as she could into the two sentences.

"Stop it, Missus Pinkwater."

"*Stop it, Missus Pinkwater.*" If anything, Bonnie piled even more ridicule into her taunt. "Shut up, girl, and pay attention. Two months ago you made a decision. You decided to lie down with Leo Quinn and create a child."

A spasm of either pain or remorse shot across Seneca's features. "That's over now. Everything's changed."

"Says who? Girl, this isn't about you anymore. This isn't some random act of sex that produced an unwanted child. This is a human being you deliberately created and now are willing to sacrifice like you sacrificed Caleb Webb."

Seneca violently shook her head. "You're twisting everything. Be quiet, and let me think."

Not on your life. Bonnie waved derisively at Gabe Trotter. "If I hear you right, all this bullshit is about honoring the memory of Leo Quinn."

Seneca's eyes flashed. "That's right!"

"Then honor him, Goddammit." She pointed to the young woman's abdomen. "You're carrying a piece of

Leo right there in your belly."

Seneca's resolve seemed to waver. A tear formed and slid down her cheek. Then as if some steel coil had been rewound, she tightened her jaw, and her grip on the pistol. "Just words. Leo's gone. That's all that matters."

Oh, shit. Think, Pinkwater.

An image of a bus ride across snowy Wolf Creek Pass appeared in Bonnie's mind. *What have you got to lose?* "Don't make these policemen kill Timothy."

Seneca turned to gape at Bonnie. "What did you say?"

Hallelujah! "I said Timothy, Seneca. Timothy Quinn. Leo's child."

"How do you—"

"Leo told me, sweetie."

Bonnie held her breath.

For a long moment, Seneca Webb remained a malevolent statue, ready to do what she'd come to do. Then, like it had suddenly grown too heavy to bear, the pistol began to lower—ten degrees, then twenty. Finally, Seneca let the gun drop to the dirt. Her hands came to her face, her entire body shaking with sobs.

From behind, Bonnie heard the sound of footfalls. Byron and the state trooper named Alvin swept past her. The trooper gathered the weapon.

Bonnie was afraid Byron would roughly slap Seneca into handcuffs. Instead he wrapped an arm around the girl and began to lead her toward the cruisers.

When she passed Bonnie, Seneca turned back, looking for all the world like an innocent child in one of Bonnie's classes. "What's going to happen to me?"

Bonnie had no more energy to expend on this murderous creature. "If you're lucky, you're going to go to jail. Probably for a long, long time."

The stark news didn't seem to faze the girl. She merely nodded her head. "And my baby?"

Bonnie touched the girl's arm. "We'll figure that one out, honey. I promise."

Seneca nodded again and let Byron lead her away.

CHAPTER 26

Bonnie smiled at the obvious cliché, but it had been a month of Sundays since she'd last occupied a church pew. Still, she wouldn't have missed this service for a year of Sabbaths. Hell, she received a personal invite from Harold T. Dobbs himself. The big man and Jason, who was still bandaged and looking a little puny—sat side by side behind the lectern while the choir went nuts, tambourines and all, on a folksy version of "A Mighty Fortress Is Our God."

I got to admit the song is growing on me.

Then there'd been the business of the twin bombshells.

Immediately following his sermon—a fine one in Bonnie's estimation, leaning heavily on Saint Paul's thirteenth chapter of Corinthians—Harold had told of his shameful behavior in Rattlesnake's bathroom and the hours after. While the air was still abuzz, he tendered his resignation in favor of his son.

Before the congregation had recovered from that

percussion grenade, Jason took the lectern and came clean about his homosexuality, although he did throw the faithful a bone by allowing that he was currently not dancing to that tune.

It was at this juncture a significant number of the SBTBPT contingent rose and exited in what had to be considered a major huff. On their way out, a few shot Bonnie scathing glares.

Remembering an obscure verse that mentioned something about not returning evil for evil and the heaping of burning coals on your enemy's head, Bonnie offered the irate members a glucose-coated smile.

When the choir finished Martin Luther's anthem, Jason took the lectern. "Ladies and gentlemen, that concludes the service. However, all of you are invited to continue our fellowship on the lawn adjacent to the church. Go with God."

Bonnie was gratified that most of the faithful returned Jason's parting valediction. She felt certain this reduced congregation would weather the storm. After all, the founder of this popular sect was known to think highly of honesty and reward same. Shoot, one Bonnie Pinkwater might even set a record and attend even another SBTBPT service within the year.

She exited her pew, and immediately adopted the polite saunter of one ensconced in the slow traffic of unhurried crowds. She promised her impatient feet she would pick up the pace once she was free.

No such luck.

On the front lawn, three of her Women in Mathematics students were waiting. Emily, the child who had become the Hypatia of Alexandria expert, caught sight of Bonnie and pointed. Oblivious that they were bucking the outward flow of traffic, the girls pressed forward.

Bonnie pointed with her head toward two long tables that were stocked with a variety of pies, ice cream, and casseroles. "Over there, you ninnies. Can't you see you're in the way?"

With the natural grace that the Maker of All Things wasted on the young, the three girls slid effortlessly through the crowd and congregated by the serving tables.

As soon as Bonnie laboriously made her way to them, Beatrice Archuleta linked her arm into Bonnie's. "So, tell us everything."

Bonnie laughed. "That's a tall order. Should I begin with several of the more popular creation myths, or do you have something particular in mind?"

Always the serious one, Yoki frowned. "You know what she means."

And Bonnie did. Still, she considered teasing the girl but then thought better of it. Girls like these were the reason she'd gone into teaching. In the end she couldn't deny them. *Besides, Pinkwater, here you are again the center of attention. While you got it, flaunt it.* "I'm assuming you're talking about Seneca Webb."

They nodded like bobble-head dolls.

"All right. I'll give in to your macabre interests." For the next few minutes, Bonnie gave her adolescent audience an abbreviated version of the incidents on Squirrel Creek Road. At several natural Q&A stopping points, Bonnie noted that her charges had been joined by select members of the congregation, so that by the time she'd finished, she'd gathered a sizable crowd. Even Jason and Harold were leaning toward her as they portioned out goodies.

"Weren't you scared?" Emily asked.

Bonnie shook her head. "Don't know the meaning of the word." She kept a straight face for all of ten seconds. "But I do know the meaning of the words *terrified*, *petrified*, *horrified*, and *frightened stiff*. Of course, I was afraid, sweetie. I'm a schoolteacher not a secret agent."

Yoki regarded Bonnie through squinted eyes, as if Bonnie might just *be* some sort of secret agent disguised as a gray-haired math teacher.

Bonnie felt someone touch her elbow. She turned to see a small white-haired man in a straw cowboy hat blinking at her. He leaned heavily on an aluminum cane.

Jason Hobbs came from behind the table. "Missus Pinkwater, let me introduce Cyrus Webb, Caleb's grandfather."

Bonnie tried to recollect just how scandalously she'd portrayed this man's murderous grandson. *Serves you right, Pinkwater, for holding court in broad daylight on such a sensitive subject.* She was getting ready to apologize when the old man drew close.

"Crazy as a bedbug," he said in a voice like desert air escaping a balloon.

Bonnie stared at the ancient specimen, not quite sure she heard him right. "Pardon?"

"He said, crazy as a bedbug," Emily offered.

Bonnie stifled a chuckle. "Thank you, honey."

As if to emphasize his pronouncement, the old man twirled a wizened index finger around his ear. "All his life, I told that boy's mama there was something not right about the scamp, that he would come to a bad end."

Bonnie shot Jason a sidelong glance to ascertain if this old man might be putting her on. The young pastor kept a straight face, giving away nothing.

Cyrus Webb clutched Bonnie's elbow. "I'm glad it's over."

This was one statement Bonnie could readily agree with. "Me, too."

Without another word, the old man hobbled away. Bonnie watched him until a middle-aged woman opened a car door for him.

Caleb's mama?

She looked up from her elderly charge, and for a long moment, she and Bonnie's eyes were locked. The woman reddened, perhaps embarrassed that her crazy-as-a-bedbug son had run amok in this close-knit community.

Bonnie turned away, not really sure how much comfort she could reasonably be expected to offer. She turned to her girls. "Ladies, do me a favor. Assist Pastor Dobbs while I have a word with this handsome young man." She laced her fingers into Jason's and patted his hand.

They'd walked a few paces in silence before Bonnie piped up. "How you holding up, youngster?"

Jason rotated his shoulder. "Still hurts like the dickens, especially when I forget to take my meds."

"I'm not talking about your arm." She waved a hand as if to take in the entire church community scene. "Is this what you really want?"

Jason chewed his lower lip, obviously considering all the ramifications of the question. "If you mean am I happy with my choices, the answer is yes. This is where I want to be right now. These people, my father, this church, they're worth the trade-off."

Bonnie studied the young man's face to see if he was being straight with her. And himself. As far back into his eyes she could see he believed what he was saying.

"And down the road? Are you being fair to yourself and to these people? Will this be enough, say, five years from now?"

The young man inhaled deeply, then with cheeks bulging, let it out. "What can I say? How does anyone know how they'll feel five or even two years in the future? My heart tells me this is right for me. If that means I have to give up some things, I'm ready to do it."

Using her thumb, she pointed back over her shoulder. "And the old man? Is he happy with all his choices?"

Jason regarded his father. The elder pastor was laughing as he and Emily dished out homemade ice cream.

"Truth be told, there's going to be some major battles in the coming weeks. In the end, I don't think the congregation will accept his resignation. Those who don't head for the hills, will want the stability."

"Will he stay?"

Jason shrugged a hard-to-say shrug. "I think so, and I'll be glad of his strong right arm when the feces hits the fan."

Bonnie wished for a world where this splendid young man didn't have to give up who he was for the love of his God and his father. She threw her arms around the young pastor. "These people are lucky to have you."

When Jason didn't answer, she pulled back and studied him.

He swiped at his eyes and looked around, obviously embarrassed at his naked emotion. "I need to get back with Dad."

Bonnie nodded her understanding. The last thing Jason Dobbs needed was one more bit of public evidence he wasn't a *real man*. She pushed him away. "Go get 'em, tiger."

Her cell phone rang. She waved good-bye to Jason

and clicked it open. "Pinkwater."

"Missus P, it's Byron."

There was something in the sound of her former student's voice that held Bonnie in check. "What's on your mind, Deputy Hickman?"

"We found Rattlesnake about an hour ago."

She was about to go into inquisition mode when she realized Byron had said, *We found Rattlesnake*—not *Rattlesnake's body*. "Is he—"

"Alive? Yeah, but don't ask me why. He had three bullets in his upper body. Lost a lot of blood. We just got him to the trauma ward. It'll be touch and go for a while, but the doctors think there's good chance he'll pull through."

"Thank God."

Even as she expressed her gratitude to a deity who'd seemed more than a little absent in the past week, Bonnie realized Rattlesnake was in deep wasabi up to his bald and tattooed head. He may not have actually killed anyone, but he made it possible for others to do so.

And how would he feel when he found out that he had been providing weapons to Leo's killer?

Bonnie made a mental note to visit the big man when she got back. He'd need a friend. She checked her Mickey Mouse watch. "Listen, Byron, thanks for the info, but I've got to go."

". . . even brought me flowers." Marjorie slapped Bonnie's knee. "Who'd have thought Lloyd Whittaker had even one romantic bone in his grizzled carcass?"

On the duct-taped bench seat of Lloyd's beat-up truck, Bonnie sat squeezed between Lloyd and his newly energized bride. Ever since Lloyd had picked Bonnie up at her house, one or the other had been nonstop about the wonderful evening they'd shared. And even though Bonnie was delighted for them, there was only so much happy-happy-joy-joy a person should be reasonably expected to endure.

Marjorie stopped to catch her breath, and Bonnie saw her opportunity. "I went to see Seneca yesterday."

The announcement had the desired effect. Both heads swiveled in her direction. She let the moment hang in the air before she spoke. "She asked me if I wanted a hand in the baby's adoption."

Marjorie leaned forward so she could look Bonnie full in the face. "You mean, you as the—"

Bonnie laughed. "Me as the mama? I don't think so. She just wanted to know if I'd be part of the process. I'm not sure what that entails, some legal business or other. I told her sure."

"What about Seneca's parents?" Lloyd asked. "Aren't they interested in keeping their grandchild?"

Bonnie shook her head. "It seems they haven't much use for the bastard child of a homosexual lover and his murderous strumpet, even if that strumpet happens to be their own daughter."

"That's so sad," Marjorie said.

And that's the third time in as many days that someone's offered that commentary. I've had to agree each time. "I'm thinking the baby's better off with people who won't judge it even before it breathes its first breath. Kid's going to have enough baggage already."

Again Marjorie slapped Bonnie's knee. "Hey, enough of that. Soooooo, are you excited?"

"Who wouldn't be? I'm going to New Jersey."

Bonnie grabbed her carry-on and stood. The two legs of the flight had been uneventful and that was just peachy with Bonnie.

Had just about all the excitement I can stand for a while.

The slow trudge from the plane reminded her of the procession she endured at the Saved by the Blood Pentecostal Tabernacle not five hours ago. *Five hours and a lifetime ago.*

As she approached the baggage claim, Bonnie scanned the waiting crowd for a familiar face. When she saw no sign, she tried to rationalize her disappointment.

Makes no sense for him to park his car and come all the way into the concourse. He'll probably be waiting by the passenger pick-up.

Then a white-bearded figure stood. The man had been stooped either picking something up or possibly tying his shoe. He was carrying a gigantic bouquet of yellow roses, her favorite. Armen Callahan's face lit up as their eyes met.

Now that's what I'm talking about. Passenger pick-up, my sagging derriere.

She waved, feeling like she might possibly be a girl of fifteen reconnecting with her boyfriend after being on vacation with her folks. It felt good. Hell, more than good, it felt right.

Forget the fact the man had lost his mind and bought her plane ticket without consulting her. They'd work through that hiccup.

Bonnie had no idea what she planned to do at the end of this couple of days. She would have to go back to Colorado. That was a given. There were the dogs to consider. Would she return to live in the big house with Armen and his dad? That was a harder one to pin down. She owed Lloyd a decision as quickly as possible so he could hire a new math teacher, if that was necessary. Right now, she didn't want to think of any of that.

I'll cross that bridge and who knows, maybe blow it up behind me.

Armen drew close, wrapped his strong arms around her. The flowers tickled the back of her head, but she didn't care. Feel-good endorphins were exploding all across her synapses. As far as she was concerned, they could stand here like this until the next plane came in. After an eternity she pulled back.

"Take me home, Mister Mouse."

THE WITCH OF AGNESI
ROBERT SPILLER

Bonnie Pinkwater is a teacher, a good one. She cares about her students. So when Peyton Newlin, a thirteen-year-old math genius, disappears, Bonnie starts nosing around.

One by one, students who were competing with the young genius start turning up dead and Bonnie suspects Peyton may be narrowing the field. Then Peyton himself turns up murdered. Bonnie's investigation ratchets up.

What she discovers is a coven of witches, a teenage comic book magnate, a skinhead Neanderthal with violent propensities, an abusive father, an amorous science teacher, and a mistranslated medieval mathematics manuscript. Somehow, all the pieces have intersected at the tragically brief life of her math protégé.

As the body count mounts, Bonnie realizes she may have bitten off more than she can chew. Because whoever is eliminating her beloved students, has now decided East Plains, Colorado would be better off without one aging math teacher.

ISBN#9781932815764
US $9.99 / CDN $13.95
Mystery
Available Now
www.rspiller.com

A Calculated Demise

The Hypatia Murders
Robert Spiller

Bonnie Pinkwater, a veteran teacher with a knack for finding trouble, is at it again.

This time sadistic wrestling coach Luther Devereaux is found murdered, and her mentally challenged aide, Matt, is found with blood on his hands. She enlists the help of Greg Hansen, student council president, to pursue her investigation and exonerate Matt ... and then Greg's marijuana-dealing brother and father are killed as well. And it looks like Matt's dwarfish brother Simon is the culprit. That is, until Simon is shot and killed by an amorous millionaire rancher pursuing Bonnie. Can it get any worse?

Oh yes. The rancher's son is now the prime suspect. And Superintendent Xavier Divine, AKA The Divine Pain in the Ass, demands Bonnie cease her investigation or lose her job.

Maybe Bonnie should have listened to him. Because things are about to get a whole lot worse. The murderer has now kidnapped Bonnie's beloved dog, and unless she wants to see him alive again, well ...

ISBN#9781933836157
US $7.95 / CDN $9.95
Mystery
Available Now
www.rspiller.com

"Fast, engaging – a fine debut." —Lee Child
NY Times bestselling author of the Jack Reacher series

GUNS
PHIL BOWIE

Sam Bass is tall and lanky, loves old western movies, wears cowboy boots and drives a beat-up Jeep Wrangler. He has a gorgeous girlfriend, Valerie, a Cherokee widow with a young son, and he's a hot shot pilot. A hot shot pilot with a past. And when Sam makes a daring and dangerous rescue of a couple lost at sea in a storm, he gets publicity he definitely doesn't need.

The Cowboy, as he's known in certain circles, has finally been located and a hit team is dispatched to take care of unfinished business. A bomb is planted in the beat-up Jeep. But it isn't Sam who drives it that day.

Grief stricken, Sam visits Valerie's grandfather in the North Carolina mountains to tell him he plans to avenge Valerie in the ancient Native American way of members of a wronged family seeking justice — with no help from the law. With only the old man's help, Sam trains his mind and body for the task ahead. And then the bloody hunt is on . . .

ISBN#9781932815597
US $6.99 / CDN $8.99
Suspense
Available Now
www.philbowie.com

MICHAEL BERES
CHERNOBYL MURDERS

1985, a year before the Chernobyl disaster. Hidden away in a wine cellar in the western Ukraine, Chernobyl engineer Mihaly Horvath, brother of a Kiev Militia detective Lazlo Horvath, reveals details of unnecessary risks being taken at the Chernobyl plant. Concerned for his brother and family, Lazlo investigates—irritating superiors, drawing the attention of a CIA operative, raising the hackles of an old school KGB major, and discovering his brother's secret affair with Juli Popovics, a Chernobyl technician.

When the Chernobyl plant explodes scores of lives are changed forever. As Lazlo questions his brother's death in the blast, Juli arrives in Kiev to tell the detective she carries his brother's child. If their lives aren't complicated enough, KGB major Grigor Komarov enters the fray, reawakening a hard-line past to manipulate deadly resources.

Now the Ukraine is not only blanketed with deadly radiation, but becomes a killing ground involving pre-perestroika factions in disarray, a Soviet government on its last legs, and madmen hungry for power as they eye Gorbachev's changes.

With a poisoned environment at their backs and a killer snapping at their heels, Lazlo and Juli flee for their lives—and their love—toward the Western frontier.

ISBN#9781933836294
US $25.95 / CDN $28.95
Thriller
Available Now

www.michaelberes.com

MICHELLE PERRY
PAINT IT BLACK

DEA agent Necie Bramhall thinks she knows a thing or two about revenge. She's devoted her life to bringing down the drug lord father who abandoned her. When she finally captures him, she thinks she'll be able to put her painful past behind her. What she doesn't realize is that she's created a brand new enemy. A deadly enemy.

Maria Barnes is beautiful, ruthless, and driven by a lifelong jealousy of the half-sister she's never known—the daughter their father could never forget. Her hatred for Necie spirals out of control following their father's arrest, and Maria vows to destroy everything Necie holds dear... starting with her marriage and her family.

When her daughter is kidnapped, new revelations reveal the man she always perceived as her greatest enemy might be the only one who can save her from her half-sister's wrath. And now her father is behind bars...

ISBN#9781933836003
US $7.95 / CDN $9.95
Romantic Suspense
Available Now

www.michelleperry.com

For more information
about other great titles from
Medallion Press, visit

www.medallionpress.com